COCKFIGHTER

by Charles Willeford

A Black Lizard Book

Berkeley • 1987

BOOKS BY *Charles Willeford*

Fiction	Cockfighter
	The Burnt Orange Heresy
	The Director
	No Experience Necessary
	The Black Mass of Brother Springer
	Pick-Up
	Until I Am Dead
	High Priest of California
	Miami Blues
	New Hope for the Dead
	Sideswipe
Short Stories	The Machine in Ward Eleven
Non-fiction	Something About A Soldier

Copyright © 1972 by Charles Willeford.
Black Lizard Books edition published 1987.

Typography by QuadraType.

ISBN 0-88739-026-9
Library of Congress Catalog Card No. 86-71888

Manufactured in the United States of America.

For Mary Jo

*What matters is not the idea a man holds, but the
depth at which he holds it.*
                                    —Ezra Pound

Chapter One

First, I closed the windows and bolted the flimsy aluminum door. Then I flicked on the overhead light and snapped the Venetian blinds shut. Without the cross ventilation, it was stifling inside the trailer. Outside, in the Florida sunlight, the temperature was in the high eighties, but inside, now that the door and the windows were locked, it must have been a hundred degrees. I wiped the sweat away from my streaming face and neck with a dishcloth, dried my hands, and tossed the cloth on the floor. After moving Sandspur's traveling coop onto the couch, I checked the items on the table one more time.

Leather thong. Cotton. Razor blade. Bowl of lukewarm soapy water. Pan of rubbing alcohol. Liquid lead ballpoint pencil. Sponge. All in order.

I lifted the lid of the coop, brought Sandspur out with both hands, turned the cock's head away from me, and then held him firmly with my left hand under his breast. I looped the noose of leather over his dangling yellow feet, slipped it tight above his sawed off spur stumps, and made a couple of turns to hold it snug. Holding the chicken with both hands again, I lowered him between my legs and squeezed my knees together tight enough to hold him so he couldn't move his wings. Sandspur didn't like it. He hit back with both feet four times, making thumping sounds against the plastic couch, but he couldn't get away.

I pinched off a generous wad of cotton between my left thumb and forefinger and clamped my fingers over his lemon-yellow beak. There was just enough of a downward curve to his short beak so he couldn't jerk his head out of my fingers. He couldn't possibly hurt himself, as long as the cotton didn't slip.

Impatient knuckles rapped on the door. Dody again. A

1

vein throbbed in my temple. At that moment I would have given anything to be able to curse.

"How long you gonna be, Frank?" Dody's petulant voice shrilled through the door. "I gotta go to the bathroom!"

I didn't answer. I couldn't. She rapped impatiently a couple of more times and then she went away. At least she didn't holler anymore.

My right hand was damp again, and I wiped my fingers on my jeans, still holding Sandspur's beak with my left thumb and forefinger. I picked up the razor blade and cut a fine hairline groove across his bill as high up as possible. This was ticklish work and I cut a trifle too deep on the right side. I dropped the razor blade back on the table and released the cock's head. I picked up the ballpoint lead pencil with my left hand and rubbed the point across my right fingertip until it was smeared with liquid lead. Pinching off more cotton with my left hand, I caught Sandspur's beak again and rubbed the almost invisible groove with my lead-smeared forefinger. I took my time, and Sandspur glared at me malevolently with his shiny yellow eyes.

As soon as I was satisfied, I unloosened the thong around his feet and put the bird on the table, washed his legs with luke-warm soapy water, and rubbed his breast and thighs. I repeated the rubdown with alcohol. I was particularly careful with his head and bill, only using cotton dipped in the pan of alcohol.

Finished, I returned the items to my gaff case and dumped the used soapy water and alcohol into the sink. Sandspur was a fine-looking fighting cock, and after his light rubdown he felt in fine feather. Holding his head high he strutted back and forth on the slick Masonite table. He was a Whitehackle cross in peak condition, a five-time winner, and a real money bird. I knew he would win this afternoon, but I also knew he *had* to win.

I stepped in close to the table, made a feinting pinch for his doctored beak and he tried to peck me. I examined his beak, and even under close scrutiny the bill looked cracked. The liquid lead inside the hairline made the manufactured crack look authentic even to my expert eyes. As a longtime professional cocker I knew the crack would fool Mr. Ed Middleton, Jack Burke, and the accordion-necked fruit

2

tramp bettors. I picked Sandspur up and lowered him gently into his coop.

I opened the door, but Dody was nowhere in sight. She was probably visiting inside one of the other trailers in the camp. After sliding up all the windows again I lit a cigarette and sat down. What I had done to Sandspur's bill wasn't exactly illegal, but I didn't feel too proud about it. I only wanted to boost the betting odds and my slender roll.

Although I knew I couldn't possibly lose, I was apprehensive about the fight coming up. Everything I had, including my old Caddy and my Love-Lee-Mobile Home, was down on this single cockfight. And Sandspur was the only cock I had left. In my mind, I reviewed my impulsive bet. I had been a damned fool to bet the car and trailer.

At four that morning I had slid out of bed without waking Dody and switched on the light. Dody slept like a child, mainly because she was a child. The girl was only sixteen. I had picked her up in Homestead, Florida, three weeks before at a juke joint near the trailer camp where I had been staying. Her parents had their trailer in the Homestead camp, and Dody was only one out of their five children. It was a family of fruit tramps, and I doubt very much if they even missed her when I took her away with me. I wasn't the first man to sleep with Dody, not by any means. There had been dozens before me, but seeing her asleep and vulnerable that morning made me feel uneasy about our relationship. She was awfully damned young. At thirty-two, I was exactly twice as old as Dody.

It was too hot in Belle Glade to have even a sheet over you, and Dody lay on her back wearing a flimsy cotton shorty nightgown. She slept with her mouth open, her long taffy-colored braids stretched out on the pillow. Her face was flushed with sleep, and she didn't look twelve years old, much less sixteen. Her body was fully mature, however, with large, melon-heavy breasts, and long tapering legs. In her clumsy, uninhibited way she was surprisingly good in bed. She was as strong as a tractor, but not quite as intelligent.

I felt sorry for Dody. She didn't have much to show for her life so far. With her parents, she had followed crops

3

all over the country—staying locked in a car by a field someplace until she was big enough to carry baskets—and this constant exposure to the itinerant agricultural worker's lackadaisical code of living had made her wise beyond her age. After spending the night with me in my trailer in Homestead, she had begged to be taken along, and I brought her with me to Belle Glade. Why I weakened I don't know, but at the time I had been depressed. I had lost four birds in the Homestead fighting, and if Sandspur hadn't won his fight, the Homestead meet would have been a major disaster. But three weeks is a long time to live with a young, demanding girl—and a stupid, irritating girl, at that.

Anyway, it was four a.m. I dressed and took Sandspur outside and around to the back of the trailer.

It was still dark and I wanted to flirt him for exercise. A cooped bird gets stale in a hurry. I sidestepped the chicken six times, gave him six rolls, and let him drink a half dip of water. He would get no more water until after the fight. When the sky began to lighten I released him. Sandspur lifted his head and crowed twice. I lit my first cigarette of the day. As I watched the cock scratch in the loose sand, a shadow fell across my face. I looked up and there was Jack Burke, a wide grin splitting his homely face. I scooped Sandspur up quickly, dropped him into the coop and closed the lid. Burke had seen him, but there still wasn't enough light for a close look.

"That the mighty Sandspur?" Burke said.

I nodded.

"He don't look like no five-time winner to me. Tell you what I'll do, Mr. Mansfield," Burke said, as though he were doing me a big favor, "I'll give you two to one."

When Burke made this offer, I had just started to get to my feet. But now I decided to remain in my squatting position. Burke is a man of average height, but I am a full head taller than he is, and my eyes are bluer. My blond hair is curly, and his lank blond hair is straight. Looking down on me that way gave him a psychological advantage, a feeling of power, and I wanted him to have it—hoping that his overconfidence would help me get even better odds that afternoon.

Burke had written me a postcard to Homestead, challenging Sandspur to the fight at even money. I had accepted by return mail, glad to get a chance at his Ace cock, Little David. Little David wasn't so little in his reputation. He was an eight-time winner and had had a lot of publicity. When my Sandspur beat Burke's Little David, his value would be doubled, and my chances for taking the Southern Conference championship would be improved.

On the drive from Homestead to Belle Glade, I had thought of the crack-on-the-bill plan, and now I didn't want even money or two to one either. After the bettors looked at the birds before the pitting, I expected to get odds of four to one, at least. I had eight hundred and fifty dollars in my wallet and I didn't want to take Burke's offer, but after accepting an even-money fight by mail, I couldn't legitimately turn down the new odds.

I snapped my fingers out four times, folded in my thumb, and held up four fingers. I nodded twice.

"You mean you've only got a hundred dollars to bet?" Burke said, with a short angry laugh. "I figured on taking you for at least a thousand!"

I pointed to the coop and lifted a forefinger to show Burke I only had the one cock. He knew very well I had lost four birds at Homestead. By this time, everybody in Florida and half of Georgia knew it.

Jack Burke followed the Cocker's Code of Conduct, and he was honest, but he disliked me. Although my luck had been mostly bad for the last three years, four years before at Biloxi my novice stag, Pinky, had killed his Ace, Pepperpot. He would never be able to forgive or forget that beating. Pinky had won only one fight against five for his cock, and Burke had taken a terrific loss at five-to-one odds. More than the money he had lost, he had resented my winning. A columnist in *The Southern Cockfighter* had unfairly blamed his conditioning methods for the loss. Actually, Pinky had only made a lucky hit. A man is foolish to fight stags, but I had needed the young bird to fill out my entry for the main—not expecting to clobber Pepperpot.

Burke studied the ground, rubbing his freshly shaven chin. He was in his middle forties, and he wore his pale, yellow hair much too long. He paid considerable attention to his clothes. Even at daybreak he was wearing a blue seersucker suit, white shirt and necktie, and black-and-white shoes. Two-toned shoes indicate an ambivalent personality, a man who can't make up his mind.

"Okay, Mr. Mansfield," Burke said at last, slapping his leg. "I'll take your hundred dollars and give you a two-to-one. I know damned well Sandspur can't beat Little David, but your cock always has a chance of getting in a lucky hit . . . the way Pinky did in Biloxi, for instance. So let's say you really get lucky—what do you have? Two hundred dollars. To give you a fighting chance to get on your feet again after Homestead, I'll put up eight hundred bucks against your car and trailer. Even money."

I chewed my lower lip, but the bet was fair. My battered Caddy was worth at least eight hundred, but I didn't know what the trailer was worth. Secondhand trailers bring in peculiar prices, and mine was fairly small, with only one bedroom and one door. If I unloaded the car and trailer through a newspaper advertisement, I could've probably sold them both together for at least a thousand. Burke wanted to beat me so bad he could taste it. And if Little David won, I'd be out on the highway with my thumb out.

I stuck out my right hand and Burke grabbed it eagerly. The bet was made.

"Too bad you haven't got anything else to lose," Burke laughed gleefully. "I'd like to make another bet that you just made a bad bet!"

My lips curved into a broad smile as I thought of Dody sleeping peacefully inside the trailer. In the unlikely event that Burke's cock did win the fight, he would also be stuck with Dody. When I pictured Burke in my mind stopping at every gas station on the road to buy Dody ice cream and Coca-Colas it was impossible to suppress my smile. On the way up from Homestead she had damned near driven me crazy.

But now the bet was made.

I consulted my wristwatch. Two thirty. It was time to go. Bill Sanders was going to meet me outside the pit at three to pick up my betting money. I stashed a hundred dollars in the utensil cupboard to cover my two-to-one bet with

6

Burke, counted the rest of my money, and it came out to an even seven hundred and fifty dollars. That was everything, except for a folded ten-dollar bill in my watch pocket. This was my getaway bread—just in case.

I put my straw cowboy hat on my head to protect my face from the Florida sun, picked up the aluminum coop and my gaff case, and stepped outside. There were fourteen trailers in Captain Mack's Trailer Camp, including mine, and if you had touched any one of them, you would have burned your hand. In the distance, across the flat, desolate country, I could see Belle Glade, three miles away. The heat waves rising off the sandy land resembled great sheets of quivering cellophane. I turned away from the trailers and started toward the hammock clump a mile away where the pit had been set up. As hot as it was, I was in no mood to unhitch my car from the trailer and work up a worse sweat than I had, and the walk was only a mile.

There was a wire gate behind the camp, with an old-timer collecting an entrance fee of three dollars. I raised my coop to show him I was an entrant, and he let me through without collecting a fee. As I passed through the gate, Dody came flying up the trail, pigtails bouncing on her shoulders. She was barefooted, wearing a pair of red silk hot pants and a white sleeveless blouse. Her big unhampered breasts jounced up and down as she ran.

"Frank!" she called out before she reached the gate. "Take me with you! Please, Frank!"

The gateman, a grizzled old man in blue overalls, raised his white brows. I shook my head. He closed and latched the gate as Dody reached it.

"Damn you, Frank!" Dody shouted angrily. "You don't let me do nothin'. You know I've never seen you cockfight. Please let me go!"

I ignored her and continued up the trail. I had enough to worry about, without her yammering around the pit and asking questions.

Captain Mack, who had made all the arrangements for the Belle Glade pitting, was talking earnestly to a Florida trooper when I reached the parking area. The trooper's state patrol car was parked directly behind a new convertible with a Dade County plate. The right door of the convertible was open, and a pretty blonde woman sat in the front seat. Her face was pale, and she had her eyes closed, breathing deeply through her open mouth. There was a wet spot in the sand outside the door. I supposed the girl had watched a couple of fights inside the pit and got sick as a consequence. Not many city women have the stomach for watching cockfights.

The pit was surrounded on four sides by a green canvas panorama made from army surplus latrine screens. There were about thirty cars in the parking area, not counting the trucks. I set down my gaff case and coop in the sparse shade of a melaleuca tree, and leaned against a parked Plymouth, watching Captain Mack argue with the trooper. Captain Mack shrugged wearily, took his wallet out of his hip pocket, and handed two bills to the trooper. Through a gap in the canvas wall, they went inside the pit. Although cockfighting is legal in Florida, betting is not, so Captain Mack had been forced to pay out some protection money.

There was excited shouting from inside the pit, followed by several coarse curses, and then the voices subsided. Mr. Ed Middleton's baritone carried well as he announced the winning cock.

"The winner is the Madigan! One minute and thirty-one seconds in the third pitting!"

Again there were curses, followed by the derisive sound of laughter. I lit a cigarette, took my notebook out of my shirt pocket, and wrote the essential information concerning Sandspur on a fresh sheet of paper. A few minutes later Bill Sanders came outside and joined me beneath the tree. I handed him my roll of seven hundred and fifty dollars and he counted it. Bill put the money in his trousers and watched my fingers. I held up four fingers on my left hand and my right forefinger.

"I doubt if I can get you four to one, Frank." Bill shook his head dubiously. "Your reputation is too damn good. You could show up with a battered dunghill, and if these rednecks thought you fed it, they'd bet on it. But I'll try."

If anybody could get good odds for me, Sanders could, and I knew he would certainly try. When I was discharged from the Army, I had spent two months in Puerto Rico with Sanders, living in the same hotel; and we had attended

8

mains at all the best game clubs—San Juan, Mayagüez, Ponce, Arecibo, and Aibonito. I had steered Sanders right on the betting, after I had gotten accustomed to the fighting techniques of the Spanish slashers, and both of us had returned to Miami with our wallets full of winnings. Bill Sanders was not a professional cockfighter like myself, he was a professional gambler. He had lost his share of the money he won in Puerto Rico at the Miami horse and dog tracks. A little bald guy with a passion for high living, he lived very well when he had money and even better when he had none. He was that kind of a man, and a good friend.

I took Sandspur out of his coop and pointed out the "cracked" beak. Bill whistled softly and his blue eyes widened.

"If that bill breaks off, you've had it, Frank." He shrugged. "But that mutilated boko should get me the four-to-one odds."

Sanders hit me lightly on the shoulder with his fist and returned to the pit.

I held Sandspur with my left hand, filled my mouth with smoke, and blew the smoke at his head. He clucked angrily, shaking his head. Blowing tobacco smoke at a cock's head irritates it to a fighting pitch, and I was smoking a mild, mentholated cigarette. I enveloped the cock's head with one more cloud of smoke and returned him to his coop. Too much smoke could make a cock dizzy.

I opened my gaff case and removed two sets of heels. I put a pair of short spurs in my left shirt pocket and a pair of long jaggers in my right shirt pocket. After shutting my gaff case, I picked up the coop and case and entered the pit.

There were only about sixty spectators inside, but this was a fairly good crowd for September. The Florida cock-fighting season didn't start officially until Thanksgiving Day, when an opening derby was held in Lake Worth. And Belle Glade isn't the most accessible town in Florida. The canvas walls successfully prevented any breeze from getting into the pit, and it was as hot inside as a barbecue grill.

I recognized a couple of Dade County fanciers and nodded acknowledgments to them when they greeted me by name. There was a scattering of Belle Glade townspeople, two gamblers from Miami who probably owned the blonde and the convertible, Burke and his two handlers, and two pregnant women I had seen around the trailer camp. The remainder of the crowd was made up from the migrant agricultural workers' camp on the other side of town.

The cockpit was made of rough boards, sixteen inches high, and about eighteen feet in diameter. The pit was surrounded on three sides by bleachers, four tiers high. Under an open beach umbrella on the fourth side of the pit, Mr. Middleton sat at a card table with Captain Mack. Behind the table there was a blackboard. I noted that Jack Burke had won both of the short-entry derbies, the first, four-one, and the second, three-two. That accounted for the glum expressions on the faces of the two Dade County breeders. Not only had they made a poor showing, their one-hundred-dollar entry fees, less Captain Mack's ten percent, had wound up in Burke's pocket as prize money.

Two men in the bleachers I didn't know called out my name and wished me good luck. I waved an acknowledgment to them, and joined Ed Middleton and Captain Mack. I removed Sandspur from the coop and handed the slip of paper to Mr. Middleton. Jack Burke and his handler, Ralph Hansen, came over. The handler was carrying Little David. Mr. Middleton produced a coin.

"Name it, gentlemen," he said.

"Let Mr. Mansfield call it," Burke said indifferently.

I tapped my forehead to indicate "heads." Mr. Middleton tossed the half dollar into the air and let it land with a thump on the card table. Heads. I reached into my left shirt pocket, pulled out the short gaffs, and held them out in my open palm. They were hand-forged steel gaffs, an inch and a quarter in length. Burke nodded grimly and turned to his handler.

"All right, Ralph," he said bitterly. "Short spurs, but set 'em low."

Burke was a long gaff man, but I preferred the short heels. Sandspur was a cutter and fought best with short gaffs. Little David was used to long three-inch heels. Winning the toss had given Sandspur a slight advantage over Little David.

The cockfight between Sandspur and Little David was an extra hack, and I had not, of course, been required to post any entry fee. However, Mr. Middleton examined both cocks with minute attention. He was acting as judge and referee and had received at least a minimum fee of one hundred and fifty dollars, plus expenses, from Captain Mack. The judge of a cockfight has to be good, and Ed Middleton was one of the best referees in the entire South. His word in the pit was law. There is no appeal from a cockfight judge's decision. As sole judge-referee, Ed Middleton's jurisdiction encompassed spectator betting as well. The referee's job has always been the most important at a cockfight. As every cocker knows, for example, honest Abe Lincoln was once a cockpit referee during his lawyer days in Illinois. Hard and fair in his decisions, and as impersonal as doom, Ed Middleton was fully aware of the traditional responsibilities of the cockpit referee.

After completing his examination of the cocks to see that they were not soaped, peppered or greased and that they were trimmed fairly, Mr. Middleton stepped back to the table.

"Southern Conference rules, gentlemen?" he asked.

"What else?" Burke said.

I nodded my head in agreement.

"Forty-minute time limit, or kill?"

I closed my fist, jerked my thumb toward the ground.

"What else?" Burke said.

Captain Mack held Sandspur while Jack Burke examined him, and I took a close look at Little David. Burke's chicken was a purebred O'Neal Red and as arrogant as a sergeant-major in the Foreign Legion. Although I had never seen Little David fight before, I had followed his previous pittings in *The Southern Cockfighter*, and I knew that he liked aerial fighting. But so did Sandspur fight high in the air, and my cock was used to short gaffs. The three additional wins Little David had over Sandspur didn't worry me when I had such an advantage.

Burke tapped me on the shoulder and grinned. "If I'd known your chicken had him a cracked bill, I'd have given you better odds."

I shrugged indifferently and sat down on the edge of the pit to arm my cock. I opened my gaff case, removed a bottle of typewriter cleaning solvent and cleaned Sandspur's spur

11

stumps. Most cockers use plain alcohol to clean spurs, but typewriter solvent is fast-drying and, in my opinion, removes the dirt easier. After fitting tight chamois-skin coverings over both spurs, I slipped the metal sockets of the short heels over the covered stumps and tied them with waxed string, setting them low and a trifle to the outside. The points of the tapered heels were as sharp as needles, and a man has to be careful when he arms a cock. I had a puckered puncture scar on my right forearm caused by a moment of carelessness seven years before, and I didn't want another one.

The betting had already started, but the crowd quieted down when Mr. Middleton stepped into the pit. They listened attentively to his announcement.

"This is an extra hack, gentlemen," he said loudly. "Little David versus Sandspur. Southern Conference rules will prevail. No time limit, and short gaffs. Little David is owned by Mr. Jack Burke of Burke Farms, Kissimmee, Florida. He's an Ace cock, with eight wins and will be two years old in November. Little David will be handled by Mr. Ralph Hansen of Burke Farms."

The crowd gave Little David a nice hand, and Mr. Middleton continued.

"Sandspur is owned by Mr. Frank Mansfield of Mansfield Farms, Ocala, Florida, and he will handle his own chicken. Sandspur is a five-time winner and a year and a half old. Both cocks will fight at four pounds even."

Sandspur got a better hand than Little David, and the applause was sustained by the two Dade County breeders who wanted him to beat Burke's cock. Mr. Middleton examined Sandspur's heels and patted me on the shoulder. Many cockers resent the referee's examination of a cock's heels, but I never have. A conscientious referee can help you by making this final check. Once the fight has started and your cock loses a metal spur, it cannot be replaced.

As Mr. Middleton crossed the pit to examine Little David, I watched the flying fingers of the bettors. The majority of the betting at cockfights is done by fingers—one finger for one dollar, five for five dollars, and then on up into the multiples of five—and I was an expert in this type of betting. I had learned finger betting in the Philippines when I was in the army and didn't understand Tagalog, and I had also used the same system in Puerto Rico, where I didn't understand Spanish very well. Little David was the favorite, getting two-to-one, and in some cases three-to-one odds.

Bill Sanders, Jack Burke and the two Miami gamblers were in a huddle next to the canvas wall. Both gamblers were staring across the pit at Sandspur while Sanders and Burke talked at the same time. Sanders had a roll of money in his hand and was talking fast, although I couldn't hear his voice from where I was sitting beside the pit.

A fistfight broke out on the top tier of seats between two fruit tramps, and one of them was knocked off backward and fell heavily to the ground. Before he could climb back into the stands, the state trooper had an armlock on him and made him sit down on the other side of the pit. When I looked back to Bill Sanders, he was smiling and holding up three fingers.

So Bill had got three-to-one. That was good enough for me. When Sandspur won, I'd be $2,250 ahead from the Miami gamblers, plus $1,000 more from Jack Burke. $3,250. This would be more than enough money to see me through the Southern Conference season, and enough to purchase six badly needed fighting cocks besides.

"Get ready!" Mr. Middleton yelled. I stood up, stepped over the edge of the pit, and put my toes on the back score. The backscore lines placed us eight feet away from each other. Ralph Hansen, holding Little David under the chest with one hand, called impatiently to the refereee:

"How about letting us bill them first, Mr. Middleton?"

Billing is an essential prelude to pitting. Ed Middleton didn't need the reminder. "Bill your cocks," he growled.

We cradled our fighters over our left arms, holding their feet, and stood sideways on our center scores, two feet apart, so the cocks could peck at each other. These cocks had never seen each other before, but they were mortal enemies. Ed allowed us about thirty seconds for the teasing and then told us to get ready. Ralph backed to his score and I returned to mine. I squatted on my heels and set the straining Sandspur with his feet on the score. The cocks were exactly eight feet apart.

I watched Mr. Middleton's lips. This was a trick I had

practiced for hours on end and I was good at it. Before a man can say the letter "P" he must first compress his lips. There isn't any other way he can say it. The signal to release the cocks is when the referee shouts "Pit" or "Pit your cocks!" The handler who releases the tail of his cock first on the utterance of the letter "P" has a split-second advantage over his rival. And in the South, where "Pit" is often a two-syllable word, "Pee-it," my timing was perfect.

"Pit!" Mr. Middleton announced, and before the word was out of his mouth Sandspur was in the air and halfway to Little David. The cocks met in midair, both of them shuffling with blurred yellow feet, and then they dropped to the ground. Neither cock had managed to get above the other.

With new respect for each other, the two birds circled, heads held low, watching each other warily. Little David feinted cleverly with a short rush, but Sandspur wasn't fooled. He held his ground, and Burke's cock retreated with his wings fluttering at the tips.

As he dropped back, Sandspur rose with a short flight and savagely hooked the gaff of his right leg into Little David's wing. The point of the heel was banged solidly into the bone and Sandspur couldn't get it dislodged. He pecked savagely at Little David's head, and hit the top of the downed cock's dubbed head hard with his bill open . . . too hard.

The upper section of Sandspur's bill broke off cleanly at the doctored crack I had made. A bubble of blood formed, and Sandspur stopped pecking. Both cocks struggled to break away from each other, but the right spur was still stuck, and all Sandspur could do was hop up and down in place on his free leg. I looked at Mr. Middleton.

"Handle!" the judge shouted. "Thirty seconds!"

A moment later I disentangled the gaff from Little David's wing and retreated to my starting line. I put Sandspur's head in my mouth and sucked the blood from his broken beak. I licked the feathers of his head back into place and spat as much saliva as I could into his open mouth. For the remaining seconds I had left I sucked life into his clipped comb. The comb was much too pale . . .

"Get ready!" I held Sandspur by the tail on the line. "Pit your cocks!"

Instead of flying into the air, Sandspur circled for the right wall. Little David turned in midair, landed running, and chased my cock into the far corner. Sandspur turned to fight, and the cocks met head on, but my injured bird was forced back by the fierceness of Little David's rush.

On his back, Sandspur hit his opponent twice in the chest, drawing blood both times, and then Little David was above him in the air and cutting at his head with both spurs. A sharp gaff entered Sandspur's right eye, and he died as the needle point pierced his central nervous system. Little David strutted back and forth, pecked twice at my lifeless cock, and then crowed his victory.

"The winner is Mr. Burke's Ace," Mr. Middleton announced, as a formality. "Twenty-eight seconds in the second pitting."

All I had left was a folded ten-dollar bill in my watch pocket and one dead chicken.

Chapter Two

There was a burial hole in the marshy ground, about four feet square and three feet deep, on the far side of the parking area. Water was seeping visibly into the mucky pit, and the dead roosters in the bottom had begun to float.

I removed the gaffs from my dead cock's spurs and added his body to the floating pile of dead chickens. As I put the heels away in my gaff case, Bill Sanders joined me at the edge of the communal burying pit.

"I just wanted to let you know that I got all your dough down, Frank," he said. "Every dollar at three-to-one, and there's nothing left."

I nodded.

"Tough, Frank, but my money was riding on Sandspur with yours."

I shrugged and emptied the peat moss out of the aluminum coop into the hole on top of the dead chickens.

"You're going to be all right, aren't you? I mean, you'll be on the Southern Conference circuit this year, and all?"

I nodded and shook hands with Sanders. As I looked

down at Bill's bald head, I noticed that the top was badly sunburned and starting to peel. The little gambler never wore a hat.

"Okay, Frank. I'll probably see you in Biloxi."

I clapped Bill on the shoulder to squeeze out a farewell. He went over to the blue Chrysler convertible and started talking to the blonde. She had evidently recovered from her upset stomach. She had remade her face, and she now listened with absorbed attention to whatever it was Bill Sanders was telling her.

I removed the bamboo handle from the aluminum coop, collapsed the sides, and made a fairly flat, compact square out of the six frames. After locking them together with the clamps, I attached the handle again so I could carry the coop folded. A machinist in Valdosta had made two of the traveling coops for me to my own specifications and design. At one time I had considered having several made, and putting them up for sale to chicken men traveling around the country, too, but the construction costs were prohibitive to make any profit out of them. My other traveling coop was at my farm in Ocala.

Carrying my gaff case and coop, I walked back to the trailer camp. Dody met me at the door of the Love-Lee-Mobile Home with a bright, lopsided smile. Her lipstick was on crooked, and there was too much rouge on her cheeks. She wanted to look older, but makeup made her look younger instead.

"Did you win, Frank?"

I leaned the folded coop against the side of the trailer and pointed to it with a gesture of exasperation.

"Oh!" she said. Her red lips were fixed in a fat, crooked "O" for an instant. "I'm real sorry, Frank."

I placed my gaff case beside the coop and entered the trailer. There was a dusty leather suitcase under the bed, and I wiped the scuffed surfaces clean with a dirty T-shirt I found on top of the built-in dresser. I unstrapped the suitcase, opened it on the bed, and began to pack. There wasn't too much to put into it. Most of my clothes were on the farm. I packed my clean underwear, two clean white shirts, and then searched the trailer for my dirty shirts. I found them in a bucket of cold water beneath the sink.

Dody had been promising to wash and iron them for the past three days, but just like everything else, she hadn't gotten around to doing it. I couldn't very well pack wet shirts in the suitcase on top of clean dry clothing, so I left the dirty shirts in the bucket.

In the tiny bathroom I gathered up my toilet articles and zipped them into a blue nylon Dropkit. When I packed the Dropkit into the suitcase, Dody began to evidence an avid interest in my actions.

"What are you packing for, Frank?" she asked.

Despite the fact that I had never said as much as a single word to her in the three weeks we had been living together, she persisted in asking questions that couldn't be answered by an affirmative nod, a negative waggle of my head, or an explanatory gesture of some kind. If I had answered every foolish question she put to me in writing, I could have filled up two notebooks a day.

I tossed two pairs of clean blue jeans into the open suitcase, and then undressed as far as my shorts. I pulled on a pair of gray-green corduroy trousers, and put on my best shirt, a black oxford cloth Western shirt with white pearl buttons. The jodhpur boots I was wearing were black and comfortable, and they were fastened with buckles and straps. I had ordered them by mail from a bootmaker in El Paso, Texas, and had paid forty-five dollars for them. They were the only shoes I had with me. I untied the red bandanna from around my neck and exchanged it for a square of red silk, tying a loose knot and tucking the ends inside my collar before I buttoned the top shirt button. It was much too hot to wear the matching corduroy coat to my trousers, so I added it to the suitcase. The coat would come in handy in northern Florida.

"You aren't leaving, are you, Frank?" Dody asked worriedly. "I mean, are we leaving the trailer?"

I nodded impatiently, and searched through a dozen drawers and compartments before I found my clean socks. There were only three pairs, white cotton with elastic tops. I usually wear white socks. Colored socks make my feet sweat. I put the socks into the suitcase.

"Where're we going, Frank? I can get ready in a second," the girl lied.

There were five packages of Kools left, a half can of lighter fluid and a package of flints. I put a fresh pack of Kools in my pocket, and tossed the remaining packs, fluid and flints into the suitcase. After one last look around I closed the lid and buckled the straps. To get my guitar from under the bed I had to lie flat on the floor and reach for it. The guitar was now the substitute for my voice, and my ability to play it is what had attracted Dody to me in the first place. When I needed a woman again, the guitar would help me get one.

I carried the guitar case and suitcase into the combination kitchen-living-dining room.

"Why don't you answer me!" Dody yelled, pounding me on the back with her doubled fists. "You drive me almost crazy sometimes. You pretend like you can't talk, but I know damned well you can! I've heard you talking in your sleep. Now answer me, damn you! Where're we going?"

I drank a glass of water at the sink, set the glass down on the sideboard, and pointed in a northerly direction.

"I don't consider that an answer! North could be anywhere. Do you mean your farm in Ocala?"

Dody had an irritating voice. It was high and twangy, and there was a built-in nasal whine. I certainly was sick of listening to her voice.

The pink slips for the Caddy and the mobile home were in the drawer of the end table by the two-seater plastic couch. I opened the drawer, removed the pink slips and insurance papers and put them on the Masonite dinette table. In the linen cupboard of the narrow hallway I found a ruled writing pad and a dirty, large brown Manila envelope. I took the five twenty-dollar bills out of the utensil cupboard and sat down at the table. Now that I had lost, I was happy about having had the foresight to hide the money from Dody to cover my bet with Burke.

Standing at the sink, her arms folded across her breasts, Dody glared at me with narrowed eyes. Her lips were poked out sullenly and drawn down at the corners. I put the insurance policies, pink slips and money into the envelope. With my ballpoint lead pencil I wrote out a bill of sale on the top sheet of the ruled pad:

To Whom It May Concern,

I, Frank Mansfield, hereby transfer the ownership of a 1963 Cadillac sedan, and one Love-Lee-Mobile Home to Jack Burke, in full payment of a just and honorable gambling debt.

(Signed) Frank Mansfield

That would do it, I decided. If Burke wanted to transfer the pink slips and insurance to his own name, the homemade bill of sale would be sufficient proof of ownership.

"Is that note for me?" Dody asked sharply.

Although I answered with a short, negative shake of my head, Dody rushed across the narrow space, snatched the pad from the table and read it anyway. Her flushed face paled as her lips moved perceptibly with each word she read.

"Oh, you didn't lose the trailer?" she exclaimed.

I nodded, curiously watching her face. The girl was too young to have control over her features. Every emotion she felt was transmitted to her pretty, mobile face. Her facial expressions underwent a rapid exchange of dismay, anger, frustration and fear, settling finally on a fixed look of righteous indignation.

"And, of course," she said, with an effort at sarcasm, "you lost all your money, too?"

I nodded again and held out a hand for the pad. She handed it to me, and I ripped off the top sheet and added it to the contents of the bulging envelope.

"You don't give a damn what happens to me, do you?"

I shook my head. I felt sorry for her, in a way, but I didn't worry about her. She was pretty, young and a good lay. She could get by anywhere. Twisting in the seat, I reached into my pocket for my key ring. I unsnapped the two car keys and the door key for the trailer. After dropping them into the envelope, I licked the flap, sealed it and squared it in the center of the table.

There was a rap on the door. I jerked my head toward the door, and Dody opened it, standing to one side as Jack Burke came inside.

"Afternoon, ma'am," Burke said politely, removing his hat. He turned to me. "I'm sorry, Mr. Mansfield, but I made the bet in good faith and sure didn't know Sandspur had him a cracked bill. But if you'd won, I know damned well you'd of come around for eight hundred dollars from me. So I'm here for the car and trailer."

Still seated, I shoved the envelope toward him. Burke unfastened the flap, which hadn't quite dried, and pawed through the contents. He put the hundred dollars into his wallet before he read the bill of sale. His face reddened, and he returned the bill of sale to the envelope.

"Please accept my apology, Mr. Mansfield. I don't know why, but I guess I expected an argument."

Either he was plain ignorant or he was trying to make me angry. A handshake by two cockfighters is as binding as a sworn statement witnessed by a notary public, and he knew this as well as I did. For a long moment I studied his red face and then concluded that he was merely ill at ease on account of Dody's presence and didn't know what he was implying.

Dody leaned against the sink, glaring angrily at Burke. "I never heard of nobody so low-down mean to take a family's home away from them!" she said scathingly.

Her remark was uncalled for, but it caused Burke a deeper flush of embarrassment. "I reckon you don't know Mr. Mansfield, little lady," he said defensively, "and not over-much about cockfighting neither. But a bet is a bet."

"For men, yes! But what about me?" Dody patted her big breasts several times with both hands and looked beseechingly into Burke's eyes. He was troubled and he scratched his head, slanting his wary eyes in my direction.

I stood up, smiled grimly, and holding out my hands with the palms up, I made an exaggerated gesture of presentation of Dody to Jack Burke. There could be no mistake about the meaning.

"Well, I don't rightly know about that, Mr. Mansfield." Burke scratched his head. "I already got me a lady friend up Kissimmee way."

I stepped out from behind the table and put on my cowboy hat. Dody came flying toward me with clawing nails. The space was cramped, but I sidestepped her rush and planted a jolting six-inch jab into her midriff. Dody sat down heavily on the linoleum floor and stayed there, gasping for breath and staring up at me round-eyed with astonished disbelief.

There are three good ways to win a fight: A blow to the solar plexus, *first*, an inscrutable expression on your face, or displaying a sharp knife blade to your opponent. Any of these three methods, singly or in combination, will usually take the bellicosity out of a man, woman or child.

The swift right to her belly and the sight of my impassive face were enough to take the fight out of Dody. Burke tried to help her to her feet, but she shrugged his hands away from her shoulders as she regained her lost breath.

"You—can—go—to—hell, Frank Mansfield!" Dody said in gasps. "I can take care of myself!" However, she prudently remained seated, supporting herself with her arms behind her back.

Burke said nothing. He ran his fingers nervously through his long hair, looking first at me and then at Dody and back to me again. He wanted to say something but didn't know what he wanted to say. I sat down at the table again and scratched out a short note.

Mr. Burke—If your Little David is still around, I challenge you to a hack at the Southern Conference Tournament—

I pushed the straw cowboy hat back from my forehead and handed him the note. After reading the message, Burke crumpled the paper and looked at me thoughtfully.

"You don't have any fighting cocks left, do you, Mr. Mansfield?"

I shook my head, and moved my shoulders in a barely perceptible shrug.

"Do you honestly believe you can train a short-heeled stag to beat Little David, a nine-time winner"—he counted on his fingers—"in only six-months' time?"

In reply, I pointed to the crumpled challenge in his hand.

"Sure, Mr. Mansfield. I accept, but it'll be your funeral. And I expect you to put some money where your mouth is when the hack's held."

We shook hands. I picked up my suitcase and guitar and went outside. As I collected my gaff case and coop together, trying to figure out how I could carry everything, Burke and Dody followed me outside. The four odd-sized pieces made an awkward double armload.

"I'll give you ten bucks for that coop," Burke offered.

The suggestion was so stupid I didn't dignify it with so much as a shrug. If Burke wanted a coop like mine, he could have one made.

Ralph Hansen had Burke's Ford pickup parked on the road about twenty yards away from the trailer. Burke strolled over to his truck to say something to Ralph. The other handler was in the truck bed with Burke's fighting cocks. The truck bed had steel-mesh coops welded to the floor on both sides, with solid walls separating each coop so that none of the cocks could see each other. A nice setup for traveling, with plenty of space down the center to carry feed, luggage and sleeping bags. I walked down the sandy road toward the open gate and the highway.

A moment later Dody caught up with me and trotted along at my side.

"Please, Frank," she pleaded, "take me with you. I don't want to stay with Mr. Burke. He's an old man!"

Burke was only forty-five or -six and not nearly as old as Dody thought. I shook my head. Dody ran ahead of me then, and planted herself in my path, spreading her long bare legs, and holding her arms akimbo. I stopped.

"I'll be good to you, Frank," she said tearfully. "Real good! Honest, I will! I know you don't like them TV dinners I been fixin', but I'm really a good cook when I try. And I'll prove it to you if you'll take me with you. I'll wash your clothes and sew and everything!" She began to blubber in earnest. Juicy tears rolled out of her moist brown eyes and flowed over her smooth round cheeks, cutting furrows in her pancake makeup.

I jerked my head for her to get out of my way. Dody moved reluctantly to one side and let me pass. At the open gate to the highway I put my luggage down and lit a cigarette. Ralph stopped the white pickup at the gate.

"I can carry you up as far as Kissimmee, Mr. Mansfield," he offered. "Mr. Burke is going to bring your Caddy and trailer up tomorrow, he said."

I shook my head friendlily, and waved him on his way. I didn't want any favors from Jack Burke. After Ralph made his turn onto the highway, I looked back toward my old trailer. Jack Burke and Dody had their heads together, and it looked like both of them were talking at the same time. A moment later, Burke held the trailer door open for Dody and then followed her inside.

It occurred to me that I didn't know Dody's last name. She had never volunteered the information and, of course, I had never asked her. I hate to write notes, and I only write them when it is absolutely necessary. What difference did it make whether I knew her last name or not? But it *did* make a difference, and I felt a sense of guilty shame.

The long blue convertible came gliding down the trail from the cockpit. The driver stopped at the gate. The blonde sat between the two Miami gamblers on the front seat, and Bill Sanders, puffing a cigar, was sitting alone in the back.

"Do you want to go to Miami, by any chance?" Sanders asked.

I shook my head and smiled.

"We've got plenty of room," the driver added cheerfully. "Glad to take you with us."

I shook my head again and waved them on. Sanders raised a hand in a two-finger "V" salute, and the big car soon passed out of sight.

I didn't want to go to Miami, and I had turned down a free ride to Kissimmee. Where did I want to go? The lease on my Ocala farm had two more years to run, and it was all paid up in advance. But without any game fowl, and without funds to buy any, there was no point in going there right now. The first thing on the agenda was to obtain some money. After I had some money, I could start worrying about game fowl.

Doc Riordan owed me eight hundred dollars. His office was in Jacksonville, and he was my best bet. My younger brother, Randall, owed me three hundred dollars, but the chances of getting any money from him were negligible. Doc Riordan was the man to see first. Even if Doc could only give me a partial payment of two or three hundred, it would be a start. With only a ten-dollar bill in my watch pocket, and a little loose change, I felt at loose ends. After collecting some money from Doc I could make a fast trip

23

home to Georgia and see my brother. I couldn't go home completely broke. I never had before, and it was too late to start now.

As I thought of home I naturally thought of Mary Elizabeth. My last visit had been highly unsatisfactory, and I had left without telling her good-bye.

On my last trip home two years before, I had been driving a black Buick convertible, and I had worn an expensive white linen suit. Although I looked prosperous, most of it was front. My roll had only consisted of five hundred dollars. That was when Randall had nicked me for the loan of three hundred. In the rare letters I had received from him since—about one every four or five months—he had never once mentioned returning the money.

Jacksonville it would be then. If nothing else, I could pick up my mail at the Jacksonville post office.

Two ancient trucks rolled through the gate loaded down with fruit tramps. They were returning to the migrant camp on the other side of Belle Glade. A couple of the men shouted to me, and I waved to them. There was a maroon Cadillac sedan about two hundred yards behind the last truck, hanging well back out of the dust. This was Ed Middleton's car. As he came abreast of the gate, I grinned and stuck out my thumb. Mr. Middleton pressed a button, and the right front window slid down with an electronic click.

"Throw your stuff in the back seat, Frank," Ed Middleton said. "I don't want to lose this cold air." The window shot up again.

I opened the back door, arranged my luggage on the floor so it would ride without shifting, slammed the door, and climbed into the front seat. A refreshing icy breeze filled the roomy interior from an air-conditioning system that actually worked.

I settled backed comfortably, and Ed pointed the nose of the big car toward Orlando.

Chapter Three

Ed Middleton is one of my favorite people. He is in his early sixties, and if I happen to live long enough, I want to be exactly like him someday. He is a big man with a big voice and a big paunch. Except for a bumpy bulbous nose with a few broken blood vessels here and there on its bright red surface, his face is smooth and white, with the shiny licked look of a dog's favorite bone.

Against all the odds for a man his age, Mr. Middleton still has his hair. It is a shimmering silvery white, and he always wears it in a thick bushy crew cut. A ghost of a smile—as though he is thinking of some secret joke—usually hovers about the corners of his narrow lips. In southern cockfighting circles, or anywhere in the world where cockers get together for chicken talk, his name is respected as the man who bred the Middleton Gray. Properly conditioned, the purebred Middleton Gray is a true money bird.

Despite his amiable manner, Ed can get as hard as any man when the time to get tough presents itself, and he wears the coveted Cocker of the Year medal on his watch fob.

"Lost your car and trailer, eh Frank?"

I nodded. Bad news has a way of traveling faster than good news.

"Tough luck, Frank." Mr. Middleton laughed aloud. "But I don't worry about you landing on your feet. If I know you, you've probably got a rooster hidden away somewhere that'll give Jack Burke his lumps."

I smiled ruefully, made an "O" with the thumb and forefinger of my left hand and showed it to him.

"I sure didn't suspect that, Frank," Mr. Middleton said sympathetically.

I opened a fresh package of cigarettes, offered them to Ed and he waved them away. He was silent for more than ten minutes, and then he fingered his lower lip and squirmed about slightly in the seat. The signs were easily recognized. He wanted to confess something; a problem of some kind was on his mind. Two or three times he opened his mouth, started to speak his mind, and then shook his head and clamped his lips together. But he would get it out sooner or later, whatever it was. Since my vow of silence I had become, unwillingly, a man who listened to confessions. Now that I couldn't talk, or wouldn't talk—no one, other than myself, knew the truth about my muteness—people often told me things they would hesitate to tell to a priest, or even to their wives. At first, it had bothered me, learning things about people I didn't want or need to know, but now I just listened—not liking it, of course, but accepting the confessions as an unwelcome part of the deal I had made with myself.

We sailed through the little town of Canal Point and hit Highway 441 bordering Lake Okeechobee.

From time to time, when the roadbed was higher than the dike, I got a glimpse of the calm mysterious lake, which was actually a huge inland sea. Small herds of Black Angus cattle were spotted every few miles between the lake and the highway, eating lush gama grass, but there were very few houses along the way. Lake Okeechobee, with its hundreds of fish and clear sweet water, is a sportsman's paradise, but the great flood of the early twenties, when thousands of people were drowned, had discouraged real-estate development, I supposed. No plush resort hotels or motels had ever been built near its banks.

"Frank," Ed Middleton said at last, lowering his voice to conspiratorial tones, "today's pitting at Belle Glade was my last appearance at a cockpit. Surprises you, doesn't it?"

It did indeed. I reached up and twisted the rear-view mirror into position so Ed could look at my face without taking his eyes off the highway too much. I looked seriously into the mirror and widened my eyes slightly.

"Nobody can keep a secret long in this business, Frank, but I've kept my plans to myself to avoid the usual arguments. I've argued the pros and cons of cockfighting thousands of times, and you know I've always been on the pro side. If there's a better way of life than raising and fighting game chickens, I haven't found it yet," he said grimly. "But I'm a married man, Frank, and you aren't. That's the difference. I'm happily married, and I have been for more than thirty years, but I can still envy a man like you. There aren't a dozen men in the United States who've devoted their lives solely to cockfighting like you have, that is, without earning their living in some other line of business.

"I suppose I've known you for ten years or more and, as a single man, you've got the best life in the world. You've earned the admiration and respect of all of us, Frank."

I was embarrassed by the praise.

"That was a clever trick you pulled this afternoon, Frank!"

I started with surprise, and Mr. Middleton guffawed loudly.

"I haven't seen anyone pull that stunt with the cracked bill to raise the odds in about fifteen years. Don't blame yourself for losing the fight. Write it off to bad luck, or face up that Jack Burke had the better chicken. But that isn't what I wanted to talk about.

"Martha has been after me to quit for years, and I finally gave in. I'm not too old, but I certainly don't need the money. I've got enough orange trees in Orlando to take care of my wants for three lifetimes. If Martha shared my enthusiasm for the game, it would be different. But she won't go on the road with me. This business of living alone in motel rooms doesn't appeal to me anymore. The two months I spent refereeing in Clovis, New Mexico, last spring were the loneliest weeks of my entire life.

"Anyway, I've sold all my Grays. Made a deal for the lot with a breeder in Janitzio, Mexico, and shipped out the last crate of April trios last week. If he fights my Grays as slashers, he'll lose his damned *camisa*, but at any rate, they won't be fighting in the States.

"If you wonder why I refereed today's fight, it was because I promised Captain Mack a year ago. But that was my last appearance in the pit, and you won't see me in the pits again, either as a referee or spectator." Ed sighed deeply, his confession completed. "Like the lawyer feller says, Frank, 'Further deponent sayeth not.'"

Several dissuading arguments came immediately to my mind, but I remained silent, of course. As far as I was concerned, what Ed Middleton did was his business, not mine, but his loss to the game would be felt in the South. We needed men like him to keep the sport clean and honest. But I didn't say anything because of my self-imposed vow of silence.

Up to this moment I've never told anyone why I made the vow. What I do is my business, but the silver medal on Ed Middleton's watch fob held the answer. Money had nothing to do with my decision to keep my mouth shut.

All of us in America want money because we need it and cannot live without it, but we don't need as much money as most of us think we do. Money isn't enough. We must have something more, and my *something more* was the Cockfighter of the Year award.

The small silver coin on Ed's watch fob was only worth, in cash, about ten or fifteen dollars, but a lot of men have settled for lesser honors. A man may refuse a clerk's job with a loan company, for instance, for one hundred dollars a week. But if this same man is put in charge of three typists and is given the exalted title of office manager, the chances are that he will work for ninety dollars a week. In business, this is a well-known "for instance."

Unlike Great Britain, we don't have any peerages to hand out, or any annual Queen's Honors List, so most of us settle for less, a hell of a lot less. In large corporations, the businessman has reached his goal in life when he gets a title on his door and a corner office with two windows instead of one. But I'm not a businessman. I am a full-time cockfighter.

My goal in life was that little silver coin, not quite as large as a Kennedy half dollar. On one side of the medal there is an engraved statement: Cockfighter of the Year. In the center, the year the award is given is engraved in Arabic numerals. At the bottom of the coin are three capital letters: S.C.T. These letters stand for Southern Conference Tournament.

To a noncocker, this desire might sound childish, but, to a cockfighter, this award is his ultimate achievement in one of the toughest sports in the world. The medal is awarded to the man Senator Jacob Foxhall decides to give it to at the completion of the annual S.C.T. held in Milledgeville, Georgia. However, Senator Foxhall doesn't always see fit to award the medal. In the last fifteen years he has only awarded the medal to four cockfighters. Ed Middleton was one of them.

In addition to the medal there is a cash award of one thousand dollars. In effect, the cocker who wins this award has the equivalent of a paid-up insurance policy. He can demand a minimum fee of one hundred and fifty dollars a day as a referee from any pit operator in the South, and the operator considers it an honor to pay him. To a cocker, this medal means as much as the Nobel Prize does to a scientist. If that doesn't convey an exact meaning of the award, I can state it simpler. The recipient is the best damned cockfighter in the South, and he has the medal to prove it.

For ten years this medal has been my goal. The S.C.T. is the toughest pit tourney in the United States, and a cockfighter can't enter his game fowl without an invitation. Only top men in the game receive invitations, and I had been getting mine for eight years—even during the two years I was in the army and stationed in the Philippine Islands.

A vow of silence, however, isn't necessary to compete for the award. That had been my own idea, and not a very bright idea either, but I was too damned stubborn to break it.

Three years before I had been riding high on the list of eligible S.C.T. cockfighters. In a hotel room in Biloxi, I had gotten drunk with a group of chicken men, and shot off my big mouth, boasting about my Ace cock, a Red Madigan named Freelance.

Another drunken breeder challenged me, and we staged the fight in the hotel room. Freelance killed the other cock easily, but in the fight he received a slight battering. The next day at the scheduled S.C.T. pitting, I had been forced to pit Freelance again because I had posted a two-hundred-dollar forfeit, and I had been too ashamed to withdraw. Freelance lost, and I had lost my chance for the award.

A few weeks later, while brooding about this lost fight, a fight that had been lost by my personal vanity and big mouth, I made my self-imposed vow of silence. I intended to keep the vow until I was awarded that little silver medal. No one, other than myself, knew about my vow, and I could have broken it at any time without losing face. But I would know, and I had to shave every day. At first it had been hell, especially when I had had a few drinks and wanted to get in on the chicken talk in a bar or around the cockhouses at a game club, but I had learned how to live with it.

On the day Mr. Middleton picked me up in his Cadillac at Captain Mack's Trailer Court in Belle Glade, I hadn't said a word to anyone in two years and seven months.

"You're a hard man to talk to since you lost your voice!" Ed Middleton boomed in his resonant baritone.

With a slight start, I turned and grinned at him.

"I mean it," he said seriously. "I feel like a radio announcer talking into a microphone in a soundproof room. I know I must be reaching somebody, but I'll be damned if I know who it is. You've changed a lot in the last two or three years, Frank. I know you're working as hard as you ever did, but you shouldn't take life too seriously. And don't let a run of bad luck get you down, do you hear?"

I nodded. Ed jabbed me in the ribs sharply with his elbow.

"You've still got a lot of friends, you big dumb bastard!" he finished gruffly. With a quick movement he snapped on the dash radio, twisted the volume on full and almost blasted me out of my seat. He turned the volume down again and said bitterly: "And on top of everything else, there's nothing on the radio these days but rock 'n' roll!"

He left the radio on anyway, and said no more until we reached Saint Cloud. We pulled into the parking area of a garish drive-in restaurant and got out of the car. It was only six thirty, but the sun had dropped out of sight. There were just a few jagged streaks of orange in the western sky, an intermingling of nimbus clouds and smoke from runaway muck fires. As we admired these fiery fingers in the sky, Mr. Middleton smacked his lips.

"How does a steak sound, Frank?"

I certainly didn't intend to spend my remaining ten dollars on a steak. In reply, I emptied my pockets and showed him a double handful of junk, and some loose change.

"I didn't expect you to pay for it," he said resentfully. "Let's go inside."

The sirloin was excellent. So was the baked potato and green salad and three cups of coffee that went with it. After three weeks of Dody's halfhearted cooking, I appreciated a good steak dinner. On regular fare, such as greens, pork chops, string beans, cornbread and so on, I'm a fairly good cook, and I enjoy the preparation of my own meals. But I never prepare food when I have a woman around to do it for me. As I ate, I wondered vaguely how Jack Burke was making out with the girl. Although I was broke, the steak restored my good spirits, and I felt a certain sense of new-found freedom now that I no longer had Dody to worry about.

We lingered over dinner for more than an hour and didn't arrive at Mr. Middleton's home until after nine. His ranch-style, concrete brick and stucco house was about three miles off the main highway on a private gravel road and completely surrounded by orange groves. An avid fisher-man, Ed had built his home with the rear terrace overlook-ing a small pond. He parked in a double carport, set well away from the house, backing in beside a blue Chevy pickup.

Before we crossed the flagstone patio, Ed flipped a switch in the carport and flooded the patio and most of the small lake with light. The pond was about forty yards in diame-ter, and there was an aluminum fishing skiff tied to a con-crete block pier at the edge of the gently sloping lawn.

"I've stocked the damned lake with fish four different times," Ed said angrily, "but they disappear someplace. Hide in the muck at the bottom, I suppose. Anyway, I've never been able to catch very many."

When the lights were turned on, Mrs. Middleton opened the back door and peered out. Her dark hair, shot through with streaks of gray, was coiled in a heavy round bun at the nape of her neck.

"Who's that with you, Ed?" she asked.

We crossed the patio to the door and Ed kissed his wife on the mouth. He gripped my upper arm with his thick fin-gers and pulled me in front of him.

"Frank Mansfield, Martha. You remember him, I'm sure. He's going to spend the night with us."

"Of course," Martha said. "Come on inside, Frank, before the mosquitoes eat you alive!"

We entered the kitchen and I blinked uncomfortably

beneath the blue-and-yellow fluorescent lights. I shook hands with Mrs. Middleton after she wiped her hands unnecessarily on her clean white apron. She was a motherly woman, about ten or fifteen years younger than her husband, but without any children to "mother."

"Have you boys had your dinner?" she asked.

"We had a little something in Saint Cloud," Ed admitted.

"Restaurants!" she said. "Why didn't you bring Frank on home to dinner when you were that close?" she scolded. "Sit *down*, Frank! How've you been? Could you eat a piece of key lime pie? Of course you can. I know you both want coffee."

As we sat down at the breakfast nook together, Ed winked at me. Mrs. Middleton bustled around in her bright and shiny kitchen, banging things together, just as busy as she could be.

"Force some pie down anyway, Frank," Mr. Middleton said in a loud stage whisper. "I'm going to eat a piece even though I hate it."

"Ha!" Martha said from beside the stove. "You hate it all right!"

After we were served and eating our pie, there was nothing else Mrs. Middleton could do for us. She stood beside the table with her hands clasped beneath her apron, working her pursed lips in and out. I had the feeling that she wanted to ask me questions, but out of consideration for my so-called affliction, she wanted to phrase her questions so that I could answer them yes or no, and yet she couldn't manage any questions of that kind. I hadn't seen Mrs. Middleton or talked to her for at least four years. As I recalled, the last time I had seen her was at a banquet held following the International Cockfighting Tournament in Saint Petersburg. My "dumbness" had been a subject that she and her husband had undoubtedly discussed between them.

"Sit down, Martha," Ed said. "Have a cup of coffee with us."

"And stay awake all night? No thanks." She sat beside her husband, however, and smiled across the table. "Do you like the pie, Frank?"

I kissed my fingertips and rolled my eyes toward the ceiling.

"Lime is Ed's favorite." She put a hand on her husband's sleeve. "How was the trip, Ed?"

Ed Middleton put his fork crosswise on his empty plate, wiped his lips with a napkin, and looked steadily at his wife. "The trip doesn't matter, Martha," he said, "because it was the last, the very last."

For a long time, a very long time it seemed to me, the elderly couple looked into each other's eyes. Mr. Middleton smiled and nodded his head, and Martha's lower lip began to tremble and her eyes were humid. An instant later she was crying. She hurriedly left the table, put her apron to her face and, still crying, ran out of the room.

Mr. Middleton crumpled the square of linen and tossed it toward the stove. The napkin fluttered to the floor, and he smiled and shook his head.

"She's crying because she's happy," he said. "Well, dammit, I promised to give up cockfighting, and a promise is a promise!" He got up from the table, doubled his right fist, and punched me hard on the shoulder. "Pour yourself some more coffee, eat another piece of pie. I'll be back in a minute."

He pushed through the swinging door and disappeared.

The lime pie was tart, tasty, with a wonderful two-inch topping of snow white, frothy meringue. I ate two more pieces, drank two more cups of coffee. I smoked two cigarettes. Just as I was beginning to wonder whether Ed was going to come back to the kitchen or not, he pushed through the door.

"Come on, Frank," he snapped his fingers, "let's go get your suitcase."

We went out to his Caddy, and after he unlocked the doors, I got my suitcase out of the back. When we returned to the kitchen, he switched off the patio lights. I followed him through the living room and into his study.

"This was supposed to be a third bedroom," he explained. "Actually, it was designed as the master bedroom, and it's a lot larger than the other two bedrooms in the back. But Martha and I decided to each take a small bedroom apiece so our snoring wouldn't bother each other. And besides, I needed a large room like this as an office. A big man needs a big room." He opened the door leading to the bathroom. "Here's the can, Frank. Take a shower if you want to. There's always hot water, and these towels are all clean in here. I'll get you some sheets."

Ed left the room and I could hear him clumping down the hallway, yelling to his wife and asking her where she kept the clean sheets hidden.

The Middletons' ranch-style home was so modern in design and color that the old-fashioned furniture in the study was out of place. The walls were painted a bright warm blue, and there were matching floor-to-ceiling drapes over both windows. The floor was black-and-white pebbled terrazzo, and there the modernity stopped. The floor was covered with an oval-shaped hooked rag rug. There was an ugly, well-scratched, walnut rolltop desk against one wall, and there was an ancient horsehair-stuffed Victorian couch against the opposite wall. Beneath one window there was a scuffed cowhide easy chair, and a shiny black steamer trunk under the other window. A red-lacquered straight chair, with a circular cane seat, stood beside the desk. Three heavy wrought-iron smoking stands completed the furnishings.

I was attracted to the framed photographs on the walls. Each photo was framed in a cheap glass-covered black frame, the type sold in dime stores. Most of the glossy photos were of gamecocks, but there were several photos of Ed Middleton and his cronies. An old cover page of *The Southern Cockfighter*, with a four-color drawing of Ed Middleton's famous cock Freddy, held the place of honor above the desk. Freddy had won nineteen fights and had died in his coop ten years before. Anywhere chicken talk is held, Freddy's name comes up sooner or later.

Mr. Middleton reentered the room, carrying sheets, a blanket and a pillow under his right arm, and a portable television set in his left hand. He tossed the bedcovers on the couch, placed the portable set on the seat of the red straight-backed chair, and plugged the cord into the wall socket.

"I told Martha you wouldn't need a blanket, but you know how women are."

I nodded. I knew how women were. I began to make up the lumpy couch with the sheets.

"To give you something to do, I brought in the TV. It isn't much good but you can get Orlando, anyway. I'd stay up and keep you company for a while, but I'm pretty tired. This has been a long day for an old man."

I soon had the couch made up, but Mr. Middleton lingered in the room. He studied a photograph of a framed cock on the wall, and beckoned to me as I started to sit down.

"Come here, Frank. Take a look at this cock. It's a phenomenon in breeding and you'll never see another like it. A bird called Bright Boy, one of the most courageous birds I ever owned. Yet it was bred from a father and a daughter. By all the rules, a cock bred that way usually runs every time, but this beauty never did. He was killed in his second fight in a drag pitting. Sorry now I didn't keep him for a brood cock to see what would have happened. I suppose there are similar cases, but this is the only one I really know is true. Did you ever hear of a real fighter bred of father and daughter?"

I shook my head. If true, and I doubted Ed's story, this was an unusual case. When it comes to cocks of the same blood, those bred from mother and son have the biggest heart for fighting to the death. Somebody had probably switched an egg on old Ed.

"Every time a man thinks he's got the answers on cock-breeding, something like this happens to teach him something new. I'm going to be pretty well lost without my chickens, Frank, but I've got a lot of stuff stored away in that trunk, old game-strain records and so on. Maybe I could write a useful book on breeding." He shook his head sadly. "I don't know. I suppose I'll find something to do with my time."

To get rid of him, I clapped him on the shoulder, sat down, and unbuckled my jodhpur boots.

I was growing weary of always being on the receiving end of personal confidences and long sad stories. The man who is unable to talk back is at the mercy of these people. He is like an inexperienced priest who listens tolerantly to the first simple confessions of impure thoughts, and then listens with increasing horror as the sins mount, one outdoing the other until he is shocked into dumbness. And, of course, the sinner takes advantage of a man's credulousness, loading ever greater sins upon him to see how far he can really go now that he has found a trapped listener who is unable to stop him. My ears had been battered by the outpourings of troubles, tribulations, aspirations, and the affairs of broken hearts for two years and seven months. Only by being rude enough to leave the scene had I evaded some of my confessors.

But Ed Middleton was wise enough to take the hint.

"Good night, Frank," he said finally, "I'll see you in the morning," and the door closed behind him.

After taking a needed shower I switched on the little television set and sat on the couch to watch the gray, shimmering images. There was a lot of snow, and jagged bars of black appeared much too often. In less than five minutes I was forced to turn it off. I'm not overly fond of television anyway. Traveling around so much I have never formed the habit of watching it. And I've never owned a set.

I was impressed by this pleasant room of Ed Middleton's. It was a man's room, and if he really wanted to write a book about cock-breeding, it was certainly quiet enough. I doubted, however, that he would ever write one. What Ed Middleton did with his remaining years was no concern of mine, and yet I found myself worried about him. He had been fighting game fowl and refereeing pit matches for thirty-odd years. Without any birds to fool around with, what could he possibly do with his time? I felt sorry for the old man.

He had a nice home, his wife was a wonderful woman, and the Citrus Syndicate took care of his orange groves. He had turned over the operation of his groves to the Central Citrus Syndicate some years back. In return, they paid him a good percentage on the crop each year, and now he didn't have to do anything with his trees except to watch them grow. By giving up cockfighting he was giving up his entire existence, and, like most elderly men who retire, he probably wouldn't live very long—with nothing to do. Martha was wrong, dead wrong, in forcing Ed to give up his game chickens.

Mary Elizabeth's opposition to the sport was the major reason we had never gotten married. Why can't the American woman accept a man for what he is instead of trying to make him over into the idealized image of her father or someone else?

There was no use worrying about Ed Middleton. I had problems of my own that were more pressing. But with a little pushing from me, my problems would somehow take care of themselves. All I knew was that I had to do what I knew best how to do. Nothing else mattered.

I switched off the light and, despite the lumpiness of the beat-up old couch, fell asleep within minutes.

Chapter Four

It seemed as if I had only been asleep for about five minutes when the lights were switched on and Ed Middleton yelled at me to get up.

"Are you going to sleep all day?" he shouted gruffly. "I've been up for more than an hour already. Come on out to the kitchen when you get dressed. I've got a pot of coffee on."

Reluctantly, I sat up, kicked off the sheet, and swung my feet to the floor. The door banged shut and I looked at my wristwatch. Five thirty. It was pretty late to be sleeping. No wonder Ed had hollered at me. I stumbled into the bathroom. After a quick shave I dug some clean white socks out of my suitcase, and put on the same clothes I had worn the day before. I joined Ed in the kitchen, and sat at the breakfast nook.

"We can eat breakfast later, Frank," he said, pouring two cups of coffee. "Coffee'll hold us for a while. I want to show you something first."

I drank the coffee black, and it was thick enough to slice with my knife.

"You want a glass of orange juice?"

I held up a hand to show that coffee was enough for now.

Ed refilled my cup, set the pot back on the stove, and paced up and down on the shiny terrazzo floor. He wore an old pair of blue bib overalls and an expensive, embroidered short-sleeved sport shirt. The bottoms of the overalls were tucked into a pair of ten-inch, well-oiled engineer boots.

His great paunch stretched the middle of the overalls tight, but the bib on his chest flapped loosely as he walked.

The second cup of coffee seemed hotter than the first, and I was forced to sip it slowly. Ed snapped his fingers impatiently, pushed open the back door, and said over his shoulder, "Come on, Frank. We can have breakfast later, like I told you already."

I gulped down the remainder of the coffee and followed him outside to the patio. The sun was just rising, and the upper rim could be seen through the trees. The tops of the orange trees across the pond were dipped in molten, golden-green fire. The oranges on the darker green lower limbs of the trees looked as if they had been painted on. A mist rose from the tiny lake like steam rising from a pot of water just before it begins to boil. Ed Middleton sat down in the center of the little skiff tied to the concrete pier, and fitted the oars into the locks. I sat forward in the prow.

"Untie the line, Frank, and let's cast off."

Mr. Middleton rowed across the lake—all forty yards of it. It would have been less trouble to take the path that circled the pond, but if he wanted to use the skiff, it didn't make any difference to me.

When we reached the other side of the pond, I jumped out, held the skiff steady for Mr. Middleton, and then both of us pulled the boat onto dry land. There was a narrow path through the grove, and I trailed the old man for about five hundred yards until we reached his chicken walks. There was a flat, well-hidden clearing in the grove, and about a dozen coop walks, each separated by approximately twenty yards. The walks were eight feet tall, about ten feet wide by thirty feet in length, with the tops and sides covered with chicken wire. The baseboards were two feet high, and painted with old motor oil to keep down the mite population.

Seeing the empty walks reminded me of my own farm in Ocala, although I had a better setup for coop-walked birds than Ed Middleton. At one time, many years before, long before he had converted his land to orange trees, he had had the ideal setup for a country-walked rooster. A pond, gently rolling terrain, and enough trees for the chickens to choose their own limbs for roosting. We walked down the row of walks to the end coop. As the rooster crowed, Ed turned around with a proud expression and pointed to the cock.

If there is anything more beautiful than the sight of a purebred gamecock in the light of early morning I do not know what it is. This fighting cock of Ed's was the most brilliantly colored chicken I had ever seen, and I've seen hundreds upon hundreds of chickens.

Middleton had devoted sixteen years and countless generations of game fowl to developing the famous Middleton Gray, and there were traces of the Gray in the cock's shawl and broad, flat chest. But the cock was a hybrid of some kind that I couldn't place or recognize. He walked proudly to the fence and tossed his head back and crowed, beating the tips of his long wings together. The tips of his wings were edged with vermilion. The crow of a fighting cock is strong and deep and makes the morning sounds of a common dunghill barnyard rooster sound puny in comparison.

The same flaming color that tipped his wings was repeated in his head feathers and thighs, but his remaining feathers, including the sweep of his high curving tail, were a luminous peacock blue. Ed was planning—or had planned—to keep him for a brood cock, because his comb and wattles hadn't been clipped for fighting. His lemon beak was strong, short and evenly met. His feet and legs were as orange and bright as a freshly painted bridge.

The floor of the cock's private walk was thickly covered with a mixture of finely ground oyster shells and well-grated charcoal, essential ingredients for a fighter's diet. The oyster shells were for lime content, and the charcoal for digestion, but against this salt-and-pepper background, the cock's colorful plumage was emphasized.

Unfortunately, coloring is not the essential factor for a winning gamecock. Good blood *first*, know-how in conditioning, and a good farm walk are the three essentials a pit bird needs to win. I knew that thirty years of cock-breeding knowledge had found its way into that cock. I could see it in every feather, and his good blood was assured by the pleased smile on Ed Middleton's thin lips.

"Except for a couple of battered Grays and an old Middleton hen I've kind of kept around for a pet, this is the only cock I've got left. I've never pitted him, and he's overdue, but I was afraid to lose him. Not really, Frank. I know damned well he can outhit any other cock in the South!"

I agreed with him, at least in theory. I spread my arms, grinned, and shook my head with admiration. Ed nodded sagely with self-satisfaction, and I didn't blame him. A flush slowly enveloped his features until his entire face was as red as his bulbous nose.

"He's got a pretty damned fancy handle, Frank," Ed said. "I call him Icarus. You probably remember the old legend from school. There was a guy named Daedalus, who had a son named Icarus. Anyway, these two—Greeks they were—got tossed into jail, and Daedalus made a pair of wings out of wax for his boy to escape. This kid, Icarus, put on the wings and flew so damned high he reached the sun and the wings melted on him. He fell to the ground and was killed. No man has ever flown so high before or since, but, anyway, that's the handle I hung on the chicken. Icarus."

Ed Middleton cracked his knuckles and clomped away from the walk and entered the feed shack. I gripped the chicken wire with my fingers and turned my attention to Icarus. For a rugged character like Ed Middleton, the high-brow name and the story that went with it were fairly romantic, I thought. Most cockers who fight a lot of cocks don't get around to naming them in the first place. A metal leg band with the cock's weight and owner number usually suffices for identification. Of course, a favorite brood cock, or a bird that has won several battles, is frequently named. But I went along with Ed all the way. As far as looks were concerned the fancy name fitted the chicken to a T. However, if I had owned the bird, I would have called him Icky, and kept the private name to myself.

I entered the feed shed, dipped into the open sack of cracked corn in the corner, and picked out a dozen fat grains. I returned to the cock's walk, opened the gate and entered. As the cock watched me with his head to one side I lined up the grains of corn on the ground about six inches apart. The cock marched toward me boldly, eating as he came, and pecked the remaining grain of corn out of my outstretched palm. He wasn't a man fighter. Ed had probably spent a good many hours talking to the cock and gently handling him. I picked Icarus up with both hands, holding him underhanded, and examined the cock's legs and feet.

They hung down in perfect alignment with his body. If a cock's legs are out of line with the direction of his body, he is called a dry-heeled cock, because he can't hit and do much harm. But if the legs are in perfect direction, the cock stands erect, and he rises high. And usually he's a close hitter. This cock's legs were perfect.

I lowered the cock to the ground, released him and opened the gate. The cock tried to follow me out, and I liked that, for some reason. Ed came out of the feed shack, and showed me the bird's weight chart, which was attached to a clipboard.

Icarus was seventeen months old and weighed 4:03 pounds. He had maintained this weight fairly well for the past three months, within two ounces either way. For a cock that wasn't on a conditioning diet, this even weight indicated that the bird was healthy enough. He was fed cracked corn twice a day, barley water, and purged twice a week with a weak solution of one grain of calomel and one grain of bicarbonate of soda dissolved in water.

The flirting and exercising sections on the chart were empty. I tapped them with a forefinger and looked questioningly at Mr. Middleton.

"I haven't done any conditioning, Frank. But as you can see, I've watched his weight closely. He should go to 4:05, maybe, or 4:07 at most—under training. That's my opinion, anyway," he qualified his estimate. For a full minute, Ed looked through the fence at the cock, and I returned the weight chart to the hook on the wall inside the shack.

"Do you want this cock, Frank?" Ed asked fiercely, when I rejoined him.

What could I say? I stretched out the fingers of my left hand and made a sawing gesture on my right forearm. I shook my head, then made the sawing motion higher up, at the shoulder.

"Okay, Frank. You can have him for five hundred dollars. I told Martha last night you'd come home with me to buy the last of my chickens. So that's the price. Pay me and take him!"

The old cock fancier dug his hands into his pockets and walked away from me, unable, for the moment, to look me in the face.

He knew perfectly well I didn't have five hundred dollars, and he also knew that the cock wasn't worth that much. For fifty dollars apiece I could purchase country-walked gamecocks, with authenticated bloodlines, from almost any top breeder in the United States. And fifty dollars was a good price. The average for a purebred cock was thirty-five, and I could buy stags for ten and fifteen dollars apiece. I've seen Ace cocks sell for a hundred, and sometimes for one hundred and fifty—but never for five hundred.

No breeder wants to sell any of his fighters to another cocker he may meet at the same pit someday. The cock he sells or gives away may possibly kill some of his own birds in a pitting. On the other hand, the breeders who raise game fowl to sell would be thought ridiculous if they attempted to peddle an untested cock for five hundred dollars!

The answer was simple. Ed Middleton didn't want to sell Icarus. He was looking for an out to keep his pet. After I left he could tell Martha I had made an offer and that he had promised to sell it to me. Anybody else who came around to buy it could be legitimately refused. "I'd be glad to sell it," he could truthfully say to a prospective buyer, "but I've promised the cock to Frank Mansfield. Sorry . . ."

The old bastard was trying to renege on his promise to his wife. Knowing that I didn't have his price and was unlikely to pay it if I did, he planned on keeping his pet cock until it died of old age. One thing I did know. If I showed up with the money, he would have to sell it. And I wanted that bird. I seemed to sense somehow that this was the turning point in my run of bad luck at the pits . . . Little Icky.

Standing by an orange tree, Ed jerked a piece of fruit from a lower limb and threw it in a looping curve over the trees. I could hear the mushy thud of the orange as it landed deep in the grove. I crossed the space separating us with an outstretched right hand.

Ed grimly accepted my promise to buy his cock with a strong handshake.

While Mr. Middleton made a mixture of barley water, I leaned against the door of the feed shack and finished my cigarette. Somehow, I was going to get the money to buy that cock. Now my impending trip to Jacksonville had a sharpened point to it. If Doc Riordan had any money at all, I intended to get it.

Ed measured out the cracked corn and fed his pet, the two battered Gray roosters, and the old hen. Although I could feel some sympathy for Martha in not wanting her husband out traveling the cockfight circuits, I could not understand her desire to make him give up cock-breeding. If she considered cock-breeding morally wrong, she could have consoled herself with the idea that Ed was doing the breeding, not her. A man like Ed Middleton could never give up his love of the game. Perhaps she was going through her menopause and, as a consequence, was losing her mind.

"Let's go get us some breakfast, Frank," Ed said, as he locked the feed shack door. Ed started down the path toward the lake, and I lingered for a last look at Icarus. He pecked away at his grain hungrily. I could see the fine breeding of the cock in his stance and proud bearing. The cock had shape, health, and an inborn stamina. Through proper conditioning I could teach him responsiveness, alertness, improve his speed, and sharpen his natural reflexes. Other than that, there wasn't much else I could do for the cock. His desire to fight was inherited. And the only way his gameness could be tested truly was in the pit.

I turned away from the walk and ran down the path to catch up with Ed.

When we entered the kitchen, Martha greeted us cheerfully and began to prepare our breakfast. Ed and I sat down across from each other at the breakfast nook and I inhaled the delicious fragrance of the frying bacon. It was quite a breakfast: crisp bacon, fried eggs, hot biscuits, grits and melted butter, orange juice, and plenty of orange-blossom honey to coil onto the fluffy biscuits.

As I sat back with a full stomach to drink my after-breakfast coffee, Ed told his wife that I was going to buy his remaining chickens.

"That's wonderful, Ed," Martha said happily. She smiled

at me and bobbed her chin several times. "You know Ed wouldn't sell those old birds to just anybody, Frank. But Ed has always had a lot of respect for you, and I know you'll take good care of them."

I nodded, finished my coffee, and slid out of the booth.

"Frank isn't taking the cocks today, Martha," Ed said, getting up from the table. "He'll be back for them later on."

"Oh, I didn't know that! I thought he was taking them now."

"These deals aren't made in an instant, sweetheart," Ed said sharply. "But we've shaken hands on the deal, and Frank'll be back, all in good time." He forced a smile and turned toward me. "Come on, Frank. I'll drive you into Orlando."

"Where're you going, Frank?" Martha asked.

I shrugged indifferently and returned her smile. This was the kind of question that could only be answered by writing it down, and I didn't feel that it required an answer. Where I was going or what I was going to do couldn't possibly have any real interest for the old lady.

"Frank can't answer questions like that without writing them down," Ed reminded his wife. "But you know we'll be reading about him in the trade magazines."

"Well, I'll pack a lunch for you anyway. Wait out on the patio. Take some more coffee out there with you. It'll only take a minute and you can surely wait that long."

While she fixed a lunch for me, I repacked my suitcase and took it out to the car. Ed unlocked the door, and I removed the coop and handed it to him before I tossed the suitcase on the floorboards.

"Sure, leave the coop with me if you like," he said, leaning it against the concrete wall.

When I returned for Icky, I could use the coop to carry him, and I didn't feel like lugging it along to Jacksonville, not hitchhiking, anyway.

A few minutes later Martha joined us on the patio and handed me a heavy paper bag containing my lunch.

"I used the biscuits left from breakfast," she said, "and made a few ham sandwiches. There's a fat slice of tomato on each one and plenty of mayonnaise. There wasn't any pie left, but I put in a couple of apples for dessert."

Rather than simply shake hands with her, I put an arm around her narrow shoulders and kissed her on the cheek. Mrs. Middleton broke away from me and returned to the safety of her kitchen. Ed called through the door that he would be back from Orlando when he got back.

We drove down Ed's private road to the highway. I didn't know where he was taking me, but I hoped he wouldn't drop me off in the center of town. With the baggage I was carrying, the best place to start hitchhiking was on the I-4 Throughway on the other side of Winter Park. Several years had passed since I had been forced to use my thumb, and I wasn't too happy about the prospect.

Orlando is a fairly large city and well spread out. The streets that morning were crowded with traffic. Ed drove his big car skillfully, and when he hit the center of town, he made several turns and then stopped in front of the Greyhound bus station. I took my baggage out of the back and started to close the door, but held it open when Ed heaved himself across the seat. He got out on my side, reached in his wallet, and handed me a twenty-dollar bill.

"You can't hitchhike with all that stuff, Frank. You'd better take a bus."

I nodded, accepted the bill and buttoned it into my shirt pocket. That made five hundred and twenty dollars I owed him, but I was grateful for the loan.

We shook hands rather formally, and Ed plucked at his white chin with his puffy fingers. "Now don't worry about Icarus, Frank," he said with an attempt at levity. "I'll take good care of him whether you come back for him or not." His eyes were worried just the same.

I held up two spread fingers in the "V" sign. It was a meaningless gesture in this instance, but Ed smiled, thinking I meant it for him. I remained at the curb and waved to him as he drove away.

I picked a folder out of the rack, circled Jacksonville on the timetable with my ballpoint pencil, shoved the folder and my twenty under the wicket, and paid for my ticket. After slipping the ticket into my hatband, I gathered my baggage around me and sat down on a bench to wait for the bus.

I thought about Icky. In reality, five hundred dollars

wasn't even enough money to get started. I needed a bare minimum of one thousand, five hundred dollars to have at least a thousand left over after paying for the cock. Two thousand was more like it.

Somehow, I had to get my hands on this money.

Chapter Five

I didn't arrive in Jacksonville until a little after three that afternoon. Instead of waiting for an express, I had taken the first bus that left Orlando, and it turned out to be the kind that stops at every filling station, general store and cow pasture along the way. A long, dull ride.

After getting my baggage out of the side of the bus from the driver I left the station and walked three blocks to the Jeff Davis Hotel, where I always stayed when I was in Jax. On the way to the hotel I stopped at a package store and bought a pint of gin.

Perhaps the Jeff Davis isn't the most desirable hotel in Jax, but it is downtown, handy to everything, the people know me there, and crowded or not I can always get a room. The manager follows cockfighting, advertises in the game-fowl magazines, and there is usually someone hanging around the lobby who knows me. The daily rate is attractive, as well—only three dollars a day for cockers, instead of the regular rate of five.

As soon as I checked in at the desk and got to my room, I opened my suitcase and dug out my corduroy coat. In September, Jacksonville turns chilly in the afternoons, and the temperature drops below seventy. Not that it gets cold, but the weather doesn't compare favorably with southern Florida. The long pull of gin I took before going out on the street again felt warm in my stomach.

I walked briskly through the streets to the post office, entered, and twirled the combination dial on my post-office box. It didn't open, but I could see that there was mail inside the box through the dirty brown glass window. I searched through my wallet, found my box receipt for the rental, and shoved it through the window to the clerk. He studied the slip for a moment, and called my attention to the date.

"You're almost ten days overdue on your quarterly box payment, Mr. Mansfield," he said. "Your box was closed out and rented to somebody else. I'm sorry, but there's a big demand for boxes these days and I don't have any more open at present. If you want me to, I'll put your name on the waiting list."

I shook my head, pointed to the rack of mail behind him. This puzzled him for a moment, and then he said: "Oh, you mean your mail?"

I nodded impatiently, drumming my fingers on the marble ledge.

"If you have any, it'll be at the general-delivery window."

I picked up my receipt and gave it to the woman at the general-delivery window. She handed me two letters and my current *Southern Cockfighter* magazine. I shoved the letters and magazine into my coat pocket and filled in change-of-address cards to transfer the magazine and post-office-box letters to my Ocala address. After mailing one card to the magazine and turning in the other to the woman at the window I returned to my hotel room.

The first letter I opened was from a pit operator in Tallahassee inviting me to enter a four-cock derby he was holding in November. I tossed the letter into the wastebasket. The other letter was the one I had been expecting. It was from the Southern Conference Tournament committee, and contained my invitation, the rules, and the schedule for the S.C.T. season.

I studied the mimeographed schedule, but I wasn't too happy about it. There wasn't a whole lot of time to obtain and keep gamecocks for the tourney.

SCHEDULE
SOUTHERN CONFERENCE

Oct. 15	—Greenville, Mississippi
Nov. 10	—Tifton, Georgia
Nov 30	—Plant City, Florida
Dec. 15	—Chattanooga, Tennessee
Jan. 10	—Biloxi, Mississippi
Jan. 28	—Auburn, Alabama

Feb. 24   —Ocala, Florida
Mar. 15-16   —S.C.T.—Milledgeville, Georgia

I was already too late for Greenville, Mississippi. The S.C.T. was unlike other invitational mains and derbies, both in rules and gamecock standards. When Senator Foxhall had organized the S.C.T. back in the early thirties, his primary purpose had been to improve the breeds and gameness in southern cockfighting. The hardest rule of the tourney was that all the cocks entered in the final round at Milledgeville had to be four-time winners. A cock can win one or sometimes two fights with flashy flies in the first pitting, and some good luck. But any cock that wins four in a row is dead game. Luck simply doesn't stretch through four wins. This single S.C.T. rule, more than any other, had certainly raised breeding standards in the South, and it kept out undesirables and fly-by-night cockers looking for a fast dollar. All the pit operators on the S.C.T. circuit were checked from time to time by members of the committee, and if their standards of operation dropped, they were dropped, in turn, by the senator.

Like the other big-time chicken men, I had fought cocks in the highly competitive six-day International Tournament in both Orlando and Saint Pete, and I intended to enter it again someday, but I preferred the more rigid policies of the S.C.T. It was possible to enter the annual International Tournament by posting a preliminary two-hundred-dollar forfeit, which was lost if you didn't show up and pay the three-hundred-dollar balance. The winning entries made big money at the International, but I could make just as much at S.C.T. pits and at the final Milledgeville meet. And the wins on the S.C.T. circuit really meant something to me.

At that moment, however, I didn't feel like a big-time cockfighter. I was at rock bottom and it was ironical to even think about fighting any cocks that season. All I had in my wallet was eighteen dollars, plus some loose change in my pockets. I owned a thirty-dollar guitar, a gaff case, a few clothes in a battered suitcase, and a lease on a farm.

Of course, the contents of my gaff case were worth a few hundred dollars, but I needed everything I had to fight cocks. I sat down on the edge of my bed, and opened my gaff case to search for the last letter Doc Riordan had sent me. I opened the letter, but before reading it again, I made a quick inventory of the gaff case to see if there was anything I could do without. There wasn't. I needed every item.

There were sixteen sets of gaffs, ranging from the short one-and-one-quarter-inch heels I preferred, up to a pair of three-inch Texas Twisters. I even had a set of slashers a Puerto Rican breeder had given me one afternoon in San Juan. With slashers, the bird is armed on one leg only. I don't believe in fighting slashers for one simple reason. When you fight slashers, the element of chance is too great, and the best cock doesn't always win. With a wicked sharp blade on a cock's left leg, the poorest cock can sometimes get in a lucky hit. Pointed gaffs, round from socket to point, are legitimate. Once a cock's natural spur points have been sawed off, the hand-forged heels fitted over the half-inch stumps are a clean substitute for his God-given spurs, and they make for humane fighting. Two cocks meeting anywhere in their natural state will fight to the death or until one of them runs away. Steel spurs merely speed up the killing process, and a cock doesn't have to punish himself unnecessarily by bruising his natural spurs.

Of course, I had fought slashers when I was a soldier in the Philippines because I had to, and I knew how to fight them. But I had never considered them altogether fair because of that slight element of chance. Cockfighting is the only sport that can't be fixed, perhaps the only fair contest left in America. A cock wouldn't throw a fight and couldn't if he knew how.

Every pair of my sixteen sets of heels was worth from twenty to thirty-five dollars, and I needed them all. The correct length of heels is a common argument, but what really determines the right length for any given cock is the way it fights. And even though I favor short heels, like they use in the North, or "short-heel country" as the North is called, I would never handicap a cock by arming him with the wrong spurs out of vain, personal preference. It is a crime not to arm a cock with the spurs which will allow him to fight his very best.

In addition to my heel sets I had a spur saw, with a dozen

extra blades, moleskin heeling tape, blade polishers, gaff pointers, a set of artificial stubs for heeling slip-leg cocks, two pairs of dubbing shears, one curved and the other straight, and two new heeling outfits, each containing pads, tie strings and leather crosspieces. There was also a brand new roll of Irish flax, waxed tie string, some assorted salves and a few gland stimulant capsules. To anybody except a cocker, this collection of expensive equipment was worthless junk. If I pawned the entire contents of my case, a pawnbroker wouldn't give me more than forty dollars for the lot.

For a few thoughtful moments I clicked the dubbing shears in my hand, and then picked up Doc's letter. I'd been carrying It around in my case for more than three months.

Dear Frank,

> *I haven't written you for some time, but I wanted you to know your investment is as good as gold. Don't be surprised if you get a stock split one of these days soon and double your eight hundred dollars. Next time you get to Jax, drop in and see me and I'll give you the details.*
>
> *Very truly yours,*
Doc Riordon

To anyone who didn't know Doc Riordan, this letter would have sounded encouraging indeed. But the letter was more than three months old and, unfortunately, I knew Doc too well. I liked the man for what he was and respected him for what he was trying to be. But unlike me, Doc lived with a big dream that was practically unattainable. All I wanted to be was the best cockfighter who ever lived. Doc, who had already reached his late fifties, wanted to be a big-time capitalist and financier.

He wasn't a real doctor, I knew that much. He was a pharmacist, and a good one, and somewhere along the years he had added Doc to his name. I had met him several years before at various Florida cockpits, and I had bought conditioning powder and ergot capsules from him when he still had his mail-order business. Conditioning powder can be made up by any pharmacist who is given the formula, but Doc was dependable, well liked by cockers, and he had also invented a salve that was a quick healer for battered cocks. However, there are a lot of businessmen who advertise the same types of items in the cocker journals. There wasn't enough big money in cocker medical supplies for Doc, and he dropped out of the field. However, he would still supply a few friends like myself when we wrote to him.

Some four years before, Doc had caught me in an amiable mood and with more than five thousand dollars in my pockets. I had put eight hundred dollars into his company—The Dixie Pharmaceutical Company—and I had never received a dividend. I had had several glowing letters from him, but not a cent in cash. In fact, I didn't even have any stock certificates to show for my investment. It was one of those word-of-mouth deals so many of us enter into in the South. A handshake is enough, and I knew my money would be returned on demand . . . providing Doc had it. But whether he had it or not was something else altogether.

It was five o'clock and I decided to wait and see him in the morning. Feeling as low as I did, I didn't want to return to my room with a turndown that evening.

I left my room, walked down the street to a café and ate two hamburgers and drank two glasses of milk. When I returned to my room, I nipped at the gin and read my new *Southern Cockfighter* magazine. The magazine had been published and mailed out before the Belle Glade derby, but there was a short item about the Homestead pitting, and my name was mentioned in Red Carey's column, "On the Gaff."

> Looks like bad luck is still dogging Silent Frank Mansfield. His sad showing at Homestead makes us wonder if his keeping methods are off the beam. Another season like his last three, and we doubt if he'll still be on the S.C.T. rolls.

The item should have irritated me, but it didn't. A columnist has to put something in his column, and I was fair game. There was nothing wrong with my conditioning methods. They had paid off too many times in the past. My problem was to get the right cocks, and when I got Icky from Mr. Middleton, I would be off to a good season. I finished the rest of the gin and went to bed.

As far back as 320 B.C. an old poet named Chanakya wrote that a man can learn four things from a cock: To fight, to get up early, to eat with his family, and to protect his spouse when she gets into trouble. I had learned how to fight and how to get up early, but I had never gotten along too well with my family and I didn't have any spouse to protect. Fighting was all very well, but getting up early was not the most desirable habit to have when living in a big city like Jacksonville.

The next morning I was up, dressed and shaved, and sitting in the lobby by five thirty. I bought a morning *Times-Union*, glanced at the headlines and then went out for breakfast because the hotel coffee shop didn't open until seven thirty. I lingered as long as I could over coffee, but it was still only six thirty when I returned to the hotel. I was too impatient just to sit around, and I soon left the dreary lobby and walked the early morning streets. The wind off the river was chilly and it felt good to be stirring about. A sickly sun rode the pale morning sky, but after an hour passed it began to get warm and promised to be a good day.

Promptly at eight I entered the Latham building to see if Doc Riordan had arrived at his office. The Latham building was an ancient red-brick structure of seven stories built in the early 1900s. Nothing had been done to it since. The entrance lobby was narrow, grimy and filled with trash blown in from the street. There was a crude, hand-lettered sign on the elevator stating that it was out of order. Doc's company was on the sixth floor.

The stairwell up was unlighted and without windows. I climbed the six flights only to discover that his office was closed. The office was two doors away from the far end of the hallway, and the frosted glass top half of the door had gold letters painted on it four inches high:

THE DIXIE PHARMACEUTICAL CO.
Dr. Onyx P. Riordan
PRESIDENT AND GENERAL MANGR.

I tried the door and found it locked. Rather than descend the stairs and then climb up again I leaned against the wall and smoked cigarettes until Doc showed up.

The wait was less than twenty minutes and I heard Doc huffing up the stairs long before I could see him. He entered the hall, red-faced, carrying a large cardboard container of coffee. The container was too hot for him to hold comfortably, and as he recovered his breath, he kept shifting it from one hand to the other as he fumbled with his key in the door lock.

"Come on in, Frank," Doc said, as he opened the door. "Soon as I set this coffee on the desk I'll shake hands."

I followed Doc into the tiny office, and we shook hands. Doc wiped his perspiring bald head and brow with a hankerchief and cursed angrily for two full minutes before he sat down behind his desk.

"I've told the superintendent before and I'm going to tell him one more time," Doc said as he ran down, "and if he don't get that damned elevator fixed, I'm moving out! That's a fact, Frank, a fact!"

I sat down in a straight-backed chair in front of Doc's desk, and surveyed his ratty little office. A single dirty window afforded a close-up of the side of a red-brick movie theater less than three feet away, and the proximity of the building didn't allow much light into the room. Doc probably had to burn his desk and ceiling lights even at midday. Doc's desk was a great, wooden, square affair, and much too large for the size of the room. In front of the fluorescent desk lamp was his carved desk sign: *Dr. Onyx P. Riordan, Pres.* (and a beautifully carved ornate job it was, too). In addition to his desk there was a low two-drawer filing cabinet, the swivel executive chair he was sitting in, and two straight-backed chairs. These simple furnishings made the room overly crowded. On the wall behind his desk was a hand-lettered, professionally done poster in three primary colors praising the virtues of a product called Licarbo. After reading the poster I studied Doc's face. He had taken two green dime-store cups out of his desk and was filling them with black coffee.

With his bald head and tonsure of thin, fine gray hair, Doc looked his fifty some-odd years, all right, but there was a certain youthfulness about his face that denied those years. His features were all small, gathered together in the center of a round, bland face. His mouth and snubby nose were small. His blue eyes were ingenuously wide and revealed the full optic circle. With his round red cheeks and freshly scrubbed look, Doc could probably have passed for thirty if he wore a black toupee and dyed his eyebrows to match.

"It's been a long time, Frank," Doc said sincerely, "and I'm really glad to see you again." He sat back with a pleased smile. "I want to show you something!"

He began to rummage through his desk. I sipped some coffee and lit another cigarette from the butt of the one I was smoking. The sight of this little hole-in-the-wall office had dashed any hopes I might have had about getting even a portion of my money back from the old pharmacist.

"Read this, Frank!" Doc said eagerly, sliding a letter across the broad surface of the desk. I read the letter. It was from a drug laboratory in New York.

President
Dixie Pharmaceutical Co.
Latham Building
Jacksonville, Florida

Dear Dr. Riordan:

We have made exhaustive tests of your product, LICARBO, at your request, and we agree that it is nontoxic, and that it will provide nonharmful relief to certain types of indigestion, such as overeating, overindulgence, etc.

However, we are not in the market for such a product at this time. Thank you for letting us examine it. Best wishes.
Very truly yours,

The signature was indecipherable, but vice-president was typed beneath the inked scribble. I put the letter down on the desk.

"Do you realize what that letter means, Frank?" Doc said excitedly. "They're interested, definitely interested! They couldn't find a single fault, and do you know why? Licarbo

54

doesn't have any, that's why! I've dealt with companies like that before. They think I'll sell out for little or nothing, but if they want Licarbo, and you can read between the lines of the letter that they're dying to get it, it'll cost them plenty!"

Doc sat back in his big chair, steepled his fingers together, and attempted to look shrewd by narrowing his eyes. His narrowed eyes only made him look sleepy, however.

"Not only do I want a flat ten thousand for my rights, Frank, I'm also holding out for a percentage on every package sold. Now what do you think of that?"

I admired Doc's spirit, but, evidently, he refused to recognize a politely worded turndown when he saw it. I shrugged my shoulders noncommittally.

"By God, I forgot!" Doc snapped his fingers. "You haven't tried Licarbo yet, have you?"

I shook my head. Doc opened the top right drawer of his desk and removed three flat packets approximately the size and shape of restaurant-size sugar packets. The name Licarbo was printed in red ink on each packet, including directions to take as needed, with or without water, following overindulgence, overeating or for mild stomach distress.

"Go ahead, Frank, open one up and taste it. There isn't a better relief for indigestion in the world than Licarbo! Take it with a glass of water and you'll belch every time. What more does a man want than a big healthy belch when his belly hurts him? Right? In the South we like our medicines in powder and liquid form. No self-respecting Southerner will take a fancy capsule for belly pains, no matter how many colors it's got."

I ripped open a packet and spilled some of the mixture into my hand. Licarbo resembled gunpowder, or a mixture of salt and black pepper, heavy on the pepper. I put my tongue to the mixture. It tasted like licorice, not an unpleasant taste at all.

"Mix it in with your coffee, Frank. Licarbo will dissolve almost instantly."

I shuddered at this suggestion, shook my head and smiled.

"Tastes good, don't it?" Doc beamed proudly, folding his short arms across his chest. "All it is, Frank, is a mixture of licorice root, bicarbonate of soda, a few secret ingredients and some artificial coloring. But the formula will make me rich, and you too, Frank. It takes time, however, to invent and develop a new product and get it out to the waiting market. The New York company isn't my only prospect, not by any means. I've got feelers out all over the nation. This is the *big* one, Frank, the one I've been working up to through thirty years in practical pharmacy. I've invented other products and sold them too, but this time I'm holding out to the last breath. Why, if I only had the capital I could manufacture Licarbo myself and literally make a fortune. A fortune!"

Doc turned in his chair, sighed deeply, and looked out the window at the rusty wall of the theater.

"People just don't have faith no more, Frank. People today don't recognize a commercial drug when they see and taste it, damn them all, anyway! But this product has got to go over, it *has* to!" Doc dropped the level of his voice, and said softly, as if to convince himself, "It's only a matter of time, Frank. Only a matter of time . . ."

I slipped the two unopened packets of Licarbo into my jacket pocket. At least I had something to show for my eight-hundred-dollar investment. Doc swiveled his chair and faced me with a bright smile.

"I made this first batch up myself, Frank, and had the sample packages printed up here in town. It costs a lot of money to get started, but you've got to admit the product is good, don't you?"

I nodded, pursing my lips. As far as I was concerned, Licarbo was as good as any one of a hundred similar products on the market. Plain old bicarbonate of soda will make you belch if a belch is required, and that was Doc's main ingredient.

"You'd like to have your eight hundred dollars back just the same. Am I right?" Doc said hesitantly.

I spread my hands, palms up, and nodded.

"Well, I just don't have it right now, Frank." Doc wet his thumb. "I just don't have it. But you'll get it back one of these days soon, every damned dime, and with plenty of interest. To be honest, I'm just hanging on these days. Don't even have a phone anymore in the office, as you can see. I've got a part-time pharmacist's job at night in a drug-store near my rooming house, and every cent I make goes into office rent, promotion of Licarbo, and I'm barely getting by on what's left. I've dropped everything else to concentrate on Licarbo, but when it hits, and it's going to, it'll be big, really big!"

Old Doc Riordan was another man like myself, riding along on an inborn, overinflated self-confidence and a wide outward smile. Deep inside, I knew he was worried sick about being unable to write me a check for my money. Well, I could relieve him from that worry in a hurry. Whether his product ever went over big or not was no concern of mine. I wasn't about to ride another man's dream; I had a big dream of my own. It was time to get the hell off Doc's back.

There was a writing tablet on his desk. I reached for it, took my ballpoint lead pencil out of my coat pocket and wrote on the pad:

President, Dixie Pharm. Co.

In return for a. ten-year supply of conditioning powder and other medicinal aids for poultry at the Mansfield Farms, the undersigned hereby turns over all his existing stock in the Dixie Pharm. Co. to the President.

After signing my name with a flourish, I smiled, and handed Doc the tablet. He read the note and frowned.

"Don't you have any faith in Licarbo, Frank?"

I looked at him expressionlessly and nodded slowly.

"Then why are you pulling out?"

I got to my feet, leaned over the desk and underlined "ten-year supply" on the note I had written.

A knowing smile widened Doc's tiny mouth, and he nodded sagely.

"You're a mighty shrewd businessman, Frank. Why, if you ever expand your farms you'll double your eight hundred dollars in five years easily! But damn your eyes, anyway!" He laughed gleefully. "I'm just going to take you up on this proposition! Whether Licarbo hits big or not, I'll either have my own lab or work in a pharmacy someplace where I can get wholesale prices on drugs. So on a deal like this, neither one of us can lose!"

We shook hands, and I turned to go. Doc stopped me at the door by putting his hand on my arm. "Just a minute, Frank. As soon as I can afford it, I'm moving to a better office. And, of course, when I get enough capital, I'm going to build my own laboratories. But meanwhile, here's the address of the drugstore where I work." He handed me a card and I slipped it into my wallet. "I'm on duty there every Friday, Saturday and Sunday night from six to midnight. And almost every Wednesday from noon till midnight. I relieve the owner, you see. So when you need anything, drop me a line there, or come by and see me yourself."

I opened the door, and returned my wallet to my hip pocket.

"You going to put an entry in the Orlando tourney, Frank?"

I shook my head and pointed north.

"Southern Conference then?"

I nodded.

"Well, I'll probably see you in Milledgeville, then. I haven't missed an S.C.T. in ten years and I don't intend to now. And when you see any of the boys on the road, say hello for me, and tell them I still send out a few things when they write."

I winked, clapped him on the shoulder, and we shook hands again. I started down the hallway toward the stairwell and Doc watched me all the way. When I reached the stairs, he called good-bye to me again. I waved an arm and descended the stairs. At the drugstore on the corner I had a cup of coffee at the counter and then returned to my room at the Jeff Davis Hotel. Fortunately, I had kept my morning newspaper.

I turned to the classified ads and looked under the Help Wanted, Male section to see what I could do about getting a job.

Chapter Six

It is a funny thing. A man can make a promise to his God, break it five minutes later and never think anything about it. With an idle shrug of his shoulders, a man can also break solemn promises to his mother, wife or sweetheart, and, except for a slight, momentary twinge of conscience, he still won't be bothered very much. But if a man ever breaks a promise he has made to himself he disintegrates. His entire personality and character crumble into tiny pieces, and he is never the same man again.

I remember very well a sergeant I knew in the army. Before a group of five men he swore off smoking forever. An hour later he sheepishly lit a cigarette and broke his vow to the five of us and to himself. He was never quite the same man again, not to me, and not to himself.

My vow of silence was much harder to maintain than a vow to quit smoking. It was a definite handicap in everything I did. I read through the want ads three times, studying them carefully, and there wasn't a single thing I could find to do. A man who can't, or won't, talk is in a difficult situation when it comes to finding a job in the city. Besides, I had never had a job in my life—except for my two years in the service.

Of course, during my year of college at Valdosta State I had waited tables in the co-op for my meals, but I didn't consider that as a job. Growing up in Georgia, I had done farm work for my father when I couldn't get out of it, such things as chopping cotton, milking a cow, and simple carpentry repair jobs around the farm. There were a good many things I was capable of doing around a farm without having to talk. But the want ads in the newspaper were no help to me at all. Unwilling to use my voice, I couldn't even ask for a job unless I wrote it down. The majority of the situations that were open in the agate columns were for salesmen. And a man who can't talk can't sell anything. I wadded the newspaper into a ball, and tossed it into the wastebasket.

One thing I could always do was walk and condition cocks for another breeder. There were plenty of chicken men in the South who would have jumped at the chance to pay me five dollars apiece for every game fowl I conditioned for them. But for a man who was still considered a big-time cockfighter throughout the South, it would be too much of a comedown to work for another cock breeder. I had never worked for anybody else in my thirty-two years on this earth, and it was too late to start now. By God, I wasn't that desperate!

Sitting in that hotel room, with only a few loose dollars in my pocket, I was beginning to feel sorry for myself. My eyes rested on my guitar case.

My guitar was an old friend. During the first few months of my self-enforced silence, the days and nights had almost doubled in length. It is surprising how much time is killed everyday in idle conversation. Just to have something to fill in time I had purchased a secondhand Gibson guitar for thirty dollars in a Miami pawnshop. The case wasn't so hot—cheap brown cardboard stamped to resemble alligator leather—but the guitar was a good one, and it had a strong, wonderful tone. The guitar served as a substitute for my lost voice, and I don't know what I would have done without it.

I opened the guitar case, removed the instrument and ran through a few exercises to limber my fingers. I hadn't played the guitar for five or six days, but the calluses on my fingers were still hard and tough. The Uncle who sold me the Gibson had also thrown in a free instruction booklet, but I had never learned how to play any regular songs. After learning most of the chords and how to tune and pick the strings, I had tossed the booklet away.

I only knew three songs, and they were tunes I had made up myself, sitting around, picking them out until they sounded like the mental images I wanted them to resemble. One was "Georgia Girl." This was a portrait in sound of Mary Elizabeth, my fiancée. The second tune I had composed I called "Empty Pockets." My pockets had been empty many times in my life, and in making up this song I had discovered a way of getting a hollow sound effect by banging the box near the hole and playing a succession of fast triplets on the lower three strings at the same time. Despite the hollow sounds, this was a gay, fast tune and I was rather fond of it. The remaining song was merely my impression of an old patchwork quilt Grandma had made many years ago, and that's what I called it—"Grandma's Quilt." I had tried to duplicate the colors and designs of that old patchwork, faded quilt in chord patterns, and I had been fairly successful.

My repertoire, then, consisted of three highly personal songs. If it was music, it was reflective music made up for my own personal enjoyment, and not for the general public. But I had to get a few dollars together, and soon, and maybe my guitar was the way? I could have pawned the Gibson for twenty dollars or so, and this sum would pay a week's rent, but if I pawned the guitar, where would I be then?

I decided to take a chance and temporarily invade the world of music. As a last resort, when push came to shove, I could pawn the instrument. I removed my wristwatch, waited until the sweep hand hit twelve, picked up my guitar and played my three songs in succession all the way through. Time elapsed: seventeen minutes, fourteen seconds. Not a lot of time for a guitar concert, but I had nothing to lose by trying, and the songs were all different. Perhaps some bar owner would put me on for a few dollars in the evening.

I shucked out of my black cowboy shirt, which was getting dirty around the collar, even though it didn't show very much, and changed into a clean white shirt. I retied my red silk neckerchief, slipped into my corduroy suit and looked at myself in the dresser mirror. I looked clean and presentable. The red kerchief looked good with a white shirt and my gray-green corduroy suit. The cheap straw cowboy hat pushed back from my forehead was just the right touch for a would-be guitar player. I had burned my name into the yellow box of my guitar with a hot wire two years before, so all I had to do was write something simple on a piece of paper and get going.

I took a fresh sheet of paper out of my notebook, sat down at the desk and looked at it, trying to figure out a strong selling point for my slender abilities. At last it came to me, a simple straightforward statement of fact. In large capital letters I wrote JOB on the page, and put the slip of paper in my shirt pocket. If a prospective owner was interested in the word JOB he would give me an audition. If I got an audition, my guitar would have to talk for me.

I checked the little square felt-covered box inside the case, and there were plenty of extra plastic picks and two new strings wrapped in wax paper. As I started toward the door, carrying my guitar, I caught a glimpse of my grim, determined expression in the mirror. I almost laughed. I made an obscene gesture with my thumb at my grinning reflection and left the room.

The time was only ten thirty. There were dozens of bars, cabarets and beer-and-wine joints in Jacksonville, and I decided to cover them all, one by one, until I found a job.

I entered the first bar I came to down the street and handed the slip of paper to the bartender. He glanced at it, gave it back and pointed to the door.

At the bar on the next corner I tried a different tactic. I had learned a lesson in the first bar. Before presenting my slip of paper to the man in the white jacket, I made the sign of the tall one, and put change on the bar to pay for the beer. Beer is the easiest drink there is to order, whether you can talk or not. No matter how noisy a place is you can always get a bartender's attention by holding stiff hands out straight, the right hand approximately one foot above the left. This gesture will always produce a beer, draft if they have it, or a can of some brand if they do not.

"Sorry, buddy," the bartender returned my slip of paper, "but I don't have a music and dancing license. I couldn't hire you if I wanted to."

I finished my glass of beer and returned to the sidewalk. A license for music and dancing had never occurred to me, but that simple requirement narrowed my search. I decided to become more selective. After bypassing several unlikely bars, and walking a half-dozen blocks, I came to a fairly nice-looking cabaret. There was a small blue winking neon sign in the window that stated Chez Vernon. The entranceway was between a men's haberdashery and a closed movie theater. To the left of the bar entrance another door opened into the package store, which was also a part of the nightclub, and there was a sandwich board on the sidewalk announcing that the James Boys were featured inside every night except Sunday.

There were four eight-by-ten photos of the James Boys mounted on the board, and I studied them for a moment before I went inside. They wore their hair long, almost to the shoulder, but they had on Western-style clothes. They were evidently a country music group. In the smiling photos two of them had Spanish guitars like mine, one held an electric guitar and the remaining member peeped out from behind a bass. I entered the bar.

The bar was in a fairly narrow corridor—most of the space it should have had was crowded out by the partitioning for the package store—but there were approximately twenty-five stools, and a short service bar at the far end. Only one bartender was on duty, and there was only one customer sitting at the first stool. The customer sat with his arms locked behind his back glaring down distastefully at a double shot of whiskey. At night, with a fair-sized crowd, a bar this long would require at least two bartenders.

Beyond the bar there was a large square room with a small dance floor, a raised triangular platform in the corner for the musicians and two microphones. There were about thirty-five small circular tables, with twisted wire ice-cream parlor chairs stacked on top of them. The walls of the large room had been painted in navy blue. Silver cardboard stars had been pasted at random upon the wall and ceiling to simulate a night sky. The ceiling was black, and the scattered light fixtures on the ceiling were in various pastel colors.

Between the bar and nightclub section there were two lavatories, with their doors recessed about a foot into the wall. A crude effort at humor had been attempted on the rest-room doors: One was labeled SETTERS and the other POINTERS. After sizing the place up, I sat down at the far end of the bar and made the sign of the tall one. As I reached for the stein with my left hand, I handed the bartender the slip of paper with my right.

"I only work here," he said indifferently, eyeing my guitar. "The James Boys are supposed to play out the month, but the boss is in the back." He pointed to a curtain covering an arched doorway near the right corner of the bandstand. "Go ahead and talk to him if you want to." His face colored slightly as he realized I couldn't talk, but he smiled and shrugged his shoulders. "His name is Mr. Vernon. Lee Vernon."

As soon as I finished my beer, I picked up my guitar, dropped a half dollar on the bar and headed for the back, pushing the curtain to one side. The hallway was short. There was a door leading to an alley, and two doors on either side. I opened the first door on the right, but it was a small dressing room. I knocked at the door opposite the dressing room and didn't enter until I heard "Come in."

For a nightclub owner, Lee Vernon was a much younger man than I expected to meet. He was under thirty, with a mass of black curls, a smiling well-tanned face, and gleaming china-blue eyes. There were three open ledgers on his gray metal desk and a few thick Manila folders. He tapped his large white teeth with a pencil and raised his black eyebrows. I removed my guitar from the case before I handed him the slip of paper.

Lee Vernon laughed aloud when he saw the word JOB and shook his head from side to side with genuine amusement. "A nonsinging guitar player!" he exclaimed, still smiling. "I never thought I'd see the day. Go ahead"—he looked at my name burned into the guitar box—"Frank, is it?"

I nodded, and wiped my damp fingers on my jacket so the plastic pick wouldn't slip in my fingers. I put my left foot on a chair, and cradled the instrument over my knee.

"Play anything, Frank," Vernon smiled. "I don't care. I've never turned down an excuse to quit working in my life."

I vamped a few chords and then played "Empty Pockets" all the way through. Mr. Vernon listened attentively, tapping his pencil on the desk in time with the music. This was the shortest of my three songs, but it sounded good in the tiny office. The ceiling was low and there was a second listen effect reverberating in the room, especially during the thumping part.

"I like the sound, Frank," Vernon said. "You're all right. All right. But I don't think I can use you right now. I'm trying to build the Chez Vernon into a popular night spot, and the James Boys pretty well fill the bill. I pay them eight hundred a week and if I pay much more than that for music, I'll be working for them instead of for myself. Do you belong to the union, Frank?"

I shook my head. The idea of any free American male paying gangsters money for the right to work has always struck me as one of the most preposterous customs we have.

"Tell you what," Vernon said reflectively. "Do you really need a job?"

I nodded seriously.

"Okay, then. The James Boys play a forty-minute set, and then they take a twenty-minute break. They play from nine till midnight, an extra hour if the crowd warrants it, and till two a.m. on Saturday nights. In my opinion, a twenty-minute break is too long, and I lose customers sometimes just because of it, but those were the terms I hired them under. If you want to sit in by yourself on the stand to fill the breaks I'm willing to try it for a few nights to see how it goes. I can give you ten bucks a night, but that's the limit."

For a few moments I thought about it, but ten dollars was too much money to give me when I only knew three songs. I held up five fingers.

"You want fifty dollars?" Vernon asked incredulously.

I shook my head and snapped out five fingers.

"You're a pretty weird cat." Vernon laughed. "Not only do you not sing, you're honest. Five bucks a night it is, Frank. But I'll tell Dick James to clean out his kitty between his sets, and any tips you get on the breaks belong to you. You'll pick up a few extra bucks, anyway."

I nodded, shook hands with my employer and returned my guitar to its case.

"Come in about eight thirty, Frank," Vernon concluded the interview, "and I'll introduce you to the James Boys."

I returned to the hotel and stretched out on my bed for a nap. Although I had taken a lower figure than the ten he offered, I still felt a little uneasy. After Lee Vernon heard me playing the same songs all evening he wouldn't be too happy about it. But during the days, maybe I could make up a few more. If so, I could ask for a raise to ten. The immediate problem was remedied. I could pay my room rent of three dollars a day, and eat on the other two until I could work my way out of the hole with an ingenious plan of some kind.

A few minutes later I was asleep.

Chapter Seven

The James Boys were very good. If Lee Vernon was paying them eight hundred dollars a week, they were worth every cent of it.

I sat at the end of the bar where I could take in the entire room, enjoying the music and the singing, and the antics of the patrons at various tables. Not many of the couples danced. It wasn't the smallness of the floor that prevented them from getting to their feet, it was just that the James Boys were more amusing to watch than they were to dance to. They wore red Western shirts with white piping on the collars and cuffs, but they didn't restrict their playing to Western music. They seemed to be equally at home with calypso and rock 'n' roll. Each of the boys, in turn, sang into the microphone, and they all had good voices.

Dick James was at the microphone, and his face had a mournful expression. He said, "It is now my sad duty to inform you, ladies and gentlemen, that for the next twenty minutes we will be absent from the stand."

He held up a hand to silence the murmurs of disappointment. "We don't want to go. Honest! It's just that we can't afford to drink here. We have to go down the street to a little place where the drinks are cheaper. And I might add," he said disingenuously, "unwatered!"

A very small ripple of laughter went through the room. Perhaps the patrons of the Chez Vernon thought their drinks were watered.

"But during our brief absence, the management has obtained for your listening pleasure, at *great* expense, one of the world's greatest guitarists! Ladies and gentlemen, I give you Frank Mansfield!"

I had been so engrossed in watching and listening, and

drinking a steady procession of beers, I hadn't realized how quickly the time had passed. To a burst of enthusiastic applause, led by the four James Boys, I threaded my way through the close-packed tables to the stand. As I sat down in a chair on the stand and removed my guitar from its case, Dick James lowered the microphone level with my waist.

"Good luck, Frank," he said, and followed the other members of the group into the hallway leading to the dressing room. I was in shirt sleeves, but wore my hat. I wished that I could have gone with them, picked up my coat in the dressing room, and made a getaway through the back door to the alley. In anticipation of fresh entertainment, the audience was fairly quiet. I felt like every eye was on me as I sat under the baby spot on the small, triangular stand.

I delayed as long as I could, well aware that I had twenty full minutes to fill before the James Boys returned, and not enough music to fill it with. I vamped a few chords, tuned the "A" string a trifle higher, and then played "Empty Pockets." The moment I hit the last chord, I got to my feet and bowed from the waist to the thin, sporadic applause. Before playing "Grandma's Quilt," I went through the motions of tuning again, and slowed the tempo of the song as I picked through it. The applause was stronger when I finished. By this time the crowd realized that my music was unusual, or, at least, different. My last number was the best, my favorite, and my nervousness had disappeared completely. There was hardly a sound from the audience as I played "Georgia Girl," but when I finished and stood up to take a bow, the applause was definitely generous.

"I could take lessons from you," Dick James said, as he climbed onto the stand. "You make some mighty fine sounds, Frankerino."

I nodded, smiled and wet my lips. The James Boys were also unaware that my repertoire only consisted of three homemade numbers. Lee Vernon, a tall drink in his hand, crossed the room and congratulated me. He whispered something to Dick, and readjusted the microphone. I had returned my guitar to the case and was halfway to the bar when Vernon's voice rasped out of the speakers in the ceiling.

"Ladies and gentlemen, there's something you don't

know about Frank Mansfield!" His voice stopped me, and I looked down at the floor. "In view of his great manual dexterity, it may be difficult to believe, but Frank Mansfield is the only deaf-and-dumb guitar player in the world! Let's give Frank another big hand? Let him feel the vibrations through the floor!"

As the drunken crowd applauded wildly and stomped their feet on the floor, I ran across the room, pushed aside the curtain to the hallway, and rushed blindly into the dressing room. I supposed Lee Vernon meant well, but I was angered by his announcement. Not only did I want to quit, I wanted to punch him in the nose. In view of his stupid announcement, he would be damned well embarrassed when I played the same three songs forty minutes later.

There was an open bottle of bourbon on the dressing table. I hit it a couple of times and smoked five cigarettes before my next appearance on the stand. Tiny James, the bass player, came and got me.

"You're on, Mansfield." He jerked his thumb. "Dick's announced you already."

I returned to the stand and got out my guitar. The room had twice as many patrons and the air was blue with smoke. Vernon's announcement had created a morbid interest. The bar crowd had pushed their way in and standees blocked the way to the service bar. The moment I picked up my instrument and strummed a few triplets, there were shushing sounds from the tables and the room was silent.

Indifferently, expertly, I played through my three numbers without pause. The applause was generous. I put the guitar back in the case and made my exit to the dressing room. When the door closed on the last James Boy I took a pull out of the open bottle of whiskey. Lee Vernon entered the room. His face was flushed and he was laughing. He held out a hand for the bottle and, when I handed it to him, freshened the drink in his left hand.

Watching him sullenly, I took another drink out of the bottle. Vernon let loose with a wild peal of happy laughter.

"Those are the only three songs you know, aren't they?" he said.

I grinned and took another short drink.

"That's wonderful, Frank," he said sincerely. "Really

wonderful!" He smiled broadly, showing his big white teeth. "Did you make them up yourself?"

I nodded.

A frown creased Vernon's flushed face, and he placed his glass down carefully on the narrow ledge in front of the mirror. He's going to fire me, I thought. The moment I put the five-dollar bill in my pocket I'm going to knock his teeth out.

"I think that's terrific, Frank. I really do. Any fool can take a few lessons and play ordinary songs on a guitar. Hell, I can play a little bit myself, and if I sing while I'm playing, I can drown out the mistakes I make. But you . . ." He shook his head comically. "To deliberately master the damned guitar the way you have and compose your own songs—well, I can only admire you for it." He picked up his glass and raised it. "To Frank Mansfield! You've got a job at the Chez Vernon for as long as you want to keep it!"

He drained his glass and opened the door. His shoulder hit the side of the door as he left, and he staggered slightly as he walked down the hall.

I closed the door and sat down, facing the back of the chair. If a man accepts life logically, the unexpected is actually the expected. I should have known he wouldn't fire me. A nightclub owner, by the fact that he is a nightclub owner, must necessarily accept things as they are. Vernon had accepted the situation cheerfully, like a peacetime soldier who finds himself suddenly in a war. There was nothing else he could do.

I had wanted to quit, but now I was unable to quit. I was in an untenable position. I had only one alternative. Every time I played my twenty-minute stint, I would have to improvise something new. If I couldn't do it, I would have to walk away and not even stop to collect the five dollars I had coming to me. It was unfair to keep playing the same three songs over and over.

I took another drink, a short one this time. I was beginning to feel the effects of the whiskey on top of the beers I had had earlier. I made my decision. When my turn came to play again I would improvise music and play something truly wonderful.

After Dick James announced me, I sat quietly in my chair, the guitar across my lap, a multicolored pick gripped loosely between my right thumb and forefinger. The room was filled to capacity. Under the weak, colored ceiling lights I could make out most of the faces nearest the stand. There was a hint of nervous expectancy in the room. Here is a freak, their silence said, a talented, deaf-and-dumb freak who plays music he cannot hear, who plays for applause he can only feel. This was the atmosphere of the Chez Vernon, caused in part by Lee Vernon's earlier announcement, and by my last session on the stand when the listeners had heard a different kind of music. Vernon sat at a table close to the platform, his face flushed with liquor, a knowing smile on his lips. On his left was a young man with long blond hair, dressed in a red silk dinner jacket, white ruffled shirt, and plaid bow tie. On Vernon's right, a tall pink drink before her, was a woman in a low-cut Kelly green evening gown. She was in her early forties, but she was the type who could pass easily for thirty-nine for a few more years.

Her lips were wet and shiny, and her dark eyes were bright with excitement as I caught them with mine and held them. She nodded politely, put long tapering fingers to her coal black hair. The woman and the young man at Vernon's table stood out from the crowd. Most of the patrons were wearing short-sleeved sport shirts. Only the younger men with dates wore coats and ties. Lee Vernon raised his glass and winked at me.

The microphone was less than a foot away from my guitar. I tapped the pick on the box. The sound, amplified by six speakers, sounded like knocking on a wooden door. Scratching the wooden box of the Gibson produced a sound like the dry rasping of locusts. The locusts reminded me of the long summer evenings in Mansfield, Georgia, and I thought about the bright silvery moths circling the lamp on the corner, down the street from Grandma's house.

I played their sound, picking them up and flying and flickering with them about the streetlight, teasing them on the "E" string.

Down the block, swinging to and fro on a lacy, metal porch swing, the chains creaking, complaining, a woman laughed, the joyful, contented laughter of a well-bred southern woman, a mother perhaps, with two young children, a boy and a girl, and the little boy said something that amused her and she laughed and repeated what the child said to her husband sitting beside her.

I played that.

And I repeated the solid rumbling laugh of her husband, which complemented her own laughter, and then my fingers moved away from them, up the staff to pick out the solid swishing whispering smack of a lawn sprinkler and a man's tuneless humming a block away. And there came a boy in knickers down the sidewalk, walking and then running, dancing with awkward feet to avoid stepping on a crack, which would *surely* break his mother's back! He bent down and picked up a stick and scampered past a white picket fence, the stick bumping, rattling, drowning out a man's lecture to a teen-aged girl on the porch of that old white house two doors down from the corner, the house with the four white columns.

And I played these things, and

then the sounds of supper and the noises, the fine good clatter in the kitchen when Grandma was still alive, and Randall and I sent to wash up before dinner in the dark downstairs bathroom where the sound of water in the pipes made the whiney, sharp, unbearable spine-tingling noise and kept it up until the other tap was turned on and modulated it, turning the groaning into the surreptitious scraping of a boy's finger on a blackboard, and sure enough, we had the schoolteacher for dinner that night and she was talking with Mother, monotonously, like always, and I hated her, and the dry, flat registers of her authoritative voice would put you to sleep in the middle of a lesson if you didn't keep pinching yourself, and Daddy pulled out his watch with the loud ticks and it was suppertime, the solid ring of the good sterling silver, the tingle-tinkle of the fine crystal that pinged with a fingernail and listen to the echo! and the rich dark laughter of Aimee, our Negro cook in the kitchen, and after supper I was allowed to go to the movie but Randall wasn't because he was three years younger and had to go to bed

so I played these things and

what a wonderful movie it was! Young Dick Powell, handsome, in his West Point uniform, and the solid ranks of straight tall men marching in the parade and only vaguely did the old songs filter through the story, *Flirtation Walk*, and the lovely girl under the Kissing Rock, and then the movie was over but I stayed to see it again, and repeated it very quickly because nothing is ever any good the second time and I was late, it was dark, and I was running down the black narrow streets, the crickets silenced ahead of my slapping feet, and the grim and heavy shadows of the great old pecan trees on our black, forbidding block. As I reached our yard, safe at last from whatever it was that chased me, Mother was on the front porch waiting with a switch in her hand, and she intended to use it, I know, but I began to cry and a moment later she pulled me in close to her warm, wonderful, never changing smell of powder, spicy lilac and cedar and sweet, sweet lips kissing me and chiding and kissing and scolding and

damned if the "G" string didn't break.

The pick fell from my fingers and I looked numbly at the guitar. The room was as silent as death. A moment later, like an exploding dam, the room rocked with the sound of slapping hands and stomping feet. I fled into the dressing room with the guitar still clutched by the neck in my left hand. The James Boys, who had been listening by the arched, curtained doorway to the hall, followed me into the small room, and Dick handed me the bottle.

"I'll be a sonofabitch, Frank," he said warmly. "I never heard finer guitar in my life. You can be a James Boy anytime you want. Go ahead, take another snort!"

I sat down, lit a cigarette and studied my trembling fingers. My throat was dry and tight and for the first time in my life I felt lonely, really lonely, and I didn't know why. I had buried all those memories for so many years, it was frightening to know that they were still in my head.

The James Boys returned to the stand, leaving the door open, and I could hear the heated strings of their first number, "The big D Rock."

"Mr. Mansfield—" I looked up at the sound of Lee Vernon's voice, and got to my feet quickly as he ushered in ahead of him the young man and the woman who had been sitting at his table out front. "I want to introduce you to Mrs. Bernice Hungerford and Tommy Hungerford." He turned and smiled at the woman. "Mr. Frank Mansfield."

"Tommy is my nephew," Bernice Hungerford said quickly, holding out her hand. I shook it briefly, and then shook hands with her nephew. His expression was studiedly bored, but he was slightly nervous.

Mrs. Hungerford was a truly striking woman, now that I could see her under the bright lights of the dressing room. A white cashmere stole was draped over her left arm, and she clutched a gold-mesh evening bag in her left hand. Her burnt sienna eyes never left my face. I was amused by the scattering of freckles on her straight nose. The freckles on her face and bare shoulders belied her age sure enough.

With a straight face, Vernon said: "Mrs. Hungerford was very impressed by your concert, Mr. Mansfield. When I told her that you had studied under Segovia in Seville for ten years, she said she could tell that you had by your intricate fretwork."

Bernice Hungerford bobbed her head up and down delightedly and shook a teasing forefinger at me. "And I recognized the tone poem, too." She winked and flashed a bright smile. Her teeth were small, but remarkably well matched and white. "You see, Mr. Mansfield," she continued, "I know a few things about music. When I hear Bach, it doesn't make any difference if it's piano or guitar, I can recognize the style. That's what I told Mr. Vernon, didn't I, Lee?" The woman turned to the implacable Lee Vernon who was covering his drunkenness masterfully. Only the stiffness of his back gave him away.

"You certainly did, Bernice. But I had to tell her, Mr. Mansfield. She thought you were playing a Bach fugue, but it was a natural mistake. She didn't know that it was a special Albert Schweitzer composition written on a theme of Bach's. Quite a natural mistake, indeed."

"If we don't get back to your guests, their throats will be dreadfully parched, Auntie dear," Tommy said lazily. "We've been gone, you know, for the better part of an hour, and that's a long time just to refurbish the liquor supply." The careless elisions of his voice were practiced, it seemed to me.

73

"But if we take Mr. Mansfield back with us, we'll be forgiven." Mrs. Hungerford patted her nephew's arm.

"I don't want to hold you up any longer, Mrs. Hungerford," Vernon said. "Why don't you and Tommy wait in the package store. Your liquor is ready, and I'll do my best to bring Mr. Mansfield along in a minute. All right?"

"But you will persuade him, won't you?" Mrs. Hungerford said.

"I'll certainly try," he replied cheerfully.

As soon as they had gone, Vernon closed the door, leaned against it and buried his face in his arms. His shoulders shook convulsively, and for a moment I thought he was crying. Then he let out a whoop of laughter, turned away from the door and sat down. Recovering, he wiped his streaming eyes with a forefinger and said, "I'm sorry, Frank, but the gag was too good to resist. When she started that talk about Bach and Segovia at the table, I had to go her one better. But it's a break for you. She has a few guests at her house, and only stopped by here to pick up some Scotch. I told her that she mustn't miss your performance, and when you came out with that tricky, weird chording and impressed her so much, I thought it might be a break for you. Anyway, the upshot is that she wants you to go home with her and play for her guests. Should be worth a twenty-dollar bill to you, at least."

I shrugged into my corduroy jacket. All through the talk about Bach and Segovia I had thought they were attempting some kind of joke at my expense, but apparently Mrs. Hungerford actually believed I had studied under the old guitarist. Vernon had gone along with the gag, which was a break for me, although I detested the condescending sonofabitch. If she wanted to pay me twenty dollars I would accept it, play my three songs, and then get out of her house. I had already made up my mind not to return to the Chez Vernon. A final concert for a group of rich people who could afford to pay for it and wouldn't miss the money would be a fitting end to my short, unhappy musical career.

"By the way, Frank," Vernon said, as soon as I was ready to go, "don't get the idea that I was trying to make fun of you by falling in with the gag. If I'd been strictly sober, I might have set her straight, but basically I poured it on so you could pick up a few extra bucks. No hard feelings?"

I ignored his outstretched hand, and brushed by him, carrying my instrument. Vernon followed me out into the club. As I stopped at the stand, to put the guitar in the case, he handed me a ten-dollar bill.

"Hell, don't be sore about it, Frank."

There was a black silhouette cutout of a plyboard cat at the end of the stand. I wadded the bill in my fist and shoved it into the open mouth of the kitty before crossing the dance floor and entering the inside door to the package store. If Lee Vernon had followed me into the package store, I would have knocked his teeth out, even if he was drunk. Although I wasn't the butt of the joke, I didn't like to be patronized by a man I considered an inferior. But Vernon was wise enough not to come outside, and I've never seen him since.

Tommy drove the Olds and Mrs. Hungerford sat between us on the wide front seat. With the guitar case between my legs, my left leg was tight against her right leg, and I could feel the warmth of her body through my corduroy trousers.

"This isn't exactly a party, Mr. Mansfield," she explained, as we drove through the light traffic of the after-midnight streets. "We all attended the Jacksonville Little Theater to see *Liliom,* and I invited the bunch home for a cold supper and a few drinks. It was a real faux pas on my part. There's plenty of food, but I didn't realize I was out of Scotch. But bringing you home to play will more than make up for my oversight, I'm sure. Don't you think so, Tommy?"

"If they're still there," he observed dryly.

"Don't worry," Mrs. Hunferford laughed pleasantly, "I know my brother!" She turned toward me and put her hand lightly on my knee. "There are only two couples, Mr. Mansfield. Tommy's father and mother, and Dr. Luke McGuire and his wife. Not a very large audience, I'm afraid, after what you're accustomed to, is it?"

In reply, I spat out the window.

"But I know you'll find them appreciative of good music."

A few minutes later we turned into a driveway guarded by two small concrete lions. Tommy parked behind a Buick on the semicircular gravel road that led back to the street. The two-story house was of red brick. Four fluted wooden columns supported a widow's walk directly above the wide, aluminum-screened front porch. The lawn slanted gradually to the street for almost a hundred yards, broken here and there with newly planted coconut palms. The feathery tips of the young trees rattled in the wind. She was wasting money and effort attempting to grow coconut trees as far north as Jax. The subtropics start at Daytona Beach, much farther downstate.

Mrs. Hungerford rushed ahead of us after we got out of the car. Tommy, carrying two sacked fifths of Scotch under his left arm and a six-pack of soda in his right hand, hurried after her. As I climbed the porch steps, Mrs. Hungerford switched on the overhead lights and opened the front doors. She held a finger to her lips, as she beckoned me into the foyer with her free hand.

"Now, you stay right here in the foyer," Mrs. Hungerford whispered excitedly, "so I can surprise them!"

Closing the front door softly, she followed her nephew into the living room. The voices greeting them contained a mixture of concern over the prolonged absence, and happiness at the prospect of a drink. Above the sound of their conversation, the clipped electronic voice of a newscaster rattled through his daily report of the late news.

The foyer was carpeted in a soft shade of rose nylon. The same carpeting climbed the stairway to the walnut-balustraded second floor. A giant split-leaved philodendron sat in a white pot behind the door. There was a spindly-legged, leather-covered table beneath a gilded wall mirror, and a brass dish on the table held about thirty calling cards. Out of long-forgotten habit I felt a few of the cards to see if they were engraved. They were. I turned my attention to a marble cherub mounted on a square, ebony base. It was about three feet high, and the well-weathered cherub looked shyly with its dugout eyes through widespread stubby fingers. A lifted, twisted right knee hid its sex, and three fingers of the left hand were missing. I removed my cowboy hat and hung it on the thumb of the mutilated hand.

The bored announcer was clicked off in midsentence, and

Mrs. Hungerford came after me a moment later.

"They're all tickled to death, Mr. Mansfield," she said happily. "Come on, they want to meet you!"

In one corner of the large living room, Tommy was engaged behind a small bar. Two middle-aged men got out of their chairs and crossed the room to greet me. Dr. McGuire was a thick-set man without a neck, and his gray hair was badly in need of cutting. Mr. Hungerford, Sr., Tommy's father, was an older edition of his blond son, except that he no longer had his hair and the top of his head was bronzed by the Florida sun. Both of the men wore white dinner jackets and midnight blue tuxedo trousers. I acknowledged the introductions by nodding my head and shaking hands. The two wives remained seated on a long, curving white sofa, and didn't offer their hands to be shaken.

"I know you're all eager to hear Mr. Mansfield play," Bernice announced to the room at large, "but you'll have to wait until he has a drink first."

Welcome news. After dropping my guitar case on the sofa I headed for the bar.

"There's plenty of gin if you don't want Scotch," Tommy suggested.

I poured two ounces of Scotch into a tall glass in reply, and added ice cubes and soda. An uneasy silence settled over the room as I hooked my elbows over the bar and faced the group. Bernice, or Tommy, one, had evidently informed them about my inability to talk, and they were disturbed by my silence. The two matrons, bulging in strapless evening gowns, had difficulty in averting their eyes from my face. I doubt if they meant to be rude, but they couldn't keep from staring at me. Dr. McGuire, standing with his back to the fireplace, lit a cigar and studied the tip through his bifocals. Only Bernice was at ease, sitting comfortably on the long bench in front of the baby grand piano, apparently unaware of her guests' discomfort. Mr. Hungerford, Sr., cleared his throat and set his glass down on a low coffee table.

"Bernice tells us you studied under Segovia, Mr. Mansfield," he said.

"Yes," Bernice replied for me, "That's what Mr. Vernon told us, didn't he, Tommy?"

"That's right. And he played a beautiful thing written by Dr. Albert Schweitzer. I hope he'll play it again for us."

"African rock 'n' roll, I suppose," Dr. McGuire chuckled from the fireplace. "That would be a treat!" When no one joined him in his laughter, he said quickly, "We're very grateful you came out to play for us, Mr. Mansfield."

I finished my drink, lifted my eyebrows for Tommy Hungerford to mix me another. I took my guitar out of the case, and started to restring it with another "G" string to replace the broken one. While I restrung the guitar, Mrs. Hungerford asked her brother and the doctor to move chairs into the center of the room and form a line. She then had her guests sit in the rearranged chairs facing me, as I stood with one foot on the piano bench. Tommy Hungerford, smiling at the new seating arrangements, remained standing at the bar. I plucked and tightened the new string, and Bernice hit the "G" on the piano for me until I had the guitar in tune. Satisfied, I put the guitar on the bench and returned to the bar for my fresh drink. The small audience waited patiently, but Dr. McGuire glowered when Tommy insisted that I have another before I began. I shook my head, picked up my guitar and played through my three-song repertoire without pause.

The moment I hit the last chord I smiled, bowed from the waist and put the guitar back in the case. Bernice Hungerford, who had hovered anxiously behind the row of chairs during my short concert, led the applause.

"Is that all he's going to play, Bernice?" the doctor asked. "I'd like to hear more."

"I think we all would," his fat wife echoed.

I shrugged, and joined Tommy at the bar for another drink.

"No, that's enough," Bernice said. "Mr. Mansfield has been playing all evening and he's tired. We shouldn't coax him. The concert is all over. Go on home. You've been fed, you've had your drinks, now go on home."

Bernice herded the two wives out of the room to get their wraps, and their husbands joined Tommy and me at the bar for a nightcap.

"You play very well, young man," Dr. McGuire said. "Did you ever play on television?"

I shook my head, and added Scotch to my glass to cut the soda.

"I think you should consider television, don't you, Tommy?"

"Not really, sir," Tommy wrinkled his brow. "I'm not so sure that the mass audience is ready for classical guitar music. I'm trying to recall, but I can't remember ever hearing or seeing a string quartet on television. If I did, I can't remember it."

"By God, I haven't either!" the doctor said strongly. "And certainly the string quartet is the most civilized entertainment in the world! Don't you agree, Mr. Mansfield?"

I shrugged my shoulders inside my jacket, and lit a cigarette.

He didn't want a reply, anyway. "But there's a definite need for serious music on TV," he continued. "And, by God, the public should be forced to listen! No matter how stupid people are today, they can be taught to appreciate good music." He banged his fist on the bar.

The two middle-aged men drained their glasses quickly as Bernice came into the room, and turned to join their wives in the foyer. Bernice crossed the room, and placed a hand on my arm. So far, she had never missed a chance to touch me.

"Mrs. McGuire would like to know if you'd consent to play for her guests next Saturday night. She's giving a party, quite a large one, and she's willing to—"

I shook my head, and crushed out my cigarette in a white Cinzano ashtray.

"It's 'no,' then?"

I nodded. She smiled, turned away and returned to the foyer to say good night to her guests and break the news to Mrs. McGuire.

"Tell me something, Mr. Mansfield," Tommy said hesitantly. "Did you really study under Segovia?"

I grinned, and shook my head. After setting my glass down, I picked up my guitar case. Tommy laughed, throwing his head back.

"I didn't think you did, but I'll keep your secret till the day I die."

Bernice Hungerford returned with a smile brightening

her jolly face. I didn't know why, but I was attracted to this graceful, pleasant woman. She appeared to be so happy, so eager to please, and yet, there were tiny, tragic lines tugging at the corners of her full lips.

"I'll drive Mr. Mansfield back into town, Auntie," Tommy said.

"Oh, no you won't!" Bernice said cheerfully. She took the guitar case out of my hand and placed it on the couch. "I'll drive him back myself. You can just run along, Tommy. I'm going to fix Mr. Mansfield something to eat—you could eat something, couldn't you?"

I shrugged, then smiled. She hadn't paid the twenty dollars yet, and I could always eat something. The cold buffet supper, however, didn't appeal to me. There were several choices of lunch meat, cold pork, three different cheese dips and pickles. I looked distastefully at the buffet table.

"Now, don't you worry," Bernice said, patting my arm with her small, white hand. "I won't make you eat the remains of the cold supper. I'll fix you some ham and eggs."

"Me, too, Auntie dear?" Tommy grinned.

"No, not you. Don't you have a job of some kind to report to in the morning?"

Tommy groaned. "Don't remind me. Well, good night, Mr. Mansfield." He shook hands with me, brushed his lips against his aunt's cheek and made his departure from the room. A few moments later the lights of his Olds flashed on the picture window as he made the semicircle to the street.

Now that we were alone in the big house, Bernice's composure suddenly disappeared. She blushed furiously under my level stare, and then took my hand. "Come on," she said brightly. "You can keep me company in the kitchen while I cook for you."

I followed her into the kitchen, and sat down at a small dinette table covered with a blue-and-white tablecloth. There were louvered windows on all three sides of the small dining alcove, but the kitchen itself, like those of most depression-built homes, was a large one. The cooking facilities were up to date, however. In addition to a new yellow enameled electric stove, there was a built-in oven with a glass door, and a row of complicated-looking knobs beneath it.

"There's coffee left, but its been setting on the warm burner so long it's probably bitter by now. I'd better make fresh coffee, if you don't mind waiting awhile, but by that time I'll have the other things ready. I think that coffee setting too long gets bitter, don't you? I've got some mashed potatoes left over from dinner, and I'll make some nice patties to go with your ham."

Bernice kept a running patter of meaningless small talk going as she cooked, and I listened thoughtfully and smoked, watching her deft, efficient movements from my chair. She had tied a frilly, ruffled white apron about her waist, and it looked out of whack with her Kelly green evening gown. She kept talking about pleasant things to eat, and I got hungrier by the second.

She wanted to please me, even though she didn't know why. She knew she was a good cook, and by cooking a decent meal for me, she knew I would be pleased. If I was pleased with her, I'd take her to bed. These thoughts probably never entered her conscious mind, but I sensed this, and knew instinctively that she was mine if I wanted her. As she chattered away, gaily, cheerfully, I learned that I did want her, very much so. She was a damned attractive woman, a little heavy in the thighs, perhaps, but I didn't consider that a detriment. I like women a little on the fleshy side. Skinny, boyish-type figures may be admired by other women, but not by most men.

I smiled appreciatively, showing my teeth, when she set the huge platter before me. The aroma of the fried ham steak, four fried eggs, and fluffy potato pancakes all blended beautifully as they entered my nose. Bernice poured two steaming cups of fresh coffee and sat down across from me to watch me eat, her face flushed from recent exertion and pleasure as I stowed the food away.

"I should have made biscuits," she said, "but I could tell you were too hungry to wait, so I made the toast instead. Would you like some guava jelly for your toast?" She started to get up, but I shook my head violently, and she remained seated.

A minute later she smiled. "I like to see a man eat," she said sincerely.

I've heard a lot of women make that trite remark:

81

Grandma, Mother, when she was still alive, and a good many others. I believe women really do like to see men eat, especially when they're fond of the man concerned, and he's eating food they have prepared for him. I have never denied any woman the dubious pleasure of watching me eat. Outside of taking care of a man's needs, women don't get very much pleasure out of life anyway.

When I finished eating everything in sight, I pushed the empty platter to one side, and wiped my mouth with a square of white damask napkin. Smiling over the lip of her cup, Bernice nodded with satisfaction. I winked slowly, returned her smile, and she blushed and lowered her eyes.

"My husband's been dead for five years, Mr. Mansfield," she said shyly. "You don't know how nice it is to cook a meal for a man again. I'd almost forgotten myself. I loved my husband very much, and still do, I suppose. My brother's always telling me how foolish I am to keep this big house and live here all alone. An apartment would be easier to keep, I know, and give me more free time, but I don't know what I'd do with more free time if I had it. I don't know what to do with myself half the time as it is.

"This old house has a lot of pleasant memories for me, and I'd miss them if I ever sold it. I can see my husband in every room. Sometimes, during the day, I pretend he isn't dead at all. He's at the office, that's where he is, working, and when six o'clock comes he'll be coming home through the front door like always, and . . ." Her voice trailed away, and two tears escaped into her long black eyelashes.

Bernice wiped them away, tossed her head impatiently and laughed.

"Morbid, aren't I? How about some more coffee?"

I nodded, took my cigarettes out of my shirt pocket, and offered them to her. She put the cork tip in her mouth, and when I flipped my lighter, she held my hand with both of hers to get a light. This was unnecessary. My hand was perfectly steady. After refilling the cups, she sat down again and described circles on the tablecloth with a long red fingernail.

"I know that you want to go, Mr. Mansfield," she said at last, "but I'm finding this a novel experience. It's a rare instance when a woman can pour her troubles into a man's receptive ear without being told to shut up!" She laughed, and shrugged comically.

"But I really don't have any troubles. As far as money goes, I'm fixed forever. My husband saw to that, God bless him. I own the house, and my trust fund is well guarded by the bank trustees. And I have a circle of friends I've known most of my adult life. So where are my troubles?" She sighed audibly and licked her lips with the point of her tongue like a cat.

"I should be the happiest woman in the world. But once in a while, just once in a while, mind you, Mr. Mansfield, I'd like to go into my bathroom and find the toilet seat up instead of down!" Color flooded into her face, and the freckles almost disappeared. She got up from the table hastily and pushed open the swinging door leading to the living room. "I'll get your money for you, Mr. Mansfield."

She had aroused my sympathy. I wondered what her husband had been like. An insurance executive probably. Every time he had gotten a promotion he had used the extra money for more protection, more insurance. It must have cost her plenty to keep up this big house. And it was a cinch she didn't have any children, or she would have talked about them instead of a man five years dead. If I could have talked, I would have been able to kid her out of her mood in no time. My sex life had really suffered since I gave up talking. Not completely, because money always talks when words fail, but a lot of women had gotten away during the last couple of years because of my stubborn vow of silence.

As I pondered the situation, how best to handle it, Bernice returned to the kitchen. She placed a fifty-dollar bill on the table. The fifty ruined everything for me.

I could have accepted a twenty, because Lee Vernon had set the fee, but I couldn't, with good conscience, accept *fifty* dollars. My concert wasn't worth that much. I knew it, and Bernice Hungerford knew it. She was trying to buy me and I resented it. I folded the bill into a small square, placed it on the edge of the table and flipped it to the floor with my forefinger. I got up from the table and left the room.

I picked up my guitar in the living room and had almost reached the foyer when Bernice caught up with me. She tugged on my arm, and when I stopped, got in front of me, looking up wistfully into my face. My jaws were tight and I looked over her head at the door.

"Please!" she said, stuffing the folded bill into my shirt pocket. "I know what you're thinking, but it isn't true! The only reason I gave you a fifty was because I didn't have a twenty. I thought I had one, but I didn't. Please take it!"

I dropped my eyes to her face, looked at her steadily, and she turned away from me.

"All right. So I lied. Take it anyway. Fifty dollars doesn't mean anything to me. I'm sorry and I'm ashamed. And if you want to know the truth I'm more ashamed than sorry!"

I retrieved my hat from the marble angel's thumb and put it on my head. But I didn't leave. I reconsidered. Damn it all anyway, the woman was desirable! I removed my hat, replaced it on the angel's thumb and dropped my guitar case to the carpeted floor. Bernice had started up the stairs, but I caught up with her on the third step, lifted her into my arms and continued up the stairs. She buried her face in my neck and stifled a sob, clinging to me with both arms like a child. As I climbed I staggered beneath her weight—she must have weighed a solid one hundred and forty-five pounds—but I didn't drop her. When I reached the balcony I was puffing with my mouth open to regain my wind.

Bernice whispered softly into my ear, "The bedroom's the first door on the right."

The first time was for me. As nervous as Bernice was, at least at first, it could hardly have gone any other way. But I was gentle with her, and providing me with satisfaction apparently gave her the reassurance she needed. There was none of that foolishness about wanting to turn off the bedside lamps, for example, and when she returned from the bathroom, she still had her clothes off.

I had propped myself up on both pillows, and I smoked and watched her as she poured two small snifters of brandy. The cut-glass decanter was on a side table, beside a comfortable wing chair. It was unusual, I thought, to keep a decanter of cognac in a bedroom, but having a drink afterward was probably a postcoital ritual that she and her late husband had practiced.

Although Bernice was a trifle on the chunky side, she had a good figure. Her heavy breasts had prolapsed slightly, but the prominent nipples were as pink as a roseate spoonbill. Her slim waist emphasized the beautiful swelling lines of her full hips, and her skin, except for a scattering of freckles on her shoulders, was as white as a peeled almond. With her thick black hair unloosened, and trailing down her back, Bernice was a very beautiful woman. To top it off, she had a sense of style. I wanted to talk to her so badly I could almost taste the words in my mouth, and it was all I could do to hold back the torrent that would become a flood if I ever let them go.

After Bernice handed me my glass, she sat cross-legged on the bed, facing me, swirling her brandy in the snifter she held with cupped hands. Her face was flushed slightly with excitement. She peered intently into her brandy glass, refusing to meet my level stare.

"I want to tell you something, Frank," she said in a soft contralto, "something important. I'm *not* promiscuous."

She said this so primly I wanted to laugh. Instead, I grinned, wet a forefinger in my brandy and rubbed the nipple of her right breast.

"And no matter what you may think, you're the first man I've let make love to me since my husband died."

I didn't believe her, of course, not for an instant. But that is the way women are. They always feel that a man will think less of them if they act like human beings. What did it matter to me whether she had slept with anyone or not for the last five years? What possible difference could it make at this moment? Now was now, and the past and the future were unimportant.

As the nipple gradually hardened beneath my circling finger she laughed, an abrupt, angry little laugh, and tossed off the remainder of her brandy. I took her glass, put both of them aside, pulled her down beside me, and kissed her.

The second time was better and lasted much longer. Although I was handicapped by being unable to issue instructions, Bernice was experienced, cooperative and so eager to please me that she anticipated practically everything I wanted to do. And at last, when I didn't believe I

85

could hold out for another moment, she climaxed. I remained on my back, with Bernice on top of me, and she nibbled on my shoulder.

"I could fall in love with you, Frank Mansfield," she said softly. "If there were only some way I could prove it to you!"

Suddenly she got out of bed, grabbed my undershirt and shorts from the winged chair, and entered the bathroom. I raised myself on my elbows, and watched her through the open door as she washed my underwear in the washbowl. She hummed happily as she scrubbed away. My underwear wasn't dirty. I had put it on clean after a shower at the hotel before reporting in at the Chez Vernon at eight thirty that evening. Women, sometimes, have a peculiar way of demonstrating their affection.

Five o'clock finally rolled around, but I hadn't closed my eyes. Bernice slept soundly at my side, a warm, heavy leg thrown over mine, an arm draped limply across my chest. She breathed heavily through her open mouth. I eased my leg out from beneath hers and got out of bed on my side. The sheet that had covered us was disarranged, kicked to the bottom of the bed. I pulled it over her shoulders, before taking my clothes from the chair into the bathroom. My underwear was still dripping wet and draped over the metal bar that held the shower curtain. I pulled on my clothes without underwear. As soon as I was dressed, I raised the toilet seat, switched off the bathroom light and tiptoed out of the bedroom, closing the door softly behind me.

At the foot of the stairs, I retrieved my hat and guitar, and made my exit into the dawn. The sky was just beginning to turn gray. I opened the guitar case, removed the instrument, and tried to scrape off my name with my knife. It was burned in too deeply, but Bernice would be able to see that I had tried to scrape it off. Then I put the neck of the guitar on the top step, and stomped on it until it broke. After cutting the strings with my knife, I placed the broken instrument on the welcome mat.

There was an oleander bush on the left side of the porch. I tossed the guitar case into the bush. Now I could keep the fifty-dollar bill in good conscience. The guitar had been worth at least thirty dollars, and the fee for the private concert was twenty dollars. We were even. The message was obscure, perhaps, but Bernice would be able to puzzle it out eventually.

I walked down the gravel driveway to the street, and noticed the number of the house on a stone marker at the bottom of the drive. 111. I grinned. I would always remember Bernice's number.

Carrying my wet underwear, I had to wander around in the strange neighborhood for almost five blocks before I could find a bus stop and catch a bus back to downtown Jacksonville.

Chapter Eight

All day long I stayed in my room. Ideas and plans circulated inside my head, but none of them were worthwhile. One dismal thought kept oozing to the top, and finally it lodged there.

I had been cheated out of my inheritance.

This wasn't a new thought by any means. I had thought about it often in the five years since Daddy died, but I had never considered seriously doing anything about it before. The telegram informing me of Daddy's death had reached me one day too late to allow me to attend the funeral. I had immediately wired Randall and given him the circumstances. Two weeks later I had received a letter from Judge Brantley Powell, the old lawyer who handled the estate, together with a check for one dollar. He had also included a carbon copy of Daddy's will. Randall, my younger brother, had inherited the four-hundred-acre farm, seven hundred dollars in bonds, and the bank account of two hundred and seventy dollars. The check for one dollar was my part of the inheritance.

With plenty of money in my pockets at the time, I had dismissed the will from my mind. After all, Randall had stayed home, and I had not. He had gone to college, earned a degree in law and passed the Georgia bar exams, returning home ostensibly to practice. I had attended Valdosta State College for one year only and had quit to go to the Southwestern Cocking Tourney in Oklahoma City. I had never returned to college and Daddy had never gotten over it. He had always wanted to keep both of us under his thumb, but no man can tell me what to do with my life.

What had happened to the lives we lived?

I had gone on to make a name for myself in cockfighting.

Sure, I was broke now, but I had firmly established myself in one of the toughest sports in the world. And what did Randall have to show for his fine education? What had he done with his inheritance?

When he was accepted for the bar he went to work as a law clerk for Judge Brantley Powell. Six months later, claiming that he was doing most of the work anyway, he asked for a full partnership in the firm. When the judge turned him down, he had quit, and he hadn't done much of anything since. He hadn't even hung out his own shingle. All day long he sat in the big dining room at home, looking for obscure contradictions in his law books, occasionally having an article published on some intricate point of law in some legal quarterly nobody had ever heard of before. To get by, he sold off small sections of the farm to Wright Gaylord, my fiancée's brother. He had also married Frances Shelby, a dentist's daughter from Macon. I suppose she had had some dowry money and a few dollars from her father once in a while, but Randall's total income from tobacco, pecans and land sales was probably less than three thousand dollars a year. He was also writing a book—or so Frances said.

By all rights, Daddy should have left the farm to me. There were no two ways about it. I was the oldest son, and there wasn't a jury in Georgia that wouldn't award the farm to me if I contested the will. They read the Bible in Georgia, and in the Holy Bible the eldest son always inherits the property.

By four that afternoon I had made up my mind. I would go home and press Randall for the three hundred dollars he owed me. If he paid me, I'd forget about the farm and never consider taking it away from him again. If he didn't, I'd see Judge Powell and do something about it. I needed money, and if I didn't get some soon I'd miss out on the cockfighting season.

I checked my bag and gaff case at the desk, wrote a message for the desk clerk to hold any mail that came for me, paid my bill, and headed for the bus station. I only planned to stay overnight at home, so my shaving kit was enough baggage. If my black shirt got too dirty, I could have my sister-in-law wash and iron it for me.

The bus pulled out at 4:45. There was a one-hour layover in Lake City to change buses, and I arrived in Mansfield, Georgia, at 3:30 a.m. The farm was six miles out of town on the state highway. I could either wait for the rural route postman and ride out with him or I could walk. After being cramped up in the bus for such a long time, I decided to stretch my legs.

I enjoyed the walk to the farm. When I had attended school in town the county had been too poor to afford a school bus. I had walked both ways, winter and summer, over a deeply-rutted red dirt road, muddy when it rained, and dusty when it hadn't rained. The road was paved now, and had been since right after the Korean war. Soldiers from Fort Benning had used a lot of the county as a maneuver area. When the war was over the county had sued the United States Army for enough money to blacktop most of the county roads.

I reached the farm a little after six. I passed Charley Smith's house first, the only Negro tenant Randall had left, but I didn't stop to see the old man, even though a coil of black smoke was curling out of his chimney. Charley was much too old to do hard farm work any longer, but his wife, Aunt Leona, helped Frances around the house four or five days a week, and she was still a good worker.

The old homestead was a gray clapboard two-story structure set well back from the road. Randall hadn't done anything to improve the looks of the place in the five years he had owned it. The ten Van Deman pecan trees, planted between the house and the road some sixty years before, had been the deciding factor when Daddy first bought the place. In another month or so, Charley, Aunt Leona and Frances would be under the trees gathering nuts. If Randall hit a good market, he would realize three or four hundred dollars from the pecans before Christmas, but I couldn't wait that long to get the money he owed me.

Old Dusty was lying on the long front gallery near the front door, but he didn't bark or lift his head when I entered the yard through the fence gate. He could neither see nor hear me. The old dog was almost sixteen years old, blind and stone-deaf. When I reached the steps, however, he felt the vibration, snuffled, and began to bark feebly. His hind legs were partially paralyzed. When he tried to struggle to his feet, I patted his head and made him lie down again. The hair of his great head was white now. Unable to hear himself, he would have continued to bark indefinitely, so I closed his mouth with my hand to shut him up. He recognized me, of course, and licked my hand, his huge tail thumping madly on the loose floorboards of the gallery. He had been a good hunting dog once, and despite his infirmities, I was grateful to Randall for not putting him away. I hadn't expected to see Old Dusty again.

Instead of entering by the front door, I took the brick walk around the house to the back. I opened the screen door to the kitchen, leaned against the doorjamb, and grinned at the expression of surprise and chagrin on my sister-in-law's face.

But I believe I was more shocked than Frances. She had begun to put on weight the last time I had seen her, but in two years' time she had gained another forty pounds. She must have been close to one hundred and eighty pounds. Her rotund body was practically shapeless under the faded blue dressing gown she wore over her nightgown. Frances's face was still young and pretty, but it was as round and shiny as a full moon. Her short brown hair was done up tight with a dozen aluminum curlers. With a grimace of dismay, Frances put a chubby hand to her mouth.

"You would catch me looking like this!" she exclaimed. "Why didn't you let us know you were coming?"

I put an arm about her thick waist and kissed her on the cheek.

"Well," she- said good-naturedly, "you can stop grinning like an ape and sit down at the table. The coffee'll be ready in a minute. I was just fixing to start breakfast."

I sat down at the oilcloth-covered kitchen table. Frances

lifted the lid of the coffee pot to look inside, and clucked her tongue disapprovingly. "You may have lost your voice, Frank," she scolded, "but you can still write! We haven't heard from you in more than six months."

I spread my arms apologetically.

"I guess I'm a fine one to talk," she said, smiling, "I never write myself, but we do enjoy hearing from you once in a while." Frances filled two white mugs with coffee, put the sugar and cream where I could reach it easily, and sat down across from me.

"Randy'll be down pretty soon. He was up late last night working on an article, and I didn't have the heart to wake him. He likes to work at night, he says, when it's quiet. But if it was any quieter in the daytime I don't know what I'd do. We never go anyplace or do anything anymore, it seems to me." She sipped her hot coffee black and then fanned a dimpled hand in front of her pursed lips. "This isn't getting your breakfast ready now, is it?"

Because Frances knew how fond I was of eating, or because she used my visit, as an excuse, she prepared a large and wonderful breakfast. Fried pork chops, fried eggs, grits, with plenty of good brown milk gravy to pour over the grits, and fresh hot biscuits. I ate heartily, hungry after walking out from town, listening with stolid patience to the steady flow of dull gossip concerning various kinfolk and townspeople. I was finishing my third cup of coffee when I heard Randall on the stairs. As he entered the room, I got up to greet him.

"Well, well," he said with false heartiness, holding onto my hand and grinning, "if it isn't the junior birdman!"

"He patted his wife on her broad rump, crossed to the sideboard and poured a shot glass full of bourbon. He swiftly drank two neat shots before turning around.

"Welcome home, Bubba," he said, "how long are you going to stay?"

He sat at the table, and I dropped into my seat again. Randall looked well. He always did, whether he had a hangover or didn't have one. His face was a little puffy, but he was freshly shaven, and his curly russet hair had been cut recently. His starched white shirt, however, was frayed at the cuffs. The knot of his red-and-blue striped rep tie was a well-adjusted double windsor, and his black, well-worn oxford flannel trousers were sharply creased.

When I managed to catch his eyes with mine, I shrugged.

"I see," he nodded, "the enigmatic response. Before I came downstairs I looked outside, both in front and out back, and didn't see a car parked. Until I realized it was you, I thought Frances was merely talking to herself again. But if you're broke, you're welcome to stay home as long as you like and close ranks with me. I've never been any flatter."

"I saved two pork chops for you, Randy," Frances said quickly.

"No, thanks. Just coffee. Save the chops for my lunch." Randall smiled abstractedly, clasped his fingers behind his head and studied the ceiling. "It isn't difficult to divine the purpose of your visit, Bubba," he continued. "When you're flush, you wheel up in a convertible, your pockets stuffed with dollar cigars. When you're broke, you're completely broke, and on your uppers. But if the purpose of your visit is to collect the honest debt I owe you, you're out of luck. Three hundred dollars!" He shook his head and snorted. "Frankly, Bubba, I'd have a hard time raising twenty!"

He leaned forward in his chair and said derisively, "But you can live here as long as you like. We can still eat, and thanks to Daddy there's a wonderful roof over our heads. And whether we pay our bills in town or not, the Mansfield credit is still good."

To drink the coffee Frances set before him, Randall gripped the large white mug with both hands. His fingers didn't tremble, but it must have taken a good deal of concentrated effort to hold them steady.

"Going to see Mary Elizabeth?" he asked suddenly.

I shrugged and lit a cigarette. I offered the pack to my brother. He held up a palm in refusal, changed his mind and took one out of the pack. He held both of his hands in his lap, after putting the cork tip in his mouth, and I had to lean across the table to light it for him.

"You kind of believe in long engagements, don't you, Bubba?" he said, smiling sardonically. "It's been about seven years now, hasn't it?"

"Eight," Frances emended. "Eight years come November."

"Well, you can't say I haven't done my part to bring you together," Randall said wryly, watching my face closely. "Five years ago our farms were almost three miles apart. But thanks to selling land to Wright Gaylord, we're less than a mile away from them now!" He laughed with genuine amusement.

I was unable to listen to him any longer. He made me feel sick to my stomach. I rose from the table, and picked up my shaving kit from the sideboard.

"There's plenty of hot water upstairs if you want to shave, but not enough yet for a bath. Lately I've taken to turning the heater off at night and not lighting it again till I get up," Frances said. "Your room is dusty, too, but when Leona comes over this morning I'll have her do it up and put fresh sheets on the bed."

I nodded at my sister-in-law and left the room. As I climbed the stairs to the second floor, Randall said, "Maybe you'd better scramble me a couple of eggs, Hon. But don't put any grease in the skillet, just a little salt . . ."

Not only was Randall weak, he was a petty tyrant to his long-suffering wife. Before she could scramble eggs she would have to pour the good milk gravy into a bowl, and wash and dry the frying pan.

My old room was at the very end of the upstairs hallway, next to the bathroom. When Daddy bought the farm and moved us out from town, I had been elated about the move because it meant having a room to myself. And somehow, Daddy had made a go of the farm when many other good farmers were half starving in Georgia. He had earned a fair sum by *not* planting things and by collecting checks from the government. But even when times were excellent, he had never made any real money out of the farm. He was a fair farmer, but a poor businessman. Daddy had only been good for giving Randall and me advice, cheap advice, and he had never found anything in either one of us except our faults.

My room was dusty all right, as Frances had said. It had also been used as a catchall storeroom during the two years I had been away. The stripped double bed had been stacked with some cardboard cartons full of books, two shadeless table lamps and two carelessly rolled carpets. Extra pieces of dilapidated furniture had been tossed haphazardly into the room, and the hand-painted portrait of Grandpa was lying flat on top of my desk. A thick layer of dust was scattered over everything. When I opened the window, dust puffs as large as tennis balls took out after each other across the floor.

For a moment or two I looked out the window at the familiar view, but it didn't seem the same. Something was missing. And then I noticed that the ten-acre stand or slash pine had disappeared—cut down and sold as firewood probably, and not replanted.

I lifted the stern-faced portrait of Grandpa off the desk and leaned it against the dresser. I wiped the surface of the desk with my handkerchief. After rummaging through the drawers, I found a cheap, lined tablet with curling edges. Sitting down at the desk, I took out my ballpoint.

It took approximately a half hour to write out a list of instructions for Judge Brantley Powell. I wanted to be sure that I covered everything completely so he wouldn't have any questions. After rereading the list, and making a few interlinear corrections, I folded the sheaf of papers and stuffed them into my hip pocket.

I went into the bathroom and shaved, planning on an immediate departure for town in order to catch the judge in his office before he went home for the day. After returning to my room, I was rebuttoning my shirt when a soft rap sounded at the door.

"Bubba," Randall's voice called through the door. "How long're you going to be?"

I opened the door and looked quizzically at my brother. He was smiling a sly, secretive smile. Whenever Mother had caught him smiling that way, she slapped his face on general principles, knowing instinctively that he had done something wrong, and also knowing that she would never find out what he had done.

"Come on downstairs," he said mysteriously. "I've got a surprise for you." Still smiling, he turned away abruptly and descended the stairs.

I slipped into my corduroy jacket, put my hat on and followed him.

The surprise was Mary Elizabeth, the last person I

wanted to see right then, standing at the bottom of the stairs, cool and crisp in a wide-necked white blouse, blue velvet pinafore and white sling pumps. Ordinarily, I would have stopped to see Mary Elizabeth first, before coming home, but I didn't want to see her at all when I was broke and without a car. My last visit home, when I had first made my vow of silence, had been a strained, miserable experience for both of us.

"Hello, Frank," Mary Elizabeth said shyly, "welcome home."

She hadn't changed a fraction in two years. She was every bit as beautiful as I remembered. Mary Elizabeth had pale golden hair, and dark blue eyes—which often changed to emerald green in bright sunlight—a pink-and-white complexion, fair, thick, untouched pale brows, and long delicate hands. Her figure was more buxom than it had been ten years before, but that was to be expected. She was no longer a young girl. She was a mature woman of twenty-nine.

A moment later Mary Elizabeth was in my arms and I was kissing her, and it was as though I had never been away. There was a loud click as Randall closed the double doors to the dining room and left us alone. At the sound, Mary Elizabeth twisted her face to one side. I released her reluctantly and stepped back.

"Your voice still hasn't come back." It was a statement, not a question.

Slowly, regretfully, I shook my head.

"And you haven't been to a doctor either, have you?" she said accusingly.

Again the negative headshake, but accompanied this time with a stubborn smile.

"I've had a lot of time to think about it, Frank," she said eagerly, "and I don't believe your sudden loss of speech is organic at all. There's something psychological about it." She dropped her eyes demurely. "We can discuss it later at The Place. Randall's telephone call caught me just as I was leaving for school, and I don't think Mr. Caldwell liked it very well when I called him the last minute that way. When I take a day off without notice, or get sick or something, he has to take my classes.

"But I've packed a lunch, and it's still warm enough to go for a swim at The Place . . ." She colored prettily. "If you want to go?"

I opened the front door and took her arm. As we climbed into her yellow Nova, she was over her initial nervousness, and she began to scold me.

"Did it ever occur to you, Frank, that even a picture post-card mailed in advance would be helpful to everybody concerned?" I rather enjoyed the quality of Mary Elizabeth's voice. Like most schoolteachers of the female sex, she had an overtone of fretful impatience in her voice, and this note of controlled irascibility amused me.

I grinned and tweaked the nipple of her right breast gently through the thinness of her white cotton blouse.

"Don't!" The sharp expletive was delivered furiously, and her blue-green eyes blazed with sudden anger. She set her lips grimly and remained silent for the remainder of the short drive to her farm, where she lived with her brother. As she pulled into the yard and parked beneath a giant pepper tree, I noticed that she had cooled off. The moment she turned off the engine, I pulled her toward me and kissed her mouth softly, barely brushing her lips with mine.

"You *do* love me, don't you, Frank?" she asked softly, with her eyes glistening.

I nodded, and kissed her again, roughly this time the way she liked to be kissed. One day, when we had first started to go together, Mary Elizabeth had asked me thirty-seven times if I loved her. At each affirmative reply she had been as pleased as the first time. Women never seem to tire of being told, again and again and again.

"Here comes Wright," Mary Elizabeth said quickly, looking past my shoulder. "We'd better get out of the car."

We got out of the car and waited beneath the tree, watching her brother approach us from the barn with his unhurried, shambling gait. Wright Gaylord hated me, and I was always uneasy in his presence because of his low boiling point. He worshiped his little sister and had put her through college. Now in his late forties, Wright was still unmarried. He had never found a woman he could love as much as he loved his sister. He hated me for two reasons. One, I could sleep with Mary Elizabeth and he couldn't.

96

After all these years he was bound to know about us, or at least suspect the best. And two, when I married Mary Elizabeth, he knew that I would take her away and he would never see her again. When our engagement had been announced and published in the paper, he had locked himself in his bedroom for three days.

"I didn't get sick or anything," Mary Elizabeth said as Wright came within earshot. "Frank came home, so I took the day off for a picnic."

Wright glared at me. His face reminded me of a chunk of red stone, roughly hewn by an amateur sculptor, and then left in the rain to weather.

"When are you leaving?" Wright asked rudely, shoving both hands into his overall pockets deliberately, to avoid shaking hands.

"Now, that's no way to talk, Wright," Mary Elizabeth chided. "Frank just got home this morning." She patted her brother's meaty arm. "We're going to The Place for our picnic. Why don't you come with us?"

"I ain't got time for picnics," he said sullenly. "I got too much work to do. Anyway, I've been meanin' to go to town all week. Give me the keys, and I'll take your car instead of the pickup."

Mary Elizabeth handed him her keys. "It might do you good to take a day off and come with us."

Wright grunted something under his breath, got into the car, and slammed the door. We entered the house, picked up a quilt and the lunch basket to take with us, and then cut across the fields for The Place.

We had called it The Place for as long as I could remember. The tiny pool in the piney woods wasn't large enough to be called a swimming hole. Fed by an underground spring that bubbled into a narrow brook about fifty yards up the pine-covered slope, the pool was only big enough for two or three people to stand in comfortably, and the water was only chest deep. The clear water was very cold, even on the hottest days. On a cruel summer day, a man could stand in the pool, his head shaded by pines, and forget about the heat and humidity of Georgia.

The Place had other advantages. There was a wide flat

rock to the right of the pool, with enough room for one person at a time to stretch out on it and get some dappled sunlight. To the left of the pool, facing up the steep hill, there was a clearing well matted with pine needles. For two people, the clearing was the perfect size for an opened quilt and a picnic. Best of all, The Place was secluded and private. Located on the eastern edge of the Gaylord farm, the wooded section merged with a Georgia state forest. The only direct access to The Place was across Wright Gaylord's property, and nobody in his right mind would have trespassed on Wright's land.

Two hours before, Mary Elizabeth and I had arrived at the pool, hot and dusty from trudging across the cultivated fields. We had stripped immediately and jumped into the water. After splashing each other and wrestling playfully in the icy water, we had allowed the sun to dry us thoroughly before we made love on the quilt stretched flat on the bed of pine needles. There had been no protest from Mary Elizabeth, despite my long absence. Her natural, animal-like approach to sex was really miraculous in view of her strong religious views. I sometimes wondered if she ever connected the physical act of love with her real life.

I don't believe she thought consciously of sex at all. If she did, she must have thought of it as "something Frank and I do at The Place," but not connected with conjugal love or as something out of keeping with her straitlaced Methodist beliefs. Perhaps it was only habit.

I had never managed to make love to Mary Elizabeth anywhere else. She had been seventeen the first time, with just the two of us at The Place. It had been an accident more than anything else. Afterward I had been ashamed of myself for taking advantage of her innocence. But the first time had led to the second, and all during that never-to-be-forgotten summer we had made daily pilgrimages to The Place.

I have never underrated Mary Elizabeth nor underestimated her intelligence, but the situation was unusual. After all, Mary Elizabeth was a college graduate now, and a teacher of high school English—she surely must have known what we were doing. But we had never discussed sex. I had an idea that the subject would be distasteful to her, and she had never brought it up on her own. And yet, every time I came home we headed for The Place like homing pigeons long absent from their coop. I had a hunch, and I had never pressed my good fortune, that as long as Mary Elizabeth never thought about it, or discussed it, we could continue to make love at The Place forever.

Once, and only once, I had asked Mary Elizabeth to drive to Atlanta with me for a weekend. She had been shocked into tears by my reasonable proposition.

"What kind of girl do you think I am?" she had asked tearfully.

Completely bewildered by her reaction, I had been unable to come up with a ready reply. I had never brought the subject up again. And besides, there wasn't a better spot in the world for making love than The Place.

Mary Elizabeth sat up suddenly, swung her long bare legs gracefully around, and sat on the rock facing me, dangling her feet in the water. I was in the pool, chest deep, and I had been studying her body as she lay flat on her back. Spreading a towel across her lap, but leaving her breasts uncovered, Mary Elizabeth looked at me sternly, and then wet her lips.

"What about us, Frank?" she said at last. "How long do we go on like this?" The tone of her voice had changed. It wasn't harsh, but it wasn't feminine either. It was more like the voice of a young boy, on the near verge of changing.

I raised my eyebrows, watching her intently.

She cupped her breasts and pointed the long pink nipples toward the sky. She narrowed her eyes, no longer greenish, but now a dark aquamarine, and caught mine levelly.

"Are they still beautiful, Frank?" she asked in this strange new voice.

I nodded, dumbly, trying to figure out what she was driving at.

"You're wrong." She smiled wanly, dropped her hands, and her plump breasts bobbed beautifully from their own momentum. "You haven't noticed, but they're beginning to droop. Not much, but how will they look in five years? Ten years? Nobody's ever seen them except you, Frank, but how much longer will you be interested? All I've ever asked you to do is quit cockfighting so we could get married. We've drifted along in a deadlock too long, Frank, and it's impossible for me to accept your way of life. I thought that as you got older, you would see how wrong it is, but now you seem to be entangled in a pattern. And cockfighting is wrong, morally wrong, legally wrong, and every other kind of wrong! You're a grown man now, Frank!"

I sloshed forward in the tiny pool, put my arms around her hips, warm from the sun, and buried my face in her lap.

"Yes, you big, dumb child," she said softly, running her fingers through my damp hair, "but I can't meet you half-way on an issue like cockfighting. My roots are here and so are yours. Give it up, please, give it up, and marry me. Can't you see that you're wrong, wrong, wrong!" She gripped my hair with both hands and tugged my head gently from side to side.

"I can't exist on postcards any longer, Frank. *'Dear M.E. I'm in Sarasota. Won the derby 4—3. I love you. Will write from Ocala. F.!'* In a few more weeks, I'll be thirty years old. I want to be married and have children! I'm tired of people snickering behind my back at our engagement. Nobody believes it anymore. If you loved me only half as much as I love you, you'd give it up. Please, Frank, stay home, marry me—"

There was a catch in her voice, and I lifted my head to look at her face. She wasn't crying, far from it. She was trying to beat me down again with an emotional appeal to my "reason." I had explained patiently to Mary Elizabeth, a dozen times or more, that cockfighting was not a cruel sport, that it was a legitimate, honorable business, and I had asked her to witness one fight, just one fight, so she could see for herself instead of listening to fools who didn't know what they were talking about. She had always refused, falling back on misinformation learned from reformers, the narrow-minded Methodist minister, and the shortsighted laws prohibiting the sport that were pushed through by a minority group of do-gooders. If she wouldn't see for herself, how could I persuade her?

"You're a brilliant man, Frank," Mary Elizabeth continued earnestly. "You could make a success out of anything you went into in Mansfield. This farm is half mine, you know, and when we're married, it'll be half yours. If you don't want to farm with Wright, I've got enough money saved that you can open a business of some kind in town. I've saved almost everything I've earned. Wright doesn't let me spend a penny, and I've been teaching for six years. And I'll help you get your voice back. We'll work it out together, you and I, Frank. We can get a book on phonetics and you—"

As she constructed these impossible feminine castles I got restless. I pulled away from her, clambered up on the opposite bank and began to dress, without waiting to get dry.

"What are you doing?" she said sharply.

As she could see for herself, I was putting my clothes on.

"You haven't listened to a single word, have you?"

I grinned, and buckled the straps on my jodhpur boots.

"If you leave, now," she shouted, "you needn't come back! We're through, d'you hear? Through! I won't be treated this way!"

When a woman starts to scream unreasonably, it's time to leave. I snatched a cold fried chicken leg out of the basket, draped my coat over my arm and started down the trail. Mary Elizabeth didn't call after me. Too mad, I reckoned.

Mary Elizabeth was stubborn. That was her problem. Anytime she truly wanted to get married, all she had to do was say so. But it had to be on my terms. I loved her, and she was a respectable woman with a good family background. I knew she would make me a good wife, too, once she got over this foolishness of wanting me to give up cockfighting and settle down in some dull occupation in Mansfield. We had been over this ground too many times, and I had a new season of cockfighting to get through. Nothing would have pleased me more than to have Mary Elizabeth as a bride at my Ocala farm, preparing meals and keeping my clothes clean. And, until she became pregnant, what would keep her from teaching school in Ocala, if that was what she wanted to do? As soon as she came around to seeing things my way, and quit trying to tell me what I could and couldn't do, we'd be married quick enough. And she knew it.

I grinned to myself, and tossed the chicken bone in the general direction of an ant nest. Mary Elizabeth had a sore point on those postcards. I'd have to do better than that. When I got back to Ocala, I'd write her a nice, interesting letter, a long newsy one for a change.

When I crossed through Wright's yard to the state road, I looked about apprehensively to see if he had returned, but he hadn't come back from town. Every time Wright caught me alone, he attempted to goad me into a fight. For Mary Elizabeth's sake, I had always refused to fight him. It would have given me a good deal of pleasure to knock a little sense into his thick head, but I knew that as soon as we started fighting he would whip out his knife, and then I would have to kill him.

I walked down the asphalt road. My biggest problem now was how to retrieve my shaving kit from the dresser in my room. If I returned to the house to get it, Randall would be curious as to why I was leaving so soon. If I wrote a note informing him I was going to take my rightful property and have him and Frances tossed out, he would attempt, with his trained lawyer's logic, to argue me out of my convictions. As I remembered, I had never really bested him in an oral argument. The only way I had ever won an argument with Randall was by resorting to force. And besides, Frances would bawl and carry on like crazy.

By the time I was level with the house, I decided the hell with the shaving kit, and continued on down the road. It would be less trouble all the way around if I bought another razor and a toothbrush when I got back to Jacksonville.

I walked about four miles before I was picked up by a kid in a hot rod and taken the rest of the way into Mansfield. When he let me out at a service station, I walked through the shady residential streets to Judge Brantley Powell's house on the upper side of town. He only went to his office in the mornings, and I was certain I could catch him at home. When I rapped with the wrought-iron knocker, I only had to wait a minute before Raymond, his white-wooled Negro servant, opened the door. Raymond peered at me blankly for a moment or so before he recognized me, and then he smiled.

"Mr. Frank," he said cordially, "come in, come in!"

It was dark in the musty hallway when he closed the door. Raymond took my hat, led the way into the dim living room and raised the shades to let in some light.

"The judge he takin' his nap now, Mr. Frank," he said uneasily. "I don't like to wake him 'less it's somethin' important."

I considered. What was important to me probably wouldn't be considered important by the old judge. I waved my right hand with an indifferent gesture, and settled myself in a leather chair to wait.

"You goin' to wait, Mr. Frank?"

I nodded, picked up an old *Life* magazine from the table beside the chair and leafed through it. Raymond left the room silently, and returned a few minutes later with a glass of ice cubes and a pitcher of lemonade. A piece of vinegar pie accompanied the lemonade. Firm, tart and clear, with a flaky, crumbly crust, it was the best piece of vinegar pie I had ever eaten.

It was almost five before the judge came downstairs. Evidently Raymond had told him I was waiting on him because he addressed me by name when he entered the room and apologized for sleeping so late. Judge Powell had aged considerably in the four or five years that had gone by since I had last talked to him. He must have been close to eighty. His head wobbled and his hands trembled as he talked. I handed him the list of instructions I had written, and he sat down in a chair close to the window to read them. He looked through the papers a second time, as if he were searching for something, and then removed his glasses.

"All right, Frank," he said grimly. "I'll handle this for you. Your Daddy was a stubborn man, and I told him he was wrong when he changed his will."

I picked up my hat from the table where Raymond had placed it.

"One more thing, Frank. How long do you expect to be at the Jeff Davis Hotel in Jax?"

I shrugged, mentally totaled my remaining money, and then held up four fingers.

"You'll hear from me before then. And when you get your money, Frank, I hope you'll settle down. A dog has fun chasing his own tail, but he never gets anywhere while he's doing it."

I shook hands with the old man and he walked me to the front door. "Can you stay for dinner, son?"

I shook my head and smiled my thanks, but when I opened the door he grasped my sleeve.

"There're all kinds of justice, Frank," he said kindly, "and I've seen most of them in fifty years of practice. But poetic justice is the best kind of all. To measure the night, a man must fill his day," he finished cryptically.

I nodded knowingly, although I didn't know what he meant, and I doubt very much whether he did either. When a man manages to live as long as Judge Powell has, he always thinks he's a sage of some kind.

I cut across town to the U.S. Highway and ate dinner in a trucker's cafe about a mile outside the city limits. Two hours later I was riding in the cab of a diesel truck on my way back to Jacksonville. I had the feeling inside that I had finally burned every bridge, save one, to the past. But I didn't have any regrets. To survive in this world, a man has got to do what he has got to do.

Chapter Nine

I was tired when I reached Jacksonville, but I wasn't sleepy. I had hoped to get some sleep in the cab of the truck on the long drive down, but the driver had talked continuously. As I listened to him, dumbly, my eyes smarting from cigarette smoke and the desire to close them, he poured out the dull, intimate details of his boring life—his military service with the First Cavalry Division in Vietnam, his courtship, his marriage and his plans for the future (he wanted to be a truck dispatcher so he could sit on his ass). He was still going strong when we reached Jax. To finish his autobiography, he parked at a drive-in and bought me ham and eggs for breakfast.

After shaking hands with the voluble truck driver, who wasn't really a bad guy, I caught a bus downtown and checked into the Jeff Davis Hotel. One look at the soft double bed and I became wide awake. If my plan was successful, I would know within three days, and I didn't have time to sleep all day. I had to proceed with a confidence I didn't actually have, as though there could be no doubt of the outcome.

After I shaved, I prepared a list for Doc Riordan. These were supplies I would need, and I intended to take advantage of our agreement. It would take a long time to use up eight hundred dollars worth of cocker's supplies.

One. Conditioning powder. Doc made a reliable conditioning powder—a concoction containing iron for vigor, and Vitamin B1. This powder, mixed with a gamecock's special diet, is a valuable aid to developing a bird's muscles and reflexes. I put down an order for three pounds.

Two. Dextrose capsules. A dextrose capsule, dropped down a gamecock's throat an hour before a fight, gives him the same kind of fresh energy a candy bar provides to a mountain climber halfway up a mountain. On my list I put down an order for a twenty-four-gamecock season supply.

Three. Doc Riordan's Blood Builder. For many years Doc had made and sold a blood coagulant that was as good as any on the market. If he didn't have any on hand he could make more. This was a blood builder in capsule form containing Vitamin K, the blood coagulating vitamin, whole liver and several other secret ingredients. Who can judge the effectiveness of a blood coagulant? I can't. But if any blood coagulants worked, and I don't leave any loopholes when it comes to conditioning, I preferred to use Doc Riordan's. Again I marked down enough for a twenty-four-gamecock supply.

Four. Disinfectants. Soda, formaldehyde, sulfur, carbolic acid, oil of tansy, sassafras, creosote, camphor and rubbing alcohol. Insects are a major problem for cockfighters. Lice are almost impossible to get rid of completely, but a continuous fight against them must be fought if a man wants to keep healthy game fowl. *Give me a plentiful supply of all these,* I wrote on my list.

Five. Turpentine. Five gallons. The one essential fluid a cocker must have for survival. God has seen fit to subject chickens to the most loathsome diseases in the world—pip, gapes, costiveness, diarrhea, distemper, asthma, catarrh, apoplexy, cholera, lime legs, canker and many others. Any one of these sicknesses can knock out a man's entire flock of game fowl before he knows what has happened to him.

Fortunately, a feather dipped in turpentine and shoved into a cock's nostrils, or swabbed in his throat, or sometimes just a few drops of turpentine in a bird's drinking water, will prevent or cure many of these diseases. When turpentine fails, I destroy the sick chicken and bury him deep to prevent the spread of his disease.

When I completed my list I sealed it in a hotel envelope, wrote Doc Riordan's name on the outside, and headed for the drugstore where he had part-time work. Doc wasn't in, but the owner said he was expected at noon. Figuring that Doc would freely requisition most of the items on my list from the owner, I decided not to leave it, and to come back later.

I walked to the Western Union office and sent two straight wires. The first wire was to my neighbor and fellow cocker in Ocala, Omar Baradinsky:

HAVE LIGHTS AND WATER TURNED ON AT MY FARM. WILL REIMBURSE UPON ARRIVAL. F. MANSFIELD.

I knew Omar wouldn't mind attending to this chore for me in downtown Ocala and inasmuch as I didn't know what day or what time I would arrive at the farm, I wanted to be certain there was water and electricity when I got there.

The other wire was to Mr. Jake Mellhorn, Altamount, North Carolina. Jake Mellhorn bred and sold a game strain called the Mellhorn Black. It was a rugged breed, and I knew this from watching Blacks fight many times.

These chickens fought equally well in long and short heels, depending upon their conformation and conditioning, but they were unpredictable fighters—some were cutters and others were shufflers—and they had a tendency to alternate their tactics in the pit. As a general rule I prefer cutters over shufflers, but I needed a dozen Aces and a fair price. Jake Mellhorn had been after me for several years to try a season with his Blacks, and I knew that he would give me a fairly low price on a shipment of a dozen. If I won with his game strain at any of the major derbies, he would be able to jack the price up on the game fowl he sold the following season to other cockers. I could win with any hardy, farm-walked game strain that could stand up under my conditioning methods—Claret, Madigan, Whitehackle, Doms—but the excellent cocks I would need would cost too much, especially after putting out five hundred dollars for Icky. It wouldn't hurt anything to send a wire to Jake and find out what he had to offer anyway.

TO: JAKE MELLHORN, ALTAMOUNT, N.C.
NEED TWELVE FARM-WALKED COCKS. NO STAGS, NO COOPWALKS WANTED. PUREBRED MELLHORNS ONLY. NO CROSSES. SEND PRICE AND DETAILS C/O JEFF DAVIS HOTEL, JACKSONVILLE, FLA. F. MANSFIELD.

If I knew Jake Mellhorn, and I knew the egotistic, self-centered old man well, I'd have a special delivery letter from him within a couple of days. And on my first order, at least, he would send me Aces.

I paid the girl for the wires, and then ate a hamburger at a little one-arm joint down the street before returning to Foster's Drugstore.

Now that the wires were on their way, I felt committed, even though they didn't mean anything in themselves. I felt like I was getting the dice rolling by forcing my luck.

I couldn't pay for the Mellhorns, no matter how good a price Jake gave me. I couldn't even repay Omar Baradinsky the utilities deposit money he would put up for me in Ocala—and yet I felt confident. Surely Judge Powell would come through with one thousand, five hundred dollars now, because I had acted as though he would. It was a false feeling of confidence, and I knew that it was bogus in the same way a man riding in a transatlantic airplane knows that there cannot possibly be a crack-up because he bought one hundred thousand dollars' worth of insurance at the airport before the plane took off.

Doc Riordan was sitting at the fountain counter, wearing a short white jacket, when I entered the drugstore. I eased onto the stool beside him and tapped him on the shoulder.

"Hello, Frank," he said, smiling. In the cramped space, we shook hands awkwardly without getting up. "Mr. Foster said there was a big man with a cowboy hat looking for me. Inasmuch as I don't know any bill collectors who don't talk, I figgered it was you."

I handed Doc the envelope. He studied the list, and whistled softly through closed teeth. "That's a mighty big order on short notice, Frank," he said, frowning. "I don't have any conditioning powder made up, and there's been so much flu going around Jax lately, I've got sixty-three prescriptions to fill before I can do anything else." He tapped the list with a forefinger. "Can you let me have a couple of days?"

I had to smile. At that stage I could have let him have a couple of months. I clapped him on the shoulder and nodded understandingly.

"Good. Come in day after tomorrow and it'll be waiting for you. All of it." He smiled. "Kinda looks like you've got your chickens for the season, and I hope you'll have a good one. Anytime you need something fast, just drop me a card here at Foster's. I know damned well I'll make the Milledgeville Tourney, but that'll be the only one this year. I've got too many feelers out on Licarbo to go to chicken fights. But then, I might get a chance to run down to Plant City—"

He had work to do, so I slid off the stool and left abruptly while he was still talking.

For the rest of the afternoon I prowled used car lots as a tire-kicker, trying to locate a pickup truck of some kind that would hold together for four or five months. Around four o'clock I discovered an eight-year-old Ford half-ton pickup that looked suitable, and the salesman rode around the block with me when I tried it out. All afternoon my silence had unnerved talkative used car salesmen. After five minutes of my kind of silence, they usually gave up on their sales talks and let me look around in peace. This fellow was more persistent. After reparking the truck in its place on the fourth row of the lot, I looked at the salesman inquisitively.

"This is a real buy for one fifty," he said sincerely. He was a young man in his early twenties, with a freckled earnest face. His flattop haircut, and wet-look black leather sports jacket, reminded me of a Marine captain wearing civilian clothes for the first time. For all I knew, he was an ex-Marine.

I looked steadily into his face and he blushed.

"But old pickups don't sell so well these days. Too many

rich farmers buying new ones. So I'll let you have it for a hundred-dollar bill."

I studied him for a moment, maintaining my expressionless face, and then got out of the cab of the truck. I started toward the looping chain fence that bordered the sidewalk, and he caught up with me before I reached the first line of cars. He put a freckled hand on my arm, but when I dropped my eyes to his hand, he jerked it away as though my sleeve were on fire.

"I'll tell you what I'll do, sir," he said quickly. "Just to move the old Ford and get it off the lot, I'll give up my commission. You can have the truck for eighty-five bucks. Give me ten dollars down, and drive it away. Here're the keys." He held out the keys, but I didn't look at them. I kept my eyes on his face.

"All right," he said nervously. "Seventy-five, and that's rock bottom."

I nodded. A fair price. More than fair. The truck had had hard use, and most of the paint had been chipped off in preparation for a new paint job. But no one had ever gotten around to repainting it. I pointed to the low sun above the skyline, and he followed my pointing finger with his pale blue eyes. To catch his wandering attention again I snapped my fingers and then held up three fingers before his face.

"Three suns?" he asked. "You mean three days?"

I nodded.

"Without a deposit, I can't promise to hold it for you, sir."

I shrugged indifferently and left the lot. I had a hunch that the pickup would still be there when I came back for it.

When I got back to my hotel room I counted my money. Twenty-three dollars and eighty-one cents. Money just seems to evaporate. I had no idea where all of it had gone, but I had to nurse what was left like a miser. Twelve dollars would be needed to pay four days' rent on the hotel room, and I would have to eat and smoke on the remainder. If I didn't get a letter from Judge Powell within three days, or four at the most, I would have to make other plans of some kind.

I spent the next three days at the public library. There was a long narrow cafe near the hotel that featured an

"Eye-Opener Early-Bird Breakfast," consisting of one egg, one slice of bacon, one slice of brushed margarine toast and a cup of coffee—all for forty-two cents. After eating this meager fare, I walked slowly to the library and sat outside on the steps until it opened, thinking forward to lunch. I read magazines until noon in the periodical room, and then returned to the hotel and checked the desk for my mail. I then returned to the library. By two o'clock I was ravenous, and I would eat a poor boy sandwich across the street, and drink a Coca-Cola. The poor boy sandwich had three varieties of meat, but not much meat. I then returned to the library and read books until it closed at nine p.m.

My taste in reading is catholic. I can take Volume III of the *Encyclopedia Americana* out of the stacks and read it straight through from Corot to Deseronto with an equal interest, or lack of interest, in each subject. *Roget's Thesaurus* or a dictionary çan hold my attention for several hours. I don't own many books. There were only a few on poultry breeding at my Ocala farm and a first edition of *Histories of Game Strains* that I won as a prize one time at a cockfight. And I also owned a beat-up copy of *Huckleberry Finn*. I suppose I've drifted down the river with Huck Finn & Co. fifty times or more.

When the library closed at nine, I ate a hamburger, returned to the hotel and went to bed.

Three days passed quickly this way. On the morning of the fourth day, however, I didn't leave the hotel. My stomach was so upset I didn't even feel like eating the scanty "Eye-Opener Early-Bird Breakfast," afraid I couldn't hold it. I sat in the lobby waiting apprehensively for the mail.

There were two letters for me, both of them special delivery. One was a thick brown envelope from Judge Powell, and the other was a flimsier envelope from Jake Mellhorn. I didn't open either letter until I reached my room. My fingers were damp when I opened the thick envelope from Judge Powell first, but when I emptied the envelope onto my bed, the only thing I could see was the gray-green certified check from the Mansfield Farmer's Trust, made out to my name for one thousand, five hundred dollars!

My reaction to the check surprised me. I hadn't realized how much I had counted on getting it. My knees began to shake first, and then my hands. A moment later my entire body was shivering as though I had malaria, and I had to sit down quickly. I was wet from my hair down to the soles of my feet with a cold, clammy perspiration that couldn't have been caused by anything else but cold, irrational fear. Of course, I hadn't allowed my mind to dwell on the possibility of failure, but now that I actually had the money, the suppressed doubts and fears made themselves felt. But my physical reaction didn't last very long. I stripped to the waist and bathed my upper body with a cold washrag, and dried myself thoroughly, before reading Judge Powell's letter. It was a long letter, overly long, typed single spaced on his law firm's letterhead, watermarked stationery:

Mr. Frank Mansfield
c/o The Jeff Davis Hotel
Jacksonville, Florida

Dear Frank:

I handled this matter personally, following your desires throughout, feeling you knew your brother Randall better than me. You did. When I called on him and informed him that you intended to break the will of your father, he laughed. If it hadn't been for your copious notes, his laughter would have surprised me.

"Is Frank willing to fight this in court?" he asked me.

"No," I told him (again following your instructions). "Your brother, Frank, said it wouldn't be necessary. 'When Randall sees that he is in an untenable position, he will sign a quitclaim deed immediately and move out.'"

Again your brother laughed as you predicted. "Do you think I'm in an untenable position, Judge?" he then asked.

"Yes, you are," I told him. "That's why I brought a quitclaim deed for you to sign."

He laughed and signed the deed. "In New York," he said, "you wouldn't have a chance, Judge." I remained silent instead of reminding him that the case, if brought to a trial, would be held in Georgia. "When does Frank want me to leave?"

"As soon as the property is sold."

"Does Frank have a buyer in mind?"

"He recommended that I try Wright Gaylord first," I said.

This statement gave your brother additional cause for merriment, because he laughed until the tears rolled down his face.

"Frank only wants a profit of one thousand, five hundred dollars," I told your brother. "He instructed me to give you any amount over that, after deducting my fee, of course."

"That's generous of Frank," he said, "but there are some taxes due, about seven hundred dollars."

"I'm aware of the taxes," I said.

"All right, Judge. You've got your quitclaim deed. Continue on down the road and sell the property to Wright Gaylord. I'll be ready to leave tomorrow morning when you bring me my share, if there's anything left over."

Wright Gaylord gave me a check the same afternoon for three thousand, five hundred dollars, which I accepted reluctantly. Given more time I am positive that your property would have sold for eight or possibly ten thousand dollars. But the sum adequately covered your required one thousand, five hundred and my fee of five hundred dollars, so I closed the sale then and there. You didn't mention it in your notes, but I realize the astuteness of selling to Mr. Gaylord, although I doubt if he did. Upon your marriage to his sister you will automatically get half your farm back and half of his as well. Mr. Gaylord is also a client of mine, and this was a fine point of legal ethics, but inasmuch as he is certainly aware of your engagement to his sister, I did not deem it necessary to remind him.

Enclosed is a certified check for one thousand, five hundred dollars. My fee of five hundred dollars has been deducted, the taxes have been paid, plus stamps, and miscellaneous expenses. I gave your brother a check for seven hundred and sixty-eight dollars and fifty cents. Randall and his wife left yesterday on the bus for Macon.

Mr. Gaylord has already begun to tear down your father's farmhouse and the outlying buildings. He hired a wrecking crew from Atlanta, and I saw some of their equipment moving through town yesterday. However, he agreed to keep your Negro tenant on the place if he wanted to stay, *per your request. But he would not consent to keep him on shares because Charley Smith is too old. Your main concern, I believe, was to maintain a home for Charley and his family, so again, in lieu of instructions to the contrary, I agreed to this condition.*

There are also some papers enclosed for you to sign on the places marked with a small X in red pencil. They have been predated, including the power of attorney, in order to send you the money without undue delay. Please return them (after you have signed them) as quickly as possible.

If your father were still alive, I know he would want you to use your money wisely, so I can only say the same. "A rolling stone gathers no moss" is an old saying but a true one nevertheless. If I can help you further do not hesitate to ask me.

Very truly yours,

BRANTLEY POWELL
BP/ bj   *Attorney-at-Law*

I didn't mind the moralizing of the windy old man, because he didn't know what I planned to use the money for, but I was irritated because he had dictated the letter to his big-mouthed old maid secretary, Miss Birdie Janes. The small initials, "bj" in the lower left-hand corner of the letter, meant that my business would be spread all over the county by now. I realized that it was a long letter, and I appreciated the details, but the old man should have written the letter personally. When I returned to Mansfield, eventually, sides would be taken—some for Randall and some for me, but the majority would take Randall's side, even though I was legally and morally right about taking what rightfully belonged to me.

The letter from Jake Mellhorn was more pressing:

Dear Frank,

Glad to see you're getting sense enough to know that the Mellhorn Black is the best gamecock in the world, bar none!!! And you're lucky you wired me just when you did. I just brought in twenty-two cocks, but if you only want a

*dozen country-walked roosters, you can have the best of the
lot, which is plenty damned good!!! I can ship you six Aces,
two to three years old. The other six are brothers, five
months past staghood, but all are guaranteed dead game,
and they'll cut for you or your money back. As you know, I
ship them wormed, in wooden coops, but they'll need
watering upon arrival. Don't trust the damned express
company to water birds en route—they'll steal the cracked
corn out of the coops and make popcorn out of it. As a special price—TO YOU ONLY!!! One dozen Mellhorn Blacks
for only seven hundred dollars. That's much less than seventy-five apiece. Let me know by return wire, because I can
sell them anywhere for one hundred to one hundred and
twenty-five dollars each.*

For a good season,
JAKE MELLHORN

An outlay of seven hundred dollars, although it was an
exceptionally fair price for Ace Mellhorns, would make a
deep dent in my one thousand, five hundred dollars, but I
had little choice. I had to have them, or others just as good.
Another five hundred to Ed Middleton, seventy-five dollars
for the truck, and I'd be down to only two hundred and
twenty-five. Luckily, I had feed at Ocala left over from last
year, and the older Flint corn is, the better it is for feeding.
And within two weeks I could win some money at the
Ocala cockpit. At least two, or possibly three, birds could
be conditioned for battle by that time.

After packing and checking out of the hotel, I cashed the
check at the bank. I wired seven hundred dollars to Jake
Mellhorn immediately with instructions to ship the cocks to
my farm. I mailed the signed papers back to Judge Powell
special delivery, and headed for the used car lot to buy the
staked-out pickup truck.

Within two hours, I was driving out of Jacksonville. The
cocker's supplies from Doc Riordan were in the truck bed,
along with my suitcase and gaff case, covered by a tarp.
The remainder of my money, in tens and twenties, was
pinned inside my jacket pocket with a safety pin.

As I turned onto Highway 17 I thought suddenly of
Bernice Hungerford. She had been in my thoughts several

times during the last three days, especially late at night when I had been trying to sleep, with hunger pangs burning my stomach. In fact, I had considered seriously going out to her house and chiseling a free meal. But I had felt too guilty to go. Leaving a broken guitar on her front porch hadn't been a brilliant idea.

There was a filling station ahead, and I pulled onto the ramp and pointed to the regular pump.

"How many, sir?"

I pulled a finger across my throat.

"Filler up? Yes, sir."

While I was still looking at the large city map inside the station, the attendant interrupted me to ask if everything was all right under the hood. The question was so stupid I must have looked surprised, because he blushed with embarrassment and checked beneath the hood without waiting for a reply. How else can a man discover whether oil and water are needed unless he looks?

I traced the map and found Bernice's street. Her house was about three miles out of my way. I didn't really owe her anything, but I knew my conscience would be eased if I repaid the woman the thirty dollars she had advanced me when I had needed it. I turned around, and drove slowly until I reached a shopping center that had a florist's shop. I parked, entered the shop, and selected a dozen yellow roses out of the icebox. The stems were at least two feet long.

"These will make a beautiful arrangement," the gray-haired saleswoman smiled. "Do you want to include a card?"

When I nodded she gave me a small white card and a tiny envelope that went with it. I scrawled a short note:

Dear Bernice:
Drop me a line sometime. RFD #1. Ocala, Fla.
Frank Mansfield

Whether Bernice would write to me or not I didn't know. I did feel, however, that the roses and thirty dollars in cash would make up for my abrupt leave-taking without saying good-bye. And I did like the woman. I tucked the money inside the little envelope, together with the card, and licked the flap.

"And where do you wish these delivered, sir?" the saleswoman asked, handing me a pink bill for twenty-five dollars and fifty cents. I put the money on the counter, and tugged at my lower lip. By having them delivered I could save time.

"We deliver free, of course," the woman smiled.

That settled it. I had to deliver the roses and the note myself. The woman was too damned anxious. Her gray hair and kindly, crinkle-faced smile didn't fool me. I had selected the twelve yellow roses with care. If I had allowed them to be delivered she would have either switched them for older roses, or changed them for carnations or something. After pocketing my change, I pointed to the stack of green waxed paper and made a circular motion with my hand for the woman to wrap them up.

When I reached 111 Melrose Avenue, I rang the bell several times, but there was no one at home. I waited impatiently for five minutes, and then left the flowers at the door. I slipped the note containing the money under the door. Maybe it was better that way.

The next move, if any, would be up to Bernice. If she had been home, I probably would have stayed overnight with her and lost another day. There was too much work ahead of me to waste time romancing a wealthy widow.

The old pickup drove well on the highway, but I was afraid to drive more than forty miles an hour. When I revved it up to fifty, the front wheels shimmied. Long before reaching Orlando I was remorseful about the grand gesture of giving the roses and thirty bucks to Bernice Hungerford. It would have been wiser to wait until I was flush again. The damned money was dripping through my fingers like water, and I'd have to win some fights before any more came in. But when I pictured the delighted expression on Bernice's jolly face when she discovered the flowers at her front door, I felt better.

I reached Orlando before midnight. I saved eight dollars by driving through town to Ed Middleton's private road, and by sleeping in the back of the truck in his orange grove. The excitement had drifted out of my mind, and, as tired as

I was, I slept as well in the truck as I would have slept in a motel bed.

The next morning, when I parked in his carport, and knocked on his kitchen door at six a.m., Ed wasn't happy to see me. Martha Middleton, however, appeared to be overjoyed by my early morning appearance. She cracked four more eggs into the frying pan and decided to make biscuits after all.

"I didn't expect you back so soon," Ed said gruffly, after he filled my cup with coffee.

I grinned at his discomfiture, took the money out of my jacket, and peeled off five hundred dollars on the breakfast-nook table. Ed glared at the stack of bills. Martha stayed close to her stove, pursing her lips. I drank half my coffee, and started in on my fried eggs before Ed Middleton said a word. In the back of my mind, I was more or less hoping he would change his mind and renege on the deal. Icarus was a mighty fine rooster, but five hundred dollars was a lot of money, and I needed every cent I could get at that moment.

"Well," Ed said thoughtfully. He counted the money twice, removed the top five twenty-dollar bills and shoved the remaining four hundred dollars back across the table.

"Here!" he said angrily. "I won't hold you to the ridiculous price we agreed on, Frank. I'll just take a hundred as a token payment. Besides, I'm sick of looking at game chickens. I'm tired of the whole business! Come on, let's go get your damned rooster!"

By the time Ed finished talking, he was almost shouting and out of the nook and fumbling at the doorknob.

"Can't you wait until Frank finishes his breakfast?" Martha said, with quiet good humor.

"Sure, sure," Ed managed to get the door open. "Take your time, Frank," he said contritely. "I'll go on out to the runs and put Icarus in your aluminum coop. Also, those two battered Grays are in good shape again. You can have them and the game hen, too. I'll have them all in coops by the time you finish eating." The door banged shut.

I wiped some egg yolk off the top twenty with a napkin and returned the money to my inside jacket pocket. The kitchen door opened again, and Ed stuck his head in. "Can you use some corn? Barley?"

I nodded.

"Good. There're about three or four partly used sacks of both in the feed shack. But if you want 'em, you'll have to carry 'em to the truck yourself. I'll be goddamned if *I'm* going to do it!" The door slammed again.

I wanted to follow him out the door but thought it best to finish my breakfast and let Ed cool off a little bit. He had never really expected me to show up with five hundred dollars for his pretty pet gamecock. But his astonishment was in my favor. He had been shamed into returning four hundred dollars, and now I was way ahead of the game. The Middleton Gray game hen was valuable for breeding, and the two Gray gamecocks were worth at least fifty dollars apiece.

"Don't you pay any mind to Ed's bluster, Frank," Martha said gently. "He's just upset and doesn't mean half of what he says. I know how much store he sets by those chickens. Someday, he'll thank me, Frank. You think I'm unreasonable, I know, making him give up his chickens and stopping him from following fights all over the country, but I'm not really. Ed's had two heart attacks in the last eighteen months. After the last one he was in bed for two weeks and the doctor told him not to do anything at all. Nothing." She shook her head.

"He isn't supposed to pick so much as an orange up off the ground. Why, the last time the doctor came out and saw that the roosters were still out there he had a fit! Now go out and get your chickens, Frank, and don't let Ed help you lift anything."

I slid out from the table and patted Martha on the shoulder. Ed Middleton certainly knew how to keep a secret. I hadn't known anything about his ailing heart.

"I know you won't say anything, Frank," Martha said, smiling, "but don't *look* anything, either!" Despite her smile and the humor in her voice, there were sparks of terror in her eyes. "Ed hasn't told a soul about his bad heart, and I know he wouldn't want me to tell you. He tries to pretend he's as strong as he ever was."

I wanted to say something, anything that would comfort the woman, but I couldn't. He was going to die soon. I could tell by her eyes.

I smiled, nodded and left the kitchen. The moment I was outside, I lit out around the little lake at a dead run to get my prize rooster before Ed Middleton could change his mind.

Chapter Ten

The scarlet cock, my lord likes best,
And next to him, the gray with thistle-breast.
This knight is for the pile, or else the Black.
A third cries no cock like the dun, yellow back.
The milk-white cock with golden legs and bill.
Or else the Spangle, choose you as you will.
The King he swears (of all), these are the best.
They heel, says he, more true than all the rest.
But this is all mere fancy, and no more,
The color's nothing, as I've said before!

This anonymous English cocking poem was thumbtacked to the wall beside my bed. I had copied it in longhand and stuck it there as a reminder that experience, rather than experiment, would be my best teacher. This poem must have been more than two hundred years old, and yet it still held a sobering truth. The best gamecock has to be of a proven game strain. Crossed and recrossed, until the color of the feathers resemble mud, if a cock can be traced to a legitimate game strain on both sides, he will fight when he is pitted and face when he is hurt. This old poem contained a particularly worthwhile truth to remember, now that I possessed Icky, the most gaily plumaged cock I had ever owned. The bettors at every pit on the circuit would be anxious to back him because of his bright blue color, and he would have to be good, because of the odds I'd be forced to give on him.

While I poured coffee into cups at the gate-legged table, Omar Baradinsky, his hairy fingers clasped behind his back, studied the poem on the wall. He must have read it three or four times, but if he moved his lips when he read, I wouldn't have known about it. Omar's pale face, which no amount of exposure to the Florida sun could tan, was almost completely covered by a thick, black, unmanageable beard. This ragged hirsute growth, wild and tangled, began immediately below his circular, heavily pouched brown eyes, and ended in tattered shreds halfway down his chest. A thick, untrimmed moustache, intermingled with his beard, covered his mouth completely. When he talked, and Omar liked to talk, his mouth was only a slightly darker hole in the center of the jet-black tangle of face hair. Out of curiosity, I had asked Omar once why he wore the beard, and his answer had been typical of his new way of life.

"I'll tell you, Frank," he had boomed. "Did you ever eat baked ham with a slice of glazed pineapple decorating the platter?"

When I admitted that I had, he had pulled his fingers through his beard fondly and continued. "Well, that's what my face looked like when I went to the office every day in New York. Like a slab of glazed, fried, reddish pineapple! For me, shaving once a day wasn't enough. The whiskers grew too fast. I shaved before leaving home in the morning, again at noon, and if I went out again at night, I had to scrape my jowls again. For as long as I can remember, my face was sore, raw in fact, and even after a fresh shave people told me I needed another. So, I no longer have to shave and I no longer shave, and I'll never shave again!"

To see Omar Baradinsky now, standing in my one-and-a-half-room shack near Ocala, wearing a pair of faded blue denim bib overalls, a khaki work shirt with the sleeves cut off at the shoulders, scuffed, acid-eaten, high-topped work shoes, and that awe-inspiring growth of black hair covering his face—no one in his right mind would have taken him for a once successful advertising executive in New York City. A closer look at his clothes, however, would reveal that Omar's bib overalls and shirt were expensive and tailored—which they were. He ordered his clothes from Abercrombie & Fitch up in New York, and they would wash and dry without needing to be ironed. In the beginning, I suspect that he had probably started to wear bib overalls as a kind of uniform, to fit some imaginary role he had made up in the back of his mind. But now they had become a part of him, and I couldn't picture Omar wearing anything else.

But Omar had been an advertising man, four years before. Not only had he been a successful executive with a salary of thirty-five thousand dollars a year, he had also owned a twenty-unit luxury apartment house in Brooklyn. He was now a breeder and handler of gamecocks in Florida, keeping Claret crosses and Allen Roundheads, and after four experimental years, slowly beginning to pull ahead. The one remaining tie Omar had with New York was his wife. She visited him annually, for one week, when she passed through central Florida on her way to Miami Beach for the winter season. So far, she had been unable to make him change his mind and return to New York. Omar's wife wasn't the type to bury herself on an isolated Florida chicken farm, so they were stalemated.

Unlike most American sportsmen, the cockfighting fan has an overwhelming tendency to become an active participant. There is no such thing as a passive interest in cockfighting. Beginning as a casual onlooker, a man soon finds the action of two game-cocks battling to the death a fascinating spectacle. He either likes it or he doesn't. If he doesn't like it, he doesn't return to watch another fight. If he does like it, he accepts, sooner or later, everything about the sport—the good with the bad.

As the fan gradually learns to tell one game strain from another, he admires the vain beauty of a game rooster. Admiration leads to the desire to possess one of these beautiful creatures for his very own, and pride of ownership leads to the pitting of his pet against another gamecock. Whether he wins or loses, once the fan has got as far as pitting, he is as hooked as a ghetto mainliner.

Of course, not every beginner embraces the sport like Omar Baradinsky—to the point of quitting a thirty-five-thousand dollar-a-year position, and leaving wife, family and friends to raise and fight gamecocks in Florida. The majority of fans are content to participate on a smaller scale—as a handler, perhaps, or as an owner of one or two gamecocks, or as a lowly assistant holding a bird for a handler while he lashes on the heels. Many spectators, unfortunately, are interested in the gambling aspects of cockfighting to the exclusion of everything else. But even gamblers must learn a lot of information about game fowl to win consistently. Whether he wins or loses, the gambler still has the satisfaction of knowing that a cockfight cannot be fixed, and not another sport in the United States will give him as fair a chance for his money.

Omar Baradinsky, however, had gone all the way, caught up in the sport at the dangerous age of fifty, the age when a man begins to wonder just what in the hell has he got out of his life so far, anyway? Omar was still as bewildered by his decision to enter full-time cockfighting now as he had been when he started.

"I can't really explain it, Frank," he had told me one idle morning, after we got to know each other fairly well, right after he had first moved to Florida. "I had done a better than average job on one of my smaller advertising accounts, and the owner invited me to his home in Saratoga Springs for a weekend. Smelling a little bonus money in the deal, you see, something my firm wouldn't know anything about, I accepted and drove to this fellow's place early on a Saturday morning.

"Just as I anticipated, he presented me with a bonus check for a thousand clams. And we sat around his swimming pool all afternoon—which was empty by the way—drinking Scotch and water and talking business. Out of nothing, he asked me if I'd like to see a cockfight that night.

" 'Cockfight!' I said. 'They're illegal, aren't they?' 'Sure, they are!' he laughed. 'But so was sleeping with that blonde you fixed me up with in New York. If you've never seen a cockfight, I think you might get a kick out of it.'

"So I went to my first cockfight. I'll never forget it, Frank. The sight of those beautiful roosters fighting to the death, the gameness, even when mortally wounded, was an exciting, unforgettable experience. Before the evening was over, I knew that that's what I wanted to do with my life: breed and fight game fowl. It was infantile, crazy maybe, I don't know. My wife thought I'd lost my mind and wouldn't even listen to my reasons. Probably because I couldn't give her any, not valid reasons. I *wanted* to do it and that was my sole reason!

"I was fed up to the teeth with advertising, and I had saved enough money to quit. I was only fifty, and although my future still glimmered on Madison Avenue, I didn't really need any more money than I already had. Still, I played it pretty cagy with the firm. I made a secret deal with one of the other vice-presidents to feed him my accounts in return for supporting my resignation on the grounds of ill health. That way, I picked up twenty-five thousand dollars in severance pay. I sold my apartment house and set up a trust fund for my wife to take care of her needs in New York. Besides, she has money of her own. Her father was a proctologist, and he left her plenty when he died. And for the first time in my life, I'm happy, really happy. Funny, isn't it?"

This was Omar Baradinsky, who owned a game farm only three miles away from mine. So far, he hadn't prospered in his adopted profession, but he was breaking even by selling trios and stags to other cockers. His gamecocks usually lost when he fought them in the southern pits. He must have been hard enough to succeed in the business world, but the stubborn streak of tenderness in his makeup didn't give him enough discipline to make Aces out of his pit fowl. He overfed them, and he didn't work them hard enough to last.

Turning away from the poem, Omar turned his huge brown orbs on me and jerked a thumb at the wall.

"Did you write that, Frank?"

I shook my head and pulled out a chair for him to sit down.

"Then what about your new cock, Icky? If that chicken wasn't bred purely for color I've never seen one."

I shrugged. Icky had been bred for color, certainly, but from a pure game strain, and his conformation was ideal for fighting. In a few days I'd see whether he could fight or not when I gave him a workout with sparring muffs in my training pit.

"Anyway, I like the looks of those Mellhorn Blacks, and especially your two Middleton Grays."

So did I. Buford, my part-time Negro helper, had gone downtown to the depot with me the night before when I picked up my shipment of Mellhorn Blacks. After helping me put the dozen cocks away in their separate stalls in the cockhouse, he had driven by Omar's place and told him about them. Omar had arrived early that morning for a look at the Mellhorns and a long admiring examination of Icky. Buford had undoubtedly given Icky a big buildup, but Omar hadn't been impressed until he saw the cock for himself.

"Tell me something, Frank, if you will," Omar said, when he finished pouring some condensed milk into his coffee. "Did you get an invitation to the Southern Conference Tourney at Milledgeville?"

In reply, I got up from the table, rummaged in the top drawer of my dresser until I found the invitation and the schedule for the S.C. pit battles, and passed them to Omar. He glanced at the forms, pulled on his shaggy beard a couple of times, and returned the papers.

"I just don't understand you people down here," he said. "It may be partly my fault, because I wrote Senator Foxhall a personal letter asking for an invitation and enclosed a two-hundred-dollar forfeit. Three days later I got the check back in the mail and no invitation. Not a damned word of explanation. What in the hell's the matter with me? I've got more than fifty birds under keep, and last season my showings hit fifty-fifty. Maybe I'm not in the same class with the S.C. regulars, but if I'm willing to lose my entry fee why should Senator Foxhall care? And here you are—I saw the date on your invitation—you didn't own a single gamecock when you got that invite! I'm not belittling your ability, Frank. I know you're a top cocker and all that, but how did the senator know you'd be able to attend? How did you receive an invitation without asking for one when I couldn't get one when I did?

"I've never attended the Milledgeville meet, and I want to go, even as a spectator. But after fighting at all the other S.C. pits this season, I'd be embarrassed to attend the tournament without an entry. Do you know what I mean?"

I knew what he meant, all right. Omar had done the normal, logical thing, and the turndown had hurt his feelings. Most of the U.S. derbies and tourneys get their entries through fees. The man who sends in a two- or three-hundred-dollar forfeit either shows up or he loses his money. A contract is returned to him by mail. When the list is filled, no more entries are accepted. I didn't really know why Omar had been turned down by Senator Foxhall. It wasn't because he was a Pole or a New Yorker.

Members of the cockfighting fraternity are from all walks of life. There are men like myself, from good southern families, sharecroppers, businessmen, loafers on the county relief rolls, Jews, and Holy Rollers. If there is one single thing in the world, more than all the others, preserving the tradition of the sport of cocking for thousands of years, it's the spirit of democracy. In a letter to General Lafayette, George Washington wrote, "It will be worth coming back to the United States, if only to be present at an election and a cocking main at which is displayed a spirit of anarchy and confusion, which no countryman of yours can understand." I carried a clipping of this letter, which had been reprinted in a game fowl magazine, in my wallet. I had told Mary Elizabeth once that George Washington and Alexander Hamilton had both been cockfighters during the colonial period, but she had been unimpressed. Nonetheless, cockfighters are still the most democratic group of men in the United States.

But the Milledgeville Tourney was unlike other U.S. meets. Senator Foxhall had his own rules, and he made his own decisions about whom to invite. I had earned my right to fight there, and I suppose the old man knew that I would be there if it was physically possible for me to be there. Maybe he didn't think Omar was ready yet. I didn't know. Surely Omar's fifty-fifty showing didn't put him into the top cocker's class. He still had a lot to learn about game fowl if he wanted to be a consistent winner.

I looked at Omar and smiled. There wasn't any use to write a note for him telling him what I thought was the reason for his turndown. His feelings would be hurt more than they were already. By writing to the senator, he had made a grave error, a social error. It was like calling a host of a party you were not invited to and asking point blank for an invitation!

I had finished my coffee, and I had work to do. I got up from the table and clapped Omar on the shoulder. Before leaving the shack, I took a can of lighter fluid off the dresser and slipped it into my hip pocket. Omar sighed audibly and decided to follow me out.

When we got to the cockhouse, I removed the Mellhorn

Blacks one at a time from their separate coops, showing off the good and bad points to Omar as well as I could before putting them back. For a shipment of a dozen, they were a beautiful lot. As Jake had promised in his letter, six were full brothers, a few months past staghood, and the other six were Aces, two to three years old, with one or more winning fights behind them. Each cock was identifiable by its web-marking, and the cardboard record sheet of each bird had been enclosed in its shipping crate when Jake had expressed them down from North Carolina. Before putting them away the night before, I had purged them with a mild plain-phosphate mixture, and they were feeling fine as a consequence.

As a conditioning bench, I used a foam-rubber double mattress stretched flat on a wooden, waist-high platform Buford and I had knocked together out of scrap lumber when I had first leased the farm. I had one of the older Mellhorn cocks on the bench showing it to Omar. The cock was a one-time winner, but he must have won by an accident. His conformation was fair, but the bird was high-stationed, with his spurs jutting out just below the knee joint. He would miss as often as he hit. A low-stationed cock would have greater leverage and fight best in long heels, but a high-stationed cock like this one would never make a first-class fighter. Jake Mellhorn hadn't gypped me on the sale. He was truly bred, and in small-time competition against strainers, the cock could often win. It had weight in its favor and was close to the shake class, but the chicken couldn't really compete in S.C. competition unless it got lucky. Luck is not for the birds. The element of chance must be reduced to the minimum if a cocker wants to win the prize money. In a six-entry derby, for instance, when the man winning the most fights takes home the purse put up by all the entries, the odd fight often provides the verdict. I couldn't take a chance with this one.

After pointing out the high spurs to show Omar what was wrong with the Black, I picked up my hatchet and chopped off the rooster's head on the block outside the doorway.

"I see," Omar said thoughtfully, as he watched the decapitated chicken flop about in the dusty yard. "You don't like to pit high-stationed cocks."

I clipped the hatchet into the block so it stuck.

"Some cockers prefer high-stationed birds," Omar said argumentatively. "And a seventy-five-dollar chicken is damned expensive eating."

True, the plateful of fried chicken I would eat that night would be a costly meal, but it would have been much more expensive to pit the cock when he would probably lose. And an owner should only bet on his own gamecock—not against it. I shrugged indifferently.

"I suppose you know what you're doing," Omar said. "But he was a purebred Mellhorn and could have been kept as a brood cock."

Except on a small scale, I've never done much breeding. I prefer to buy my gamecocks. Conditioning and fighting them are what I do best, but I would never have bred the high-stationed Black. Like begets like, and the majority of the chicks sired would have been high-stationed.

I shook my head and grinned at Omar. He was well aware of the heredity factor—his head was crammed with breeding knowledge he had learned through reading and four years' experience. Omar was still sore about the Milledgeville Tourney.

"What about the six brothers? How do you know they're game? The Aces have been pit-tested, but if one of the brothers is a runner they all may be runners."

Unfortunately, there is no true test for gameness. Only a pit battle can decide gameness. There are various tests, however, a cocker can try which will give him an indication of a cock's gameness. In the case of the six brothers, I was stymied by a lack of knowledge concerning the father and mother. If the father had been a champion, Jake Mellhorn would have said so, and charged a higher price for them. The six cocks were obviously Mellhorn Blacks. I could tell that by looking at them. But only one drop of cold blood from a dunghill will sometimes cause a cock to run when it is hurt. One of the young cocks had to be tested for gameness, and I had planned on doing it this morning before Omar came over. If the cock I tested proved to be game, I could then assume that the others were equally game. But in the testing I would lose the gamecock. Another seventy-five bucks shot.

127

One rigid test for gameness is to puncture a cock all over his body with an ice pick, digging it in for a quarter to half an inch. If the injured cock will still attempt to fight another cock the next morning, even if all he can do is lie on his back and peck, it is considered game. The ice-pick method of testing is fairly popular with cockers because they can usually salvage their bird after it recovers from its injuries. I don't consider this test severe enough. The Roman method I use is more realistic than a halfhearted jabbing with an ice pick, even though the cock is lost during the process.

For the test, I selected one of the brothers with the poorest conformation. The choice was difficult because all of the brothers were fine Mellhorn Blacks. For an opponent, I used the largest of the two Middleton Grays. Omar held the Gray when I heeled it with sparring muffs. The Black would be practically helpless, and I didn't want him killed until he had suffered sufficiently to determine his gameness.

My homemade pit is crudely put together with scrap lumber, but it meets the general specifications. I've also strung electric lights above it in order to work my birds at night, and it's good enough for training purposes. Omar put the Gray under one arm, after I completed the heel-tying of the muffs, and headed for the training pit in front of my shack.

The young Black was a man fighter and pecked my wrist twice before I could get a good grip around his upper legs with my left hand. A moment later I had his body held firmly against my leg where he couldn't peck at me anymore. In this awkward position, I stretched his legs out on the block outside the cockhouse and chopped them off at the knee with the hatchet.

When I joined Omar at the pit, his brown eyes bulged until they resembled oil-soaked target agates. "Good God, Frank! You don't expect him to fight without any legs, do you?"

I nodded and stepped over the pit wall. I cradled the Black over my left arm, holding the stumps with my right hand, and raised my chin to indicate that we should bill them. Omar brought the Gray in close and the Black tore out a beakful of feathers.

We billed the cocks until their ingrained natural combativeness was aroused, and then I set the Black down on the floor of the pit and took the Gray away from Omar. The Gray was anxious to get to his legless opponent, but I held him tightly by the tail and only let him approach to within pecking range. When the Black struggled toward him, I pulled him back by his tail. Without his feet, the Black was unable to get enough balance or leverage to fly, and his wildly fluttering wings couldn't support him in an upright position. He kept falling forward on his chest, and after a short valiant period of struggling, he gave up altogether. I let the Gray scratch into range, still holding him by the tail. The Black pecked every time, although he no longer tried to stand on his stumps. Finally, I let the Gray go, and he described a short arc in the air and landed, shuffling, in the center of the Black's back. Getting a good bill hold on the prostrate cock, the Gray shuffled methodically in place, hitting the padded muffs hard enough to make solid thumping sounds on the Black's body. This was the first time I had seen the Gray in action. I realized that Ed Middleton had really done me a favor when he gave me the once-battered fighter. Any cock that could shuffle with the deadly accuracy displayed by the Middleton Gray would win a lot of pit battles.

The Black was too helpless to fight off the Gray, so I picked up the muff-armed bird and gave him to Omar to hold for a moment. I took the can of lighter fluid out of my hip pocket, and sprinkled the liquid liberally over the Mellhorn Black. Flipping my lighter into action, I applied the lighter to the cock, and his feathers blazed into oily flames.

When Omar returned the Gray I pitted him against the burning bird from the score on the opposite side of the pit. He walked stiff-winged toward the downed Black with his long neck outstretched, holding his head low above the ground. The fire worried and puzzled him, and he was afraid to hit with his padded spurs. The Gray pecked savagely at the Black's head, however, even though it was on fire, and managed to pluck out an eye on his first bill thrust.

The Black tried to stand again, fluttering his smoldering wings, but his impassioned struggles only succeeded in increasing the flames. The smell of scorching feathers filled the air with a pungent, acid stench. As I grabbed the Gray's tail with my right hand, I held my nose with my left. As the flames puffed out altogether, the Black lay quietly. The charred quills resembled matchheads or cloves dotting his undressed body, and for a moment I thought he was dead. But as I allowed the straining Gray to close the gap between them, the dying Mellhorn raised his head and pecked blindly in the general direction of the approaching Gray. With that last peck, a feeble peck that barely raised his head an inch above the ground, he died.

I put the Gray under my arm and turned around to see what Omar thought of this remarkable display of gameness. But Omar had gone inside the shack. I cut the sparring muffs away from the Gray's spurs and returned him to his coop.

Omar sat at the table, staring at his open hands, when I joined him inside the shack. I opened a pint of gin I had stashed away behind the dresser—because of Buford—and put the bottle on the table. Omar took a long pull, set the bottle down, and I took a long one myself. I needed that drink and felt a little sick at my stomach. And I knew that Omar felt as badly as I did. But what else could I do? I had lost a wonderful gamecock, but I could now assume that his five brothers would be as game as he had been. The unfortunate part of the testing was that I didn't really know if the brothers were equally game. But I could now *assume* that they were.

"I couldn't treat a gamecock like that, Frank," Omar said, without looking at me, keeping his eyes on his open hands. "Sure, I know. A chicken is supposed to be an insensitive animal and all that crap. But *I* couldn't do it! I could no more set a cock on fire than I could—" His mind searched for something he could no more than do, and then he shrugged his heavy shoulders and took another shot of gin.

I took another short one myself.

"Was he game, Frank? It was too much for me. I couldn't stick around to see."

I nodded glumly and lit a cigarette.

"Unbelievable, isn't it! Burning like a damned torch and still trying to fight! A man couldn't take that kind of punishment and still fight. Not a man in this world could do it."

I stubbed out the cigarette. It tasted like scorched feathers, despite the menthol and filter tip.

"Well, Frank," Omar said pensively, "there're a lot of things I don't like about cockfighting, but a cocker's got to take the bad with the good."

I nodded in agreement and pushed the bottle toward him.

Omar studied my face and, ignoring the bottle, leaned forward.

"You and I need each other, Frank," he said suddenly. "Why don't we form a partnership for the season?"

For some reason his suggestion startled me, and I shook my head automatically.

"Don't decide so hastily," he continued earnestly, leaning over the table. "I've picked up twenty cocks already, and I've still got better birds to pick up on walks in Alabama. Between the two of us, if you conditioned and handled, and I took charge of the business end, we could have one hell of a season. I know how tough it's been since you lost your voice. I still remember how you used to holler and argue and knock down the odds before the fights. What do you say, Frank?"

I was tempted. Two of my cocks were gone before I started. I only had thirteen birds left for the season, and my cash was low. If we combined our gamecocks we could enter every money main and derby on the circuit, and if Omar didn't interfere with my conditioning—

"Let it go for now," Omar said carelessly, getting to his feet. "Just think about it for a while. I don't like to mention my money, but I'm lousy with capital. I've got a lot more than you have, and if you had a partner putting up the forfeits, entry fees, and doing all the betting, you could concentrate on conditioning and handling. And on a partnership we can split everything we take in right down the middle."

He turned in the doorway and his shadow fell across my face. "No matter what you decide," he said cheerfully, "come over to my place for dinner tonight. I'll take that high-stationed Mellhorn home with me. I've always wanted to eat a Mellhorn Black with dumplings." He laughed. "Chicken and dumplings for two! That's about

131

thirty-seven, fifty a plate, isn't it?" Omar waved from the door and disappeared from sight.

I remained seated at the table. A few minutes later I heard the engine of his new Pontiac station wagon turn over, and listened to the sounds as he drove out of the yard. The pot of coffee on the hot plate burbled petulantly. I poured another cup, and a cock crowed outside, reminding me of all the work still to be done that morning. I couldn't put off the dubbing of Icky any longer.

Ordinarily, the deaf ears, wattles and comb are trimmed away when the bird is a young stag of six or seven months. Ed Middleton, for reasons known only to himself, had failed to dub Icky. He probably meant to keep Icky as a pet and brood cock and had never intended to pit him. But I was going to pit him, and he had to be dubbed for safety in battle. With his lovely free-flowing comb and dangling wattles, an opposing cock could get a billhold and shuffle him to death in the first pitting. I had been putting off the dubbing, afraid that he might bleed to death. With a stag the danger is slight, but Icky was fully matured, more than a year-and-a-half old. And it had to be done.

I got my shears, both the straight and the curved pairs, and went outside to Icky's coop room.

He was a friendly chicken, used to kindness and handling, and ran toward me when I opened the gate. I picked him up, sat on the bench in front of the shack, and went to work on his comb. With my experience I don't need a man to hold a chicken for me. I've dubbed as many as fifty stags in a single morning, all by myself, and I've never had one die from loss of blood yet. But I was extra careful with Icky.

Gripping his body firmly between my knees, and holding his head with my left hand, I clipped his comb with the straight shears as close to the head as possible. Many cockers leave about an eighth of an inch, believing erroneously that the slight padding will give the head protection from an opponent's pecking. But I've never known a cock to be *pecked* to death. I trim right down to the bone because the veins are larger close to the head and there isn't as much bleeding. I cut sharply, and with solid, quick snips, so the large veins were closed by the force of the shears. Luckily, Icky's head bled very little. I then cut away the wattles and deaf ears with the curved shears, again taking my time, and did a clean job. As an afterthought I pulled a few short feathers out of the hackle and planted them in Icky's comb. The little blue feathers would grow there and ornament his head, until they were billed out by an irate adversary.

When I completed the dubbing I turned him loose in his coop. He had held still nicely, and because he had been so good about it, I caught the Middleton Gray game hen running loose in the yard, and put her into his coop. The dubbing hadn't bothered him. He mounted the hen before she had taken two steps. A moment later he flew to his roosting pole and crowed. Within a week his head would be healed completely, and he would be ready for conditioning.

Omar had taken the decapitated Ace Black with him, but the charred Mellhorn was still in the pit. I buried the dead chicken and the other cock's severed head in the sand before eating lunch.

If I had been completely broke, or without any gamecocks of my own, I wouldn't have considered a partnership with Omar. But I had enough Ace chickens to hold up my end. Omar had excellent, purebred gamecocks. All he needed was a man like me to work the hell out of them. The idea of forming a partnership with anybody had never occurred to me before, although partnerships were common enough in cockfighting circles. Besides, I had a good deal of affection for Omar, almost a paternal feeling toward him, despite the fact that he was more than twenty years older than me. He wanted success very much, and there were many things he had to learn. And there was a lot that I could teach him.

After feeding the chickens that evening, I drove to Omar's farm for supper. His farm was on the state road, and his house was a two bedroom-den structure with asphalt-tile floors. It was a luxurious house compared to my one-and-a-half-room shack. There was an arch above the entrance gate, and a sign painted with red letters on a white background stated:

THE O.B. GAME FARM
"Our Chickens Lay Every Night!"

Omar had been in advertising too many years to pass up

a good slogan. In addition to the arch sign, there was a smaller sign nailed to the post of the gate at the eye level of passing motorists.

EGGS. $15 PER DOZEN

At least once a week, some tourist driving down the highway toward Santos or Belleview would stop and attempt to buy eggs from Omar, thinking that the sign was in error and that the eggs were fifteen cents a dozen. Omar enjoyed the look of surprise on their faces when he told them that there was indeed no mistake. Of course the eggs were fifteen dollars a dozen and worth a hell of a lot more! And of course, Allen Roundhead and Claret setting eggs were a bargain indeed at fifteen dollars a dozen.

Smiling at the sign, I turned into Omar's farm. A man like Omar Baradinsky would be a good partner for me. Why not? I couldn't think of a single valid objection.

That evening after supper, when Omar brought out the bottle of John Jameson, a partnership was formed.

Chapter Eleven

For the next three days Omar and I lived out of his station wagon, driving through southern Alabama and picking up his country-walked roosters from various farmers. The back of the station wagon had been filled with young stags before we left, each of them in a separate coop. Every time we picked up a mature cock we left a stag to replace it.

Omar paid these Alabama farmers ten dollars a year for the privilege of leaving one of his gamecocks with the farmer's flock of hens. In addition to the board bill, he also had to buy up and kill all the farmer's stags each year. Selecting the right farm walk for a fighting cock is an art, and Omar had done a careful, thorough job. All his Alabama walks were more than adequate.

A gamecock is a bird that loves freedom of movement. With his harem at his heels, a cock will search for food all day long, getting as far as three or more miles away from his chicken house on the farm. The more difficult his search for food, the greater his stamina becomes. At night, of course, once the chickens are asleep, the farmer must sneak out and scatter enough corn in the yard to supplement the diet. But he must never put out enough feed to completely satisfy the chickens. Like members of a welfare state, chickens who don't have to get the hell out and scratch for their living will soon learn to stand around waiting for a free handout, getting fat and useless.

The hillier the farmland, the better it is for the cock's legs. Trees to roost in at night, green fields, and, whenever possible, a fast-flowing brook for fresh water are the requisites for a good walk. Florida is too flat for good walks, and Omar had been wise to put his roosters out in southern Alabama.

To assist us in picking up the half-wild, country-walked gamecocks, I had brought along my big Middleton Gray. He had a deep, strong voice and an exceptionally aggressive disposition. We had little difficulty in getting the half-wild cocks to come back to the farmyards.

First, we drove into a farmer's yard, and Omar told him we were there to pick up the rooster, and that we had another to replace him.

"Well, now, Mr. Baradinsky," the farmer said, invariably scratching his head, "I ain't seen your rooster for two or three days now."

"Don't worry," Omar would laugh. "He'll be here in a minute."

By that time, I would have the big Gray heeled with a pair of soft sparring muffs. As soon as I dropped the Gray in the yard, he would begin to look for hens, crowing deep from his throat. Within seconds, an answering crow would echo from the fields or woods a mile away. As we watched, the cock we came for would be running toward us as fast as his strong legs could carry him, his harem scattered and trailing out behind him. He often crowed angrily as he ran— *Who is this threat to my kingdom? This interloper who would steal my hens?*—he seemed to say. When he reached the yard, he attacked immediately, and the Gray, seeing all those pretty hens, piled right into him with the sparring muffs. Omar would catch the wild country-walked cock, and I'd put the Gray back into his coop.

After closely examining the wild gamecock, I'd saw off his natural spurs a half inch from the leg, and arm him with the other pair of sparring muffs. We pitted the two cocks then and there to see how the bird fought. It is very difficult to spot a runner on his own domain—often a useless dunghill rooster will fight to protect his own hens—but I could always get a fair idea of the bird's fighting ability. If the cock was satisfactory, we left a young stag to take over the harem and placed the cock in the stag's coop. Before leaving, Omar would pay the farmer ten dollars in advance for the next year's board and warn the man against clipping the new stag's wings. We never took the farmer's word either. Before leaving we always checked personally to see that there weren't any other full-grown roosters, turkeys, or guinea fowl around. A stag must be in complete control of the yard. If there was a mature rooster on the farm, dunghill or otherwise, the stag might have been intimidated and gone into hack, submitting to the dunghill's rule.

Omar had developed a firm, gruff manner with these farmers who loaned their farms for walks. Despite his strong New York accent, which rural southerners distrust instinctively, he had won them over completely during four years of contact. He didn't merely leave a stag and forget about it until the following season. He wrote letters periodically during the year, asking how his rooster was getting along, enclosing a stamped, self-addressed postcard to make sure he would get a reply. The farmers responded cheerfully to Omar's active interest, and, if nothing else, they were awed by his impressive jet-black beard.

Most farmers, once they accept the idea of having a gamecock instead of a dunghill ruling their hens, are well pleased by the setup. Why shouldn't they be? The eggs they obtain are bigger and better-tasting, the offspring of a gamecock have more meat, and the small payment of ten dollars a year is money from an unexpected source. And any farmer who keeps a few hens has to have a rooster. Why not a game rooster?

Every time we picked up another country-walked rooster my heart swelled with pleasure. Their feathers were tight and their yellow eyes were bright and alert. Their exercised bodies were firm to the touch, and their dubbed combs usually had the dark red color of health. Out of the twenty-eight cocks Omar had on country walks, we picked up twenty-one. The other seven, in my considered opinion, needed another full year of exercise in the country.

I was happy to get back to Ocala and anxious to get to work. The little town of Ocala has always been my favorite Florida city, combining, as it does, the best aspects of Georgia and the worst side of Florida. A small city, of about twenty thousand permanent residents, and some one hundred miles below the Georgia state line, Ocala is where the state of Florida really begins.

As a driver enters town on the wide island-divided highway, the first sight that hits his eyes is the banner above the road: OCALA—BIRTHPLACE OF NEEDLES! This famous racehorse will be remembered by the Ocala townspeople forever.

To his left, six miles away, is Silver Springs, one of the most publicized tourist attractions in the world. On either side of the highway there are weird attractions, displays and souvenir shops. Commercial Florida also begins at Ocala. But the town itself is like a small Georgia town. Decent, respectable and God-fearing. The townspeople are good southerners—they provide their services to the rural residents and to themselves, and take only from the vacationing tourists with cameras dangling from their rubber necks.

Two miles outside the city limits in gently swelling country is my small leased farm of twenty-three acres, a small house to live in, an outhouse and outside shower, a well-constructed concrete brick cockhouse and some thirty-odd coop walks. My shack, as I called it, was unpainted but comfortable. The man who built it had started with concrete bricks, but ran short before the walls had reached shoulder height. The remainder of the house had been completed with rough, unfinished pine, and roofed over with two welded sheets of corrugated iron. In a downpour, the heavy pounding of raindrops on the corrugated iron had often driven me out of the shack.

Omar dropped me off first and then drove to his own farm. He had much better facilities to take care of the cocks than I had, and, upon his suggestion, I had agreed to alternate between our farms for conditioning purposes.

Buford ran out of the cockhouse as I entered the yard, a big white smile shining in the middle of his ebony face.

"Mr. Frank," he said happily, taking my bag, "I sure is happy to see you! My curiosity's been drivin' me near crazy for two days. Just wait till you see them big packages I put in the house!"

I entered the shack, followed closely by Buford, and the first thing I did was reach behind the dresser for my pint of gin. As I had suspected, the bottle contained less than two ounces, and it had been almost half full when Omar had picked me up three days before. I looked sternly at Buford, but he was pointing innocently to the two large cardboard boxes on my bed.

"I don' know what they is, Mr. Frank," he said quickly. "The man from the express brought 'em out day before yesterday, and I signed your name. What do you reckon's in there?"

I finished the gin, and handed the empty to Buford. Buford had had his share while I was gone—the man had an unerring instinct for discovering where I hid my bottle. He thought that finding my bottle was some kind of a game.

I took out my knife and slit open the two cardboard boxes. One box contained a speaker, and the long box held an electric guitar. But *what* a guitar! The instrument was fashioned out of some kind of light metal, painted a bright lemon yellow and trimmed in Chinese red. On the box, above the strings, there were two sets of initials, encircled by an outline of a heart.

If I thought I had made the grand gesture when I sent Bernice a dozen yellow roses, she had certainly topped me. The electric guitar and its matching yellow amplifying speaker must have set her back four or five hundred dollars. I searched through the excelsior in both cartons for a note of some kind, but there wasn't even a receipt for the instrument. The initials inside the heart contained her message.

Buford looked admiringly at the guitar, shaking his head with feigned amazement. As soon as I looked at him he laughed the professional laugh of the American Negro.

"Whooee!" he exploded with false amusement. "You got yourself a guitar now for sure, Mr. Frank!"

I pointed to the door. Out in the yard I gave Buford a ten-dollar bill in payment for looking after the place for three days. Buford had his own farm, a wife and four children, but he spent more time with me than he did with his family. When I happened to think about it, I'd slip him a five or a ten, but I didn't keep him on a regular salary because I didn't need him around in the first place. He knew as much about the raising and handling of gamecocks as any Negro in the United States, if not more. Unfortunately, because of his color, he was barred from almost every white cockpit in the South. He would have been an invaluable assistant for me on my trips to circuit cockpits, but I couldn't take him along. However, he helped me out around the place, handled opposing cocks in my own training pit and made himself fairly useful during conditioning periods. He loved game-cocks. That much I knew about him. And I believe he would have sacrificed an arm or a leg for the opportunity to fight them. Because I knew this much about the man, I was well aware that his rich and easy laughter was insincere.

What in the hell did Buford have to laugh about?

"I fixed up all them sun coops the way you showed me, Mr. Frank," Buford said. "And I put some new slats in the cockhouse stalls. But they ain't much else to do, so I won't be back around till Saturday."

I nodded, and Buford climbed into his car.

"Whooee!" he laughed through his nose. "You got you a git-fiddle now, sure enough! Will you play some for me come Saturday?"

Again I nodded. As Buford made a U-turn onto the gravel road toward the highway, I entered the shack.

The wonderful and unexpected gift had made my heart sing with delight, although I had controlled my inner excitement from Buford. As soon as he was gone, I connected the various electrical cords, following the directions in the illustrated instruction booklet. I plugged the cord into the wall outlet and tuned the strings. The full tones, amplified by the speaker set at full volume, reverberated in the small room and added a new dimension to my playing. After experimenting with several chords, banging them hard and listening to them echo metallically against the iron ceiling, I tried a song.

Halfway through the song I stopped playing and placed the guitar gently on the floor. Unconsciously, I had played "Georgia Girl" first. The rich amplified tones brought suppressed visions of Mary Elizabeth flooding into my mind, and I dropped the plastic pick.

In the sharp silence, following so closely on the sound of the echoing song, I pictured Mary Elizabeth in my mind, still in the same position where I had left her at The Place. She sat quietly, feet below the surface of the pool, and with dancing dappled sunlight reflecting on her pale nude body. Her blue-green eyes looked at me reproachfully, and her ordinarily full lips were set in a tight grim line.

To make her disappear I shook my head.

This was a recurrent vision of Mary Elizabeth. Whenever I happened to think of the woman, a guilty, sinking feeling accompanied the thought. She was always nude, always at The Place. I never thought of her as fully clothed—that was a Mary Elizabeth I didn't want to think about—the spinster-ish, school-teacherish, Methodist kind, with a reproving expression on her face. As a rule, when I hadn't seen Mary Elizabeth for several months, her features became indistinct, except for her hurt blue? green? eyes. But her body was always as clear in my mind as a Kodachrome color print. I remembered every anatomical detail, the way her right shoulder dipped a quarter of an inch lower than her left, the round, three-eyed shape of her button navel, and every golden pubic hair.

I loved her and I had always loved her and I always would love her, and the dark guilty shadows erased her pink-and-white body from my mind. No man had ever treated a woman any shabbier than I had Mary Elizabeth!

Suppose, I thought blackly, she just says the hell with

you, Frank Mansfield, and marries a nice stay-at-home
Georgia boy . . . a bloated bastard like Ducky Winters, for
instance, the manager of the Purina Feed Store? Why not?
He's single and over thirty. What if his bald head does look
like a freshly washed peach and the roll of fat around his
waistline resembles a rubber inner tube half filled with
water? He's got a good job, and he's a member of the Board
of Stewards of the Methodist church . . . well, isn't he? His
mother can't live forever, and he did pinch Mary Elizabeth
on the ass at the box social that time . . . remember? You
wanted to take him outside, but Mary Elizabeth wouldn't
let you.

How many good prospects does she have? Ducky Winters, no matter what you may think, is one of the *better*
prospects. Suppose she marries one of those red-necked
woolhat cronies of her brother's? Wright doesn't want her
to get married, but he would approve of some farmer who
would keep her close to home, just so he would be assured
of seeing her every day. What if she married Virgil Dietch,
whose farm is only three miles down the road? Virgil's only
forty, a widower with two half-grown boys, and he'd be
damned happy to marry a woman like Mary Elizabeth.
With his growling German accent—despite three generations in Georgia—and his lower lip packed chock-full of
Copenhagen snuff, she wouldn't be able to understand half
of what he said, but Wright liked Virgil and ran around
with him. And Wright wouldn't object to a marriage
between them.

For more than an hour I tortured myself, mulling over the
list of eligible suitors in the county Mary Elizabeth could
marry if she wanted to spite me. There weren't many left.
Most of the men in rural Georgia get married young, and
divorces are rare. The remaining eligibles were a sorry lot,
especially when I considered the widowers who had
worked their wives into an early grave.

It was exquisite torture to consider these ignorant wool-
hatters who shaved only on Saturday, who wore a single
suit of long johns from October 15th to May 15th, and who
didn't take a bath until the Fourth of July. And yet, as far as
husbands were concerned, every one of these men would
make a better husband than I would. As a woman, she was

entitled to a home and children and a husband who stayed with her at all times.

I had provided Mary Elizabeth with eight years of nothing. A quickly scrawled line on the back of a picture postcard, and on one of my rare, unscheduled visits, a quick jump in a woodland glen. To make matters worse, I hadn't even talked to her on my last two visits. But I had never been able to talk to her anyway. She had consistently resisted every explanation I had tried to give her concerning my way of life and had never consented to share it with me. Perhaps I could write her a letter, a really *good* letter this time, a letter that would make her think?

This year was going to be my year. I could sense it, and my new partnership with Omar was the turning point in my run of ill fortune. I knew this. My prospects had been as good before, but they had never been any better. I couldn't continue through life silent and alone, and I couldn't keep Mary Elizabeth dangling on a thread—the thread would break, and both of us would be lost. If there was to be a break, it would have to be now—Her way or My way—and *she* could make the choice!

I sat down at the table to write Mary Elizabeth a letter:

Dearest Darling,

I love you! How inadequate are written words to tell you of my feelings! To be with you and yet to be unable to speak, to tell you again and again that I love you is unbearable. To leave without saying good-bye, as I did, hurt me more than you can ever know. And yet, I had to leave silently, like a thief in the night. If I had written you a note with a bare "Good-bye," you would have rightfully demanded an explanation I couldn't give because I couldn't speak! But an explanation is due, my Love, and on the blankness of this page I shall attempt the impossible. Never, never doubt my love!

First, I was home to obtain my rightfully owned property. You know this now, of course, because your brother bought my farmhouse and land from me. What you don't know is that Judge Powell was instructed to sell only to Wright. Whether I was right or wrong in turning Randall out of his home depends upon how you want to look at it. In the Holy Bible the eldest son gets the inheritance of his father, as you know. In the eyes of the Lord, and I recognize no other Master, I was right. But even so, I only sold my land because I had to.

For ten years my goal has been to be the best cockfighter in the United States. Several, not many, times I've tried to explain cockfighting and my ambitions to you, but you have never listened. Read this, now, and then decide. Our future happiness, yours and mine, depends upon your decision. Closing your ears to all rational argument, you have always said that cockfighting was cruel and therefore wrong. But you have never SEEN a cockfight, and you said that you never intended to. At last I say you must!

The only way that you can find out that cockfighting is not a cruel sport is to see for yourself. I am now engaged in my very last try to reach the top. To continue fighting year after year without success is no longer possible. If I don't win the two-day Milledgeville Tourney this year, I promise you that I'll quit forever! We will be married immediately, and I'll enter any profession or endeavor YOU decide upon!

However, if I do win, and I want you physically present at the Milledgeville pit, win or lose, I intend to follow cock-fighting as a full-time profession for the rest of my natural life. If you can accept this way of life, we will get married immediately and go to Puerto Rico on our honeymoon.

The remaining alternative, of course, is to tear this letter to bits and put me out of your mind and life forever. If this latter course is your decision, I'll abide by it, and I'll never, I promise, write or see you again, but my heart will be completely broken!

Don't write and tell me what your decision is. If you do write, I won't open your letters. Two seats will be reserved in your name at the Milledgeville Tourney (bring your brother if you like) from March 15 to March 16. I won't write again, and will pray daily to the good Lord above that you will TRY—and please let your heart decide—to be there at Milledgeville.

I love you. I always have and always will!

Frank

I read the letter twice before sealing it into an envelope, and I thought it was a damned good letter. The little religious touches were particularly well done, and so was the part about going to Puerto Rico for our honeymoon. There are many luxury hotels in San Juan, and March is a good time to see slasher fights at the Valla Piedros. The pit opens daily at two p.m. and the cockfights are continuous until the cocktail hour. After dinner we could hit the casinos, shoot craps or even play a little blackjack.

Of course, there was always the chance that Omar and I wouldn't win the tourney. With ten entries scheduled, a lot of things could happen, but the main idea of the letter was to ensure Mary Elizabeth's physical presence at the pit. Once she saw for herself how well organized the tourney was, and how fair the pit decisions were, I was positive she would like the sport. A lot of ministers follow cockfighting zealously without conflict with their religious beliefs. After all, the cock that crowed after Peter denied Jesus Christ thrice was a gamecock! That was right in the Bible and a damned good point.

I considered rewriting the letter and mentioning this fact to Mary Elizabeth, but it was too late. I had already sealed the envelope. A better idea, perhaps, would be to introduce her to a couple of the ministers who attended the Milledgeville Tourney every year and let them talk to her. I knew little about the Bible and hadn't read any scripture in fifteen years, maybe more.

Suppose she didn't show up? My stomach tightened at the thought. I had to risk it. If she couldn't see my side of things after reading a letter like that, there was no hope left for the two of us anyway. Feeling better about our relationship than I had in months, I picked up the guitar again and strummed it gently, enjoying the amplified sounds.

The tablet was still on the table, and I decided to write Bernice Hungerford a letter. She was entitled to a thank-you note after giving me such an expensive gift. A letter was the least I could do. Perhaps Bernice would like to see the tournament? She thought I was some kind of modern-day minstrel. What a terrific surprise it would be for her to learn that I was a professional cockfighter!

Dear Bernice:

What a wonderful surprise, what a wonderful guitar! There is only ONE way you could have pleased me more, and I intend to get into that later. This may come as a shock to you, but I'm a professional cockfighter, not a musician. For the next few months I'll be out on the circuit and won't be able to see you, but two seats will be reserved for you at the Milledgeville, Georgia, S.C.T., March 15–16. Please come. Bring your nephew, Tommy, along to keep you company, because I'll be too busy during the meet to sit with you. I know it's a long time off and I don't know how I'll be able to wait that long without seeing you again, but I must.

I have reason to hope that my voice will come back within the next few months. A letter is not the best way to tell you how I feel about you—I would prefer to tell you in person, whispering into your pretty ear! Perhaps I've written too much already, but you should have a FAIR idea of how I feel about you. All my love—till March 15.

Frank

P.S. The Milledgeville pit is north of town. Check at any gas station in town for directions.

After sealing and addressing the envelope to Bernice, it occurred to me that she might not know anything about cockfighting or what the initials S.C.T. stood for—most of the people in the U.S. thought that because cockfighting was illegal it had been abolished. I should have spelled it out in detail, I supposed. But if she made any inquiries at all, she could find out about it easily enough. Her nephew could do the investigating for her, and my name was certainly well known in cockfighting circles. The letter was better this way. If she attended the Milledgeville meet, I'd be able to determine if she was as interested in me as she appeared to be.

I walked down the gravel road to the highway and put the two letters and some change for stamps into my R.F.D. mailbox. The night was warm and soft for late September, and a gentle breeze blew steadily across the fields. There was a steady hum from a million insects communicating with each other in their own little ways.

When I switched on the overhead lights in the cockhouse to check the chickens, the Mellhorn Blacks jumped up and down nervously in their coops, clucking and crowing almost in unison. They were all hungry, and I intended to keep them that way. I filled the water dips with water and returned to my shack. Without turning on the lights again, I sat in the dark strumming away on my new guitar until way past midnight.

This was one of the most pleasant evenings I have ever spent by myself. Although I was tired after three hectic days on the road with Omar, I was much too happy to sleep.

Chapter Twelve

We were unable to make the first Southern Conference meet, October 15, at Greenville, Mississippi, but there was ample time to prepare our gamecocks for the six-cock, November 10 derby in Tifton, Georgia.

During the interim, Omar wrote to Pete Chocolate at Pahokee and arranged a hack match at the Ocala cockpit to be held on a Sunday afternoon in two weeks. Pete Chocolate was a worthy opponent, although he was eccentric in many ways. He was a top cockfighter and a longtime Southern Conference regular and usually fought Spanish game fowl and Spanish crosses. He also had the distinction of being the first Seminole Indian to graduate from the University of Florida with a master's degree in Asian Studies. I don't know why he wanted a degree in Asian Studies, but I know how he got it. A rich Chinese pawnbroker who had made all his money in Miami left an annual scholarship to the university in Asian Studies for any Seminole who wanted to take it. The Chinaman had been dead for more than fifteen years, and Pete Chocolate had been the first and only Seminole to take advantage of the free degree.

Another peculiarity about Pete was his habit of wearing a black tuxedo suit at all times, even when he handled in the pit. He didn't always wear a white shirt and black tie with the tuxedo. Sometimes he did, but he occasionally wore a sport shirt, a blue work shirt, or, as often as not, no shirt at all.

His master's degree and tuxedo had nothing to do with his ability as a cockfighter. He was a top handler and feeder, and a tough opponent to face in the pit.

The check weights for the hacks were 4:02, 5:00, 5:06 and 5:10. This early in the season, Pete only wanted to fight these weights, and we had to meet them in order to get the match. Each hack was to be a separate pit battle, and we were to put up fifty dollars a fight. With the wide selection of cocks we had, it was easy to meet the weights. I selected two of Omar's Roundheads, one Ace Mellhorn Black, and my 5:00 Middleton Gray. Although Icky's weight was only 4:02, I put him on the conditioning program too, in case I could get an extra hack for him. Before I could enter Icky in the Milledgeville Tourney against my old rival Jack Burke, he had to win at least four fights. In my opinion, Icky was the cock to beat Burke's Little David. With this eventual goal in mind, I intended to select Icky's four preliminary matches with care.

For the first few days of our partnership, Omar was often sullen, but he gradually came around to my way of conditioning. To prepare a gamecock for the pit is tough enough if he is in good feather already, but if the conditioner has to work off excess fat at the same time, his task is doubly difficult. When I worked out a regular diet for Omar's flock of Roundheads and Clarets, he objected bitterly.

"Damn it, Frank," he said, shoving my list of feeding instructions back into my hand, "I feed my cocks three times as much as that!"

We were looking over Omar's chickens at the runs on his farm, so I tried to show him why the new feeding schedule was necessary. I picked one of his Claret roosters out of a nearby coop, felt his meaty thighs with a dour expression on my face, handed him to Omar, and nodded for him to do the same.

"He's hard as a brick," Omar said defensively, squeezing the Claret's legs.

I shook my head, picked up a stick and printed FAT! on the ground with the point of it. Omar rubbed out the word with his toe, returned the cock to the coop, and pawed through his beard.

"All right. If you say so, Frank. But he doesn't feel fat to me!"

Although Omar had been fighting cocks for four years, it was evident that he had never "felt" a truly conditioned game-cock. The right *feel* of a gamecock is indescribable. Maybe it is an instinct of some kind, but if a man ever gets the right feel of a perfectly conditioned gamecock in his fingers, his fingers never forget. The exact right *feel* is an incorporeal knowledge, and once the fingers memorize it, they are never satisfied until they find it again. When a game-cock has the right feel, it is ready for the pit. Omar thought my regular diet was drastic, but I had to get the excess fat off his birds before I could put them on my special conditioning diet.

I checked the list again: *1 tablespoon of ⅔ cracked corn and ⅓ whole oats, once a day, tossed into scratch pen. One-fourth of an apple every four days. Two ounces of hamburger every ten days. Plenty of grit and oyster shells available at all times. Keep the water cups full.*

This was a good diet, a practical feed I had learned through long apprenticeship. The chickens wouldn't starve, and they wouldn't get fat. If they had any fat when they were put on it, they would lose it in a hurry. And as long as this diet was maintained, any cock could be switched to a battle-conditioning diet and be ready to fight within ten days. By weighing them daily, any sudden, dangerous weight loss would be detected, and the feed could be increased slightly. But Omar had to begin somewhere, and the new diet was the first step forward in his professional education. I returned the list to my unhappy partner, and this time he accepted it. The Claret crowed deeply, anxious to get some more attention.

"You'd better crow now," Omar shouted at the game-cock. "By this time next week you'll be too damned hungry to crow!"

The conditioning of game fowl is not a job for a lazy man. To condition five gamecocks for the hack coming up was easy for me, but I don't think Omar had ever worked as hard in his life. The way he groaned and complained was downright funny. Just wait, I thought, until we start conditioning twenty or thirty at a time. In order to get six cocks ready for the Tifton derby, we would have to condition at least twenty.

After I rousted Omar out of bed at his farm at four thirty two mornings in a row, he brought a cot and his sheets over to my shack and bunked there. There was an old Negro couple, Leroy and Mary Bondwell, who looked after Omar at his farmhouse. During the two weeks Omar lived with me, Leroy fed Omar's cocks with the new diet. Every afternoon Omar drove home to check and weigh his birds, returning to my place for the evening conditioning sessions.

Buford dropped by for an hour or so every day, and I would put him to work changing straw in the coops, painting coop walks with creosote, or give him some other kind of odd job. But Omar and I, on a strict time schedule, did everything else.

I wakened Omar daily at five. I shaved and Omar fixed breakfast. By five thirty, at the latest, we were in the cockhouse.

During the entire conditioning period, the cocks were each kept in a separate stall in the cockhouse. The wooden slats on each door were close enough together so the chicken couldn't stick his neck between them and jump up and down. They were so hungry, they thought they were going to be fed every time a man entered the cockhouse. If they were allowed to bounce up and down, with their necks between the slats, they would bruise the top of their dubbed heads.

While Omar crushed two hard-boiled eggs, shells and all, into the feed pan, I measured out cracked Flint corn and pinhead oats. When the mixture was blended, each of the five cocks got one heaping teaspoonful. We never mixed more than enough for one feeding, and they all got a second feeding that night. Every other morning I tossed three or four large chunks of marble grit on the floor of their stalls.

When the chickens finished eating, and they ate fast, a cup of water was put in each coop. As long as they were drinking they were left strictly alone, but the moment they quit drinking or lost interest in the water, the cup was removed.

By six thirty they were ready for the foam-rubber mattress workbench. It was firm and only slightly springy, and it was covered with an Army surplus shelter half. I ran the cocks first, one at a time, of course, from one end to the other, and then back again, twenty times the first day, thirty the second day, increasing the number of runs ten each day until they reached a hundred. A cock fights fast so I ran them as fast as I could up and down the workbench.

Following the runs, the cocks were flirted. Flirting forces a cock to flap his wings to maintain his balance, and his wing muscles are strengthened. Like the runs, they started with twenty flirts the first day, and were increased ten flirts every day until they reached a hundred. Once a man gets the hang of it, flirting isn't really difficult. A conditioner must remember to always be as careful as he can so the cock won't get bruised. If a cock is flirted roughly, he will soon get stiff, even if he doesn't get bruised. Omar was good at flirting, so I usually took the runs and let him fly them back and forth between his big hands. It was a pleasure to relax with a cigarette and watch Omar work.

With his left hand on the cock's breast, he would toss the bird deftly back for about a foot and a half, catch him with his right hand, and then toss him back. Omar started slowly, but once he caught the rhythm the cock was flying back and forth from one hand to the other so fast it looked like the cock was running in place. He had a definite flair for careful flirting, and he was proud of his ability.

Every other day, following the flirting period, we heeled a pair of the cocks undergoing conditioning with sparring muffs, and let them fight each other in the pit for about a minute and a half.

If one of the cocks appeared to be too tired, I didn't spar him. There is always risk involved in sparring. Even when a bird is armed with soft chamois muffs he can get hurt. But by watching two sparring cocks closely, I can observe how well their stamina is building up.

After the sparring period, the cocks were allowed to rest for fifteen minutes, and then we washed them with warm soapy water. To help relieve soreness, I rubbed their legs down gently with a sponge dipped in rubbing alcohol. When the birds were all washed and rubbed down, they were placed in separate sun coops for twenty minutes. There was a roosting pole in each sun coop, and if the cocks were still active enough to have a fine old time jumping up to the pole and then down again with animated eagerness, I made a note to increase their runs and flirting for the next day.

The drying-off period gave Omar and me enough time to have a coffee break.

Before we returned the cocks to the cockhouse for the day, each bird was given two flies. Two daily flies not only bring out the aggressive spirit of a gamecock, they get him used to the idea that the best way to reach his opponent is to use his wings and fly to him. For the fly, Omar held out one of the cocks with his arm extended, with the tail of the bird facing me. I held the flying cock on the ground until Omar was ready, and then I'd let him go. When I released his tail he would take to the air, but before he could reach the bird Omar was holding out toward him, Omar would twist slightly to one side, causing the flying bird to extend himself to fly higher. After a few days of flying, a mature cock could rise eight or ten feet into the air from a standing position. If a cock could remember that he knew how to fly this well, it could save his life when pitted.

The flies completed the morning conditioning. A record sheet was kept on a clipboard beside each coop, and I filled in the cock's weight, number of runs, flirts, flies, and made a note of his color. The well-conditioned cock has a dark red face and comb. When the color turns pinkish something is wrong. In the space for comments I jotted down any observed weaknesses, or changes to be made in the diet due to gains or losses that were unexpected.

Like people, every gamecock has to be handled a little differently. A chicken's brain is about the size of a BB, but within those tiny brains there is an infinite variety of character and personality traits. I've seen personalities that ranged from lassitude to zealousness, from anarchy to obedience, from friendliness to indifference. Luckily, a chicken can't count. If they could count, they would have resented the daily raising of the number of flirts and runs we gave them.

A gamecock is the most stupid creature on earth and, paradoxically, the most intelligent fighter.

When my chart notations were completed, I dropped a canvas cover over the slatted doorway of each coop, and the darkness kept the birds quiet until it was time for the evening training periods.

The other cocks, not under conditioning, were fed, watered, examined and weighed, and I was through for the morning. Omar and I would then play chess until time for lunch. When Buford was around, I drove to Omar's farm for lunch, and inspected his gamecocks before returning home. If Buford failed to drop by, I would cook either a potful of canned beef stew or pork and beans and fix a pan of hoecakes.

"How come you've never gotten married, Frank?" Omar asked me one day, as he looked unhappily at his heaping platter of hot pork and beans. "By God, if I didn't eat something else besides stew or beans every day, I'd marry the first woman who came along!"

Omar was so used to my silence by now that he answered his own questions. "I don't suppose many women would want to marry a professional cockfighter, though. Most of the women I've known want their husband home every night, whether they like him or not, just so they can have somebody to complain to. But canned beans—ugh!"

In the afternoon, after Omar went home, I took a walk with one of my gamecocks that wasn't undergoing conditioning. When taken out of their runs, some of the cocks would follow me around. They liked attention, but they also hoped that I would drop a grain of corn on the ground now and then. And sometimes I did.

Mary Bondwell either fixed supper for us at four thirty at Omar's farm, or we drove into Ocala for a steak or barbecued ribs. By five thirty, we were ready to start the conditioning all over again—the feeding, weighing, flies, flirts, runs and recording. Not many game strains can stand up to the hard conditioning I give them, but my two cocks—the Mellhorn and the Gray—came along fast, and Icky thrived on it. Omar's Roundheads had a tough time for the first three days, but as soon as their excess fat disappeared, they came up nicely.

At night, to get our gamecocks used to lights and noise, because they would be fighting at night later on in the season, I turned on the overhead lights of the cockpit, and played sound-effects records on a portable phonograph. The records weren't loud enough to suit Omar. He charged around the outside of the pit, shouting out bets at the top of his voice.

"Hey! Who'll give me an eight to ten! I got a blinker here, half dead already! Who'll lay twenty to ten!"

He then accepted preposterous bets in a mincing falsetto, managing to make enough noise for a major cockpit. It was comical to watch his wild antics, charging around the pit, flopping his big bare arms loosely, his black beard glistening under the lights. I could never picture Omar in a homburg and gray flannel suit walking down Madison Avenue. He fitted in with a cocker's life as though he had been born to it.

After only a few nights of noise and lights, every one of the cocks could stand quietly and patiently in the center of the pit, and pay no mind either to the records or Omar.

And of course, we had a bottle every night, either gin or bourbon, and we passed it back and forth. Omar would tell me stories about New York, the advertising business, or anecdotes about radio and television people he had known.

Quite suddenly he would stop relating a story in midsentence—"Frank, do you want to know something? You and I, you big, dumb, silent son-of-a-bitch, we've got the best life in the entire world! I wouldn't trade my life now if I was given every filter-tip account in the United States and fifty percent of the stock!"

He would reach for the bottle, take a healthy swig and pass it to me.

"I know you're tired of listening to me ramble on. Why don't you get out that electronic monster of yours and play us something?"

I had rigged an extension cord from the shack, and I would play for an hour or so, sitting on the bench beside the lighted cockpit. I never played songs, I more or less played with the guitar instead, trying out chord progressions, or attempting to express a mood of some kind. Omar never said whether he liked my music or not, but he listened attentively.

One night Buford drove over with a big pot of greens his

wife had cooked for me. Omar told Buford to get his enamel cup from the hook above the faucet where he kept it, and then filled it with whiskey. Before Buford had finished the cupful of whiskey he got mellow and sang for us—old-time blues and field hollers. When he held a note long enough for me to catch it, I would hit the corresponding chord on my guitar. I might have been a little drunk, but I thought Buford had the greatest voice I had ever heard.

These were all pleasant evenings for me. I have always guarded my aloneness jealously. But Omar didn't encroach on my solitude, he complemented it. For the first time in my life, I realized that companionship between two kindred spirits is not impossible—as long as each man respects the other's rights.

On the eighth day of conditioning, the exercising of each cock was cut in half. On the morning of the ninth day my Mellhorn Black got moody and refused to eat. He wasn't sick, he was mean and sulky. I put the Gray game hen in his coop with him for a couple of hours and he snapped out of his lethargy. When I removed the hen and dumped a spoonful of feed on the floor of his coop, he gobbled it up in no time.

Omar thought this was funny. "Maybe that's what's wrong with me, Frank," he laughed. "If somebody dropped a blonde into my bed for two hours every night, I could probably eat those beans of yours and like them."

On the twelfth day, the cocks were taken off exercise and food together. They weren't given any water, but they didn't want water. This was a good sign, and meant they were ready for the pit. They would fast right up until pit time. All five cocks were in the peak of condition. I made Omar "feel" every one of them, and his fingers learned the difference.

"If I didn't know better, Frank," he said, "I'd think these cocks were made out of stone."

Sunday afternoon we put the cocks into traveling coops and drove to the cockpit in Omar's station wagon. The Ocala Game Club wasn't really in Ocala—it was closer to Martel, eight miles west of the city. But it was called the Ocala pit because out-of-town cockfighters stayed in Ocala motels when the February 24 S.C. derby was held. During the entire season, the pit operator, an old retired farmer named Bandy Taylor, held hack matches almost every Sunday.

Bandy Taylor was in his late sixties, with brown leathery skin and enough deep wrinkles on his face to resemble a relief map. His legs were so bowed, he couldn't have caught a pig in a trench.

Although Bandy's pit was not an elaborate setup, all of the Lownes County cockfighters liked to meet there. His wife maintained a small stand outside the pit area, where she sold coffee, Coca-Colas and hamburgers, and Bandy charged a reasonable, one-dollar admission fee. The old man, an authorized S.C.T. referee, never bet on the fights, but he made enough money on admission fees and the food his wife sold to get by. Any wins I had there could be signed by Bandy on the official records, and they would be acceptable by the Milledgeville judges for qualifying purposes.

The crowd was small, considering that four hacks between Pete Chocolate and our new partnership had been scheduled. There were thirty some-odd spectators, including a nervous Yankee tourist from Silver Springs. There were only a half dozen other cockers, looking for extra hacks. I wanted to get an extra hack for Icky, but the prospects weren't too good. I wrote my name and Icky's weight on the blackboard and hoped for the best.

Pete Chocolate won the toss and decided to fight from bottom weights up. His fighters were all Spanish crosses, and they were in fine feather. Omar held for me while I heeled the 4:02 Roundhead, and then he tried to rustle up a few bets in the bleachers. I considered fighting Icky against the other 4:02 opponent, but the Spanish Ace looked too formidable. I had made a good decision. Omar was also lucky in the stands, because the only bet he could get was a ten-dollar even money wager.

The Spanish cock uncoupled my Roundhead, breaking his spine, in the first pitting. He was counted out, paralyzed and unable to move a feather. Omar paid Pete Chocolate the fifty-dollar loss, and paid off the fan in the stands. Because of our quick loss in the first fight, Omar was able to lay a thirty-dollar bet on the outcome of the second hack.

In the second fight, I showed the 5:00 Middleton Gray, and he finished his opponent in the fourth pitting. My Gray shuffler got above the Spanish every time.

The third battle was one of those fights that never appear to get anywhere. The two cocks were evenly matched, and very little damage was done until the eighteenth pitting. By the twenty-third pitting we were alternating on calling for the count. On my count, however, the Spanish developed a rattle from an earlier wound, refused to face, and the hack was mine. Our Roundhead was well battered and wouldn't be able to fight again for at least two months.

The fourth hack was a miracle win. My 5:10 Mellhorn Black had been in fights before, and he smothered the Spanish in the first two pittings. In the third pitting, the Black attacked furiously the moment I released his tail. The Spanish was bowled over and fell back close to the wall. He leaped high into the air, and landed on the ground outside the pit. The Spanish was game—he wasn't a runner by any means—but he was outside the pit and my Black was still inside.

It was a tense moment. I held my breath, and none of the spectators made a sound. If Pete's Spanish had jumped back into the pit, the fight would have been continued. He didn't. Confused, twisting his head about in search of my gamecock, the Spanish darted under the bleachers in bewildered retreat. The hack was mine by default.

I had known Pete Chocolate for several years, but this was the first time I ever saw him get really angry. He caught his gamecock, removed the heels, and swung the cock's neck against as upright post. He then jerked off the cock's head. This isn't easy. It takes a strong man to pull a chicken's head off with his bare hands. He tossed the dead chicken on the ground and came back to the pit.

"That's the first runner I ever had, Frank," Pete said blackly. "A Spanish don't run! That same cock won two fights before. Is that a runner? D'you ever hear of me showing a runner?"

I shook my head solemnly. Blood had dripped from the dead chicken's neck onto the white polo shirt Pete was wearing with his tuxedo, and his white tennis shoes were splashed with blood.

"He didn't run, Pete," Omar said. "He was confused and didn't remember where the pit was, that's all."

"He won't get confused again!" Pete said with satisfaction. He whipped out his wallet and paid Omar off. We were ahead one hundred dollars from Pete Chocolate, and Omar had won eighty dollars more in side bets. We had lost one cock, and our Roundhead had been battered so badly he might not ever win another fight. We were just about even.

A good first day, I thought, as Omar joined me at the lunch stand.

"Frank," he said, "there's a kid at the cockhouse with a Gray cross of some kind who wants to fight Icky. His name is Junior Hollenbeck. D'you know him?"

I nodded and finished my Coke. I didn't actually know Junior, but his father, Rex Hollenbeck, was a real-estate man in Ocala. He had introduced himself to me one day in town. Mr. Hollenbeck was a fan, he said, and he had seen me handling at the Orlando International Tourney.

"Do you want to fight him, Frank? The kid's only about nineteen, and his Gray shades Icky two full ounces."

I started toward the cockhouse to see whether I did or not. Junior was waiting in front of Icky's coop, cradling his Gray gamecock in his arms. He was a well-dressed young man, wearing buckled shoes, charcoal-flannel Daks, and a gaily colored body shirt. His tangled chestnut hair was worn long, all the way to his shoulders, and his face was sunburned. He had a sparse straggly moustache, and the pointed chin whiskers of a young ram goat. Evidently his nose had peeled, because it was smeared with a thick covering of white salve.

"This is Mr. Mansfield, Junior," Omar introduced us.

"I know. I saw the 4:02 weight on the blackboard, Mr. Mansfield," Junior said, all business, "and thought I'd challenge you. My cock's won two fights this year and has a couple of ounces over yours, but I'm willing to cut away some feathers for the chance to fight you."

I stared impassively at the kid, and he blushed through his sunburn.

"That is," he added, "the man I bought him from *said* he won two fights in Tallahassee."

I took the Gray out of Junior's arms and felt him. The bird

went in and out like an accordion. I turned to Omar, winked, and moved my chin down a fraction of an inch.

"You've got a hack, Junior," Omar said. "And you don't have to cut any feathers. The Southern Conference allows a two-ounce leeway either way on hacks. But you'll have to fight short heels. Got any?"

"No, sir. I don't have any heels at all. I thought I might borrow a set. And I want to bet twenty-five dollars, even money."

"Fair enough. I'll lend you a pair. D'you want me to heel him for you?"

"I know how to heel him," Junior said defensively. "I've heeled cocks plenty of times. Just lend me the heels and hold him for me."

Omar laughed good-naturedly. "Sure. Wait'll I tell Bandy there's an extra hack, before his crowd gets away."

There had been two hacks held before the four between Pete Chocolate and me. After our last hack, a few of the spectators had departed, including the nervous tourist, but there were still a dozen or more standing around discussing the fights. When Bandy announced that there was going to be another hack, they scrambled hurriedly into the bleachers and began making bets.

We heeled with inch-and-a-quarter gaffs. To my surprise, Junior did a good job of heeling his Gray. By the way he handled his chicken, I could see he knew his way around the pit, and I felt a little better about the fight coming up.

While Bandy examined both cocks prior to the fight, I listened to the bettors. Although the Gray was announced as a two-time winner, and the Blue—as Icky was called—was announced as a short-heel novice in his first fight, most of the bettors were taking Icky and offering five to one. The odds were caused, in part, by my reputation, but they really preferred my gamecock because of his color. This kind of thinking was like betting on the color of a jockey's eyes instead of on the record of the horse at a racetrack. At any rate, Omar had a hard time getting bets. Even with the high odds, only a few men were willing to back the Gray. But Omar finally managed to lay three ten-dollar wagers.

Junior was nervous during the billing, but he handled fairly well.

When Bandy told us to "get ready" in his reedy old man's voice, Junior squatted behind his score, and held the Gray's tail like a professional.

"Pit!"

Icky took two short steps forward and then flew six feet into the air. The Gray ran forward on the ground at the same time, and Icky landed behind him. They wheeled simultaneously and mushed, breast against breast, engaged in a shoving contest. The Gray backed off, and then tried a short rushing feint that didn't work. Icky got above him, shuffled, and the two went down with Icky's right gaff through the Gray's left wing.

"Handle!"

Junior disengaged the heel from the Gray's wing bone, and we retreated to our respective scores for a thirty-second rest. The boy worked so furiously over the Gray I had to grin. He blew on the cock's back, stretched and jerked the neck, spat into its mouth, rubbed the thighs vigorously between his hands, and licked the head feathers and hackles with his tongue.

These were all legitimate nursing techniques, but to use them, any of them, after the first pitting was ridiculous. Over-nursing does more harm than good. Unless a gamecock is in drastic need of help, the handler can help him best by letting him rest between pittings. I laced Icky away from the Gray and let him stand quietly so he could get the maximum benefit from the rest period.

"Get ready," Bandy said, watching his wristwatch sweephand.

"Pit!"

We dropped them on their scores. Because of rough over-nursing, more than for any other reason, the Gray was slow in getting started. Icky made a forward dash with raised hackles, took off in a low, soaring flight, fanning in midair, and cut deeply into the Gray's neck with blurred gaffs. The left heel stuck, and the two cocks tumbled over, coupled.

"Handle!" Bandy said quickly.

The instant Junior removed Icky's gaff from the Gray's neck, his gamecock strangled. When a cock's long neck fills with blood, the strangling sound is unmistakable. Except for going through the motions in accordance with the rules, the fight was over. Until the Gray actually died, or refused to fight through three twenty-second counts, or unless his handler picked him up and carried him out, we still had to go through the routine pittings and counts.

Junior had heard the strangle, but he nursed the Gray furiously. He sucked blood out of the Gray's throat and rubbed its chest hard enough to dislodge the tight feathers. He held the feet, placed the cock on its chest and pressed his mouth against the back, blowing his breath noisily into the feathers to warm the Gray's circulation. The Gray was down, his neck stretched flat, and his eyes were glazed. Blood bubbled from his open beak, but he wasn't dead. And then, right before my astonished eyes, Junior inserted his right forefinger into the downed Gray's vent and massaged the cock's testicles!

I snapped my fingers in Bandy's direction, but he had witnessed the foul as soon as I had.

"Foul!" Bandy yelled. "The Blue wins in the second pitting!"

I picked Icky up and held him tail first toward Bandy so he could cut the tie strings away from the heels with his penknife. None of the spectators complained about the ruling. The Gray had obviously lost before the foul was called anyway. With his sunburned face redder than it had been before, Junior pushed between us.

"What do you mean, foul!" he shouted at Bandy.

"Mr. Mansfield and I both saw you put your finger in the vent, son," Bandy said quietly. "And so did everybody else, if they had any eyes." Omar joined me in the pit and I handed Icky over to him.

"That's no foul," Junior protested. "Nursing's allowed, ain't it?"

"Legitimate nursing, yes. Not that kind!"

"I was told if you rubbed the balls with your finger you could put new life in your chicken—" Junior argued futilely.

"Who told you that, son?" Bandy cut him off.

"My dad told me," Junior replied. We were all three staring at him now, and he looked at us worriedly. "Is that considered a foul?"

"Your daddy told you wrong, Junior," Bandy said quietly.

"You rub a cock's balls and you take every speck of fight right out of him. It's a deliberate way of throwing a fight."

"Well, I didn't know it," Junior said. "I want to apologize, Mr. Mansfield," he said, with evident sincerity.

"Too late for that now," Bandy told him. "You're through. I got to send in a report on this to the Southern Conference. As of now, you're blacklisted at every cockpit in the S.C. I reckon that's what your daddy wanted or he wouldn't have told you no lie. But you've pitted your last gamecock at this game club, Junior."

Junior's sun-reddened face was reduced to a pink glow. "How long's the blacklist last, Mr. Taylor?" he asked.

"Forever. Whether you knew what you were doing or not don't make no difference. You threw the fight and there was people with bets on your Gray. I don't want you comin' out here no more, and you tell your daddy that he ain't welcome out here neither!"

Bandy turned away, his speech over, but Omar took a grip on his arm. "Now, just a minute, Bandy," Omar said good-humoredly, "aren't you carrying this thing too far? The kid said he didn't know about the rule, and he apologized. Isn't that enough? The Gray had strangled anyway."

"Are you arguing with me, Mr. Baradinsky?" Bandy said testily. "You'd better read up on the rules before you try! My decision's final, and if you want to argue you just try it! I'll suspend you from this pit for thirty days so fast your head'll spin!"

Omar started to say something else. I managed to catch his eye, and put a finger to my lips. Bandy turned away and headed for the cockhouse, walking as dignified as a bandy-legged man is capable of walking. I took out my notebook and pencil, scribbled the word *Apologize!*, and handed the open notebook to Omar.

"The hell with that crusty old bastard," he said, returning my notebook. "Why should I apologize?"

"Please don't get into trouble on my account, Mr. Baradinsky," Junior said humbly. "I've learned a lesson today I'll remember all my life."

"I agree. But it's a hard lesson. Bandy meant what he said, you know. You're washed up when it comes to cockfighting."

"I know it, sir. But I still want to apologize to you both." Junior hung his head, and started to leave the pit. I snapped my fingers, and held out my hand, palm up.

"Oh, that's right!" Junior smiled winningly. "I owe you twenty-five dollars, don't I? Well, to tell you the truth, Mr. Mansfield, I don't have any cash with me. I was so sure I'd win I didn't think I needed any. But I've got some money at home, and just as soon—"

I grabbed Junior's wrist, twisted his arm behind his back and put some leverage on it. He bent over with a sharp cry of pain, and then whimpered. I took his wallet out of his right hip pocket with my left hand and passed it to Omar who promptly put Icky on the ground. Omar opened the wallet and counted seventy-eight dollars. After taking twenty-five dollars from the sheaf of bills, he returned the remainder and threw the wallet disgustedly on the floor of the pit.

As I released Junior's wrist, I coordinated nicely and booted him with the pointed toe of my jodhpur boot. He sprawled awkwardly on the hard ground, and his head made a solid "thunk" when it bounced against the low pine wall of the cockpit. Without a word of protest, Junior picked up his wallet and broke for his car in the parking lot at a dead run. I picked Icky up and grinned.

For a moment, Omar stared at the bills in his hand, and then cleared his throat. "Well, Frank," he said, "I guess I'd better find old Bandy Taylor and apologize. If anybody learned a lesson today, it was me."

Omar headed reluctantly toward the cockhouse, his hands shoved deep in his pockets. Omar might have been a big shot in the advertising business, but he certainly had a lot to learn about people if he wanted to make a name for himself in cockfighting.

Chapter Thirteen

To prepare our cocks for the six-cock Tifton derby, I found it more practical to move myself and my game-cocks to Omar's farm. I was made comfortable there. I had my own bedroom, there was an inside shower and bathroom, and the meals prepared by Mary Bondwell were a lot tastier than the bachelor meals I had been cooking for myself.

I was so anxious to win the Tifton meet, I put thirty cocks into conditioning just to shape up six top fighters. Working thirty cocks daily rarely gave me a free hour to myself during the day, and I was usually asleep by eight thirty. Sunday is not a holiday for a cockfighter when he has birds to condition for a derby. There were too many things I had to do on Sunday to fight at the Ocala pit, but I sent Omar to the pit to fight some of the cocks that peaked fast. He didn't lose a single hack out of the eight battles he fought.

Our wallets were growing fatter.

On the morning of November 9, we left for Tifton, Georgia, at five, and arrived at the Tifton game club at three the same afternoon. We signed the derby contracts and were assigned to a cockhouse and given a padlock for the door.

Jack Burke was an entry in the Tifton derby, and he looked me up that evening after supper. Omar had stayed in our motel room to watch television, but I was edgy and drove out to the pit to take a final look at the twelve cocks we had brought along. The birds were roosting all right. As I locked the door and lit a cigarette, Jack Burke approached me through the dusk.

"Evenin', Frank," he greeted me cordially. "It's nice to see you again." Jack looked prosperous in a double-breasted blue worsted suit, a wide paisley necktie, and black-and-white shoes.

I shook hands with the man. Jack rubbed his chin nervously, and I could sense that something was on his mind. He fixed his eyes on an imaginary point to the left of my head.

"I don't suppose you heard the good news," he said, smiling bleakly.

I waited patiently for him to tell it.

"I got married!" He laughed. "Bet that surprises you, don't it? Yes, sir! Sooner or later they catch up with the best of us, Frank!" He hesitated. "I married Dody White, Frank," he added softly.

I felt sorry for Jack, but I shook hands with him again

163

anyway. So White was Dody's last name. I had wondered about that. And now she was Mrs. Dody Burke.

"I wanted to bring Dody along to the derby, Frank, but she wouldn't come because you were here. I tried to tell her you weren't the kind who would rake up the past, but she wouldn't believe me. She seems to have the idea that you can talk, and she's afraid you'll say something about her. I know you can't talk, but I couldn't convince Dody." He hesitated. "*Can* you use your voice, Frank?"

I smiled and flipped the butt of my cigarette in an arc to the ground. The idea that I would ever say anything about Burke's wife whether I could talk or not was patently ridiculous. And Burke knew it. Dody had undoubtedly forced him to ask me to keep quiet about our former alliance. For an instant I felt sorry for him, and then I despised him for being so damned weak and pussy-whipped.

"I feel like a fool!" Burke blushed. For a man in his mid-forties, the ability to blush is quite a feat.

"Well," Burke said, "I'll bring her along to the Plant City derby, and introduce you all just like you'd never seen each other before. That way, Dody's mind'll be at ease. All right?"

I nodded and looked away. I could almost smell the rancorous acid burning Jack's insides. What a comedown for Jack Burke, to let a little tramp like Dody humiliate him this way.

"Now, to business!" Jack said briskly, in his regular voice. "D'you think you and that new partner of yours can show enough cocks after the Plant City meet to fight me in an old-fashioned main?"

The decision was up to me. I was positive Omar would'nt object to the challenge. Burke fed almost twice as many cocks as we did, but I had a fierce hankering to beat him in a two-entry main. I lowered my chin a fraction and spat between his feet.

"Good! I'll make the necessary arrangements to get the pit on the thirty-first, the day after the derby. How does two hundred dollars a fight sound, with a thousand on the odd fight?"

For the third time in as many minutes, I shook hands with Burke.

He started to say something else, changed his mind, and

walked away through the deepening dusk toward the parking lot. Burke was still a damned good man. In time he would learn how to handle Dody. But the memory of this humiliating episode would rankle him forever. I knew this, and I knew just as well that he would eventually blame me instead of himself. That's the way men are.

The next day we lost only one fight in the six-cock derby, but it was one fight too many. Jack Burke didn't lose a single fight, and picked up the thousand-dollar purse. Getting close only means something when it comes to pitching horseshoes. But despite the lost fight, Omar had placed enough judicious bets to add nine hundred dollars to our bankroll.

The money was welcome, of course, but the Tifton loss was made even more depressing by the sad news that Martha Middleton, Ed Middleton's wife, had died of a heart attack. Her obituary appeared in the same issue of *The Southern Cockfighter* that carried the announcement of Ed Middleton's retirement from the sport.

I had liked the old lady, and I tried to write Ed a letter of condolence. But after a futile attempt to write a decent letter that didn't sound banal or morbid, I gave up on the idea and sent him a commercial condolence card by special delivery. Not much of a writer himself, Ed Middleton acknowledged receipt of my condolences by thanking me on the back of a picture postcard of Disney World. His card was waiting for me when I returned to Ocala.

There was also a letter waiting for me in my mailbox from Frances, my fat sister-in-law. Frances was the last person I ever expected to hear from. After two stiff drinks and a wait of one hour, I made myself open the letter.

Dear Frank,

Only a few short weeks ago I hated you and would have been glad to shoot you. But now I see your wisdom in getting Randall out of the terrible rut he was in. He won't write you, because he's too proud. But he loves you and he's your very own brother and I want you to write him soon.

It was an awful shock to move out of what I considered my home for life, especially knowing that wreckers were going to tear it down the next day.

But I forgive you, Frank, for what it did for Randy.

We could have moved in with Daddy in Macon, but Randy wouldn't do it. We rented a room in a boarding-house in Macon instead—and Frank, Randy hasn't had a single drink since the morning we left the farm!

He found a position right away. You remember how he used to dig through those law books day after day? Well, he took some of his findings down to the White Citizen's Council and they were actually amazed at some of the loopholes he found in the new bussing laws. Anyway, they hired him as a full-time WCC counselor with a retainer of eight thousand dollars a year! And it's all been so wonderful for me, too. Randy takes me to all the meetings and I've met ever so many nice new people! His speeches are just wonderful, Frank, and he gets one hundred dollars and expenses every time he talks. Next Monday, we're going to the WCC rally in Atlanta and Randy is going to talk about the black-power movement. I'm proud enough to bust and his picture will be in the paper! Next Monday, in the Constitution, *but I'll cut it out and send you a copy.*

I can't tell you how happy I am about Randy's success. Make up with your brother, Frank. Please?

He loves you and so do I!

All my love, Frances.

I had no intention of writing Randall and making up with him. But I appreciated the news from Frances. I had feared that the two of them would appear at my Ocala farm some morning, begging to be taken in—and I would have been forced to shelter them. Now that Randall was finally on his own, he could go his way and I would go mine. I didn't answer Frances either, but I saved the envelope because it had their Macon address.

When Christmastime came, I would send them a card. *Peace on Earth. Good Will toward Men!* Anytime Randall really wanted to make up with me, all he had to do was to send me the three hundred dollars he owed me.

It was my fault that we lost the Plant City derby, although no one can win them all, no matter how good his game-cocks are. But I had concentrated on the selection and the conditioning of the cocks for the post-derby main with Jack Burke, and Omar had done most of the conditioning for the derby. I can't blame Omar for the loss. He did a good conscientious job. I did feel, however, that if I had helped him more we would have come out better than third place. There was some consolation in the fact that Jack Burke finished fourth. Like me, Jack had undoubtedly concentrated his efforts on preparing for our main.

The Texas entry of Johnny McCoy and Colonel Bob Moore were the winners of the derby, and it was no disgrace to lose to them. These partners are two of the biggest names in U.S. cockfighting.

Like a bridge player, who can remember every important hand he held in a rubber of bridge five or ten years back, a cockfighter can remember the details of every pitting in an important cockfight. The details of the two-entry main between Jack Burke and myself are still as vivid in my mind as if it were held ten minutes ago. But I like the way Tex Higdon reported the event in *The American Gamefowl Quarterly.*

Tex had been reporting cockfights for game-fowl magazines for twenty years or more, and he's a topflight pit reporter. And yet, hardly a season goes by when Tex doesn't get into one or two fistfights for his pains. His way of writing rubs a lot of high-strung cockfighters the wrong way, especially when they are on the receiving end of his sarcasm. But his reporting is conscientious when it comes to accuracy. It takes a damned good eye to catch fast action in the pit. The following is a tear sheet of his article from *The American Gamefowl Quarterly:*

Red Heels At Plant City!
by Tex Higdon

Plant City Florida, November 31—If you're looking for the results of the Southern Conference Plant City Derby, held November 30th, you'd better look elsewhere in these pages. This Texan is reporting the Main between the two master cockers, Jack Burke and silent Frank Mansfield. By the way, folks, Frank has gone out and got himself a partner after all these

years, a New York country boy with the worst look-ing black beard your reporter has seen in a month of Sundays. It's a good thing Frank don't talk anymore. His new sidekick, Omar Baradinsky, does enough talking for *three* cockfighters!

The Main was a real old-fashioned-type event, well worth staying over for in Plant City another day. I wish we had more mains like this one, or at least more mains. This is an old cockpit, but there's plenty of room for three hundred people. The main pit is below ground, the way they ought to be; there are plenty of cockhouses, and clean latrines for visitors, plus a drag pit that's better than most regular pits I've seen at supposedly high-class game clubs. Pit operator-referee Tom Doyle sells toasted cheese sandwiches for a dollar apiece, and that's an outrage, but as long as people buy them, he'll probably keep the same price. Next time I visit Plant City, this Texas boy will bring his own lunch!

Referee Tom Doyle announced right off: "If you people violate our rules, have yourself a few too many drinks and get tough, you're just right for me to handle!" Tom Doyle is big enough for the crowd to believe him. They were downright cowed, and hip pints were well hidden.

There were three checkweights, 5:00, 6:05, and shake, as set up by Jack Burke. Frank won the toss and decided to fight from bottom weights up. Twenty-six cocks were shown by both cockers and thirteen fell in.

No. One. Both show 5:00 cocks, Burke a Brady Roundhead, Mansfield an Allen Roundhead. Frank broke through early and then slowed up about the 12th pitting. He was blinded in the 20th right after they went to breast on the time call. The Brady was a hardhead that kept trying, took plenty of punish-ment, and broke counts as fast as the Allen Round-head took them. In the 48th pitting Jack Burke won with a down cock that got the count and kept it while his opponent breathed gently down his neck but quit pecking.

No. Two. **Burke a 5:01 Claret cross; Mansfield a 5:02 Mellhorn Black. This was a bang-up 1st pitting,** followed by a dozen dirty buckles in the 2nd. Frank had the best cutter, and in the 18th Jack stayed put on his score. When they went to breast in the 25th the Mellhorn Black kicked like a taxpayer and won in the 30th when Burke carried his bird out.

No. Three. **Burke showed an Alabama Pumpkin (if I ever saw one) bred by his brother Freddy in Vero Beach. 5:08. Mansfield a Middleton Gray, 5:06.** Frank had a great shuffler that wasn't even touched. He was over the Burke chicken in the 1st pitting like a short-circuited electric blanket, uncoupled him in the 2nd, and won in the 5th when Burke carried out a dead one. This made the Gray a five-time winner, according to Mr. Baradinsky—who made a special trip to the press box to relieve me of fifty dollars— and I could very well believe it.

No. Four. **Burke showed a 5:08 Blackwell Round-head, Mansfield a 5:07 Claret. This was the most even and best match so far.** The two cocks mixed like sand and cement every time they met until the 10th when Burke got tired. The Roundhead was down on his score in the 18th, and taken out in the 19th unable to face.

No. Five. **Burke a Blue-Spangle cross, Mansfield a green-legged Allen Roundhead with the widest wingspread I've seen outside of Texas. Both scaled 5:09.** Two ring-wise roosters met in this battle and it was truly the best fight of the whole Main. Mansfield rattled in the 6th and then came back strong after I don't know how many changed bets. Burke was killed in the 19th after the Rouudhead regained vigor and shuffled all over the Cross a dozen times. Folks, there was money lost on this fight!

No. Six. **Both showed 5:10 cocks. Burke a Tulsa Red and Mansfield a Claret cross.** The light-footed Tulsa Red was truly a great cutter that uncoupled the Claret in the 2nd pitting. Frank carried him out in the 3rd.

No. Seven. **Both showed 5:12 cocks. Burke an**

O'Neal Red, Mansfield a low-stationed Mellhorn Black. Jack was rattled in the 3rd and down on his score in the 14th. The Mellhorn Black who spiked the steel with unerring accuracy in every pitting won for Frank in the 20th.

No. Eight. Both showed 5:13 cocks. Burke a Butcher Boy and Frank an Allen Roundhead. The steel was tossed from every angle in the 1st and 2nd pittings as sudden squalls hit Middle Florida. The Butcher Boy weakened in the 3rd but grew stronger in the 7th and hurt the Roundhead in the next two pittings. In the 9th the Roundhead slowed and the Butcher Boy put him out of the running. Frank carried him out after the 10th.

No. Nine. Both showed 5:14 cocks. Burke a battle-wise Whitehackle, Mansfield a fine-colored Claret. Frank was smiling all over the place up to the 8th pitting when the Whitehackle got down to business and changed his smile to a frown. His Claret was counted out in the 12th.

No. Ten. Both showed six-pounders. Mansfield a side-stepping Mellhorn Black that skipped constantly to the right, and Burke a black-and-white Spangle. The Black broke the Spangle's leg in the 3rd and Burke carried his cock out. Frank had a real Ace here, and his way of fighting bewildered the Spangle. This was the sidestepper's fourth win this season.

No. Eleven. Two more six-pound cocks, Burke with an Ace Kansas Cutter, and Mansfield with a three-year-old Alabama-walked Claret. The Kansas chicken hung every time he got close to the Claret, and Frank had to take him out in the 9th.

No. Twelve. Burke showed a 6:02 Sawyers Roundhead and Mansfield gave him two ounces with the Claret he showed. These cocks came out with plenty of gas, and buckled hard for the first five pittings. An even match, one in and then the other. Mansfield was cut down on his score in the 13th. A few fast shuffles by the Sawyers Roundhead and the blood-sodden Claret was carried out helpless.

The score was tied six to six!

Odd fight. Shakes. No weights were given, of course. Burke looked determined to win the odd fight when he showed an enormous Shawlneck. My educated guess gave the Shawlneck at least ten ounces over Mansfield's oversized Roundhead. But Jack needed more than weight. In Frank's hands the Roundhead showed a furious style of fighting that befuddled the heavier bird. Burke was down in the 18th with a broken leg and Frank won in the 23rd.

But there was an even better fight to come!

As Jack Burke, great sportsman that he is, was counting out the greenbacks into Frank's eager hand, Mrs. Dody Burke, Jack's beauteous young bride, decided to put on a hack of her own! Weighing approximately 125 pounds, and armed with red shoes (with three-inch heels), she flew across the pit and gaffed silent Frank in the shins. She also tried a right-cross to Frank's jaw with a free-swinging red leather purse, but was blocked by her handler, Jack Burke, and carried out of the pit screaming. A fine ending to a fine main! We wonder what kind of conditioning Mr. Burke is giving his new bride?

Chapter Fourteen

"When the pressure's on, a promoter's got to do the best he can," Fred Reed said petulantly for the fourth time during his sales talk. He ought to make a recording, I thought to myself.

Fred Reed had done the best he could all right, but I didn't like the setup, not any part of it. Including Mr. Reed, there were nine of us sitting around in the plush pink-and-white bridal suite of the new Southerner Hotel in Chattanooga. Johnny Norris, Roy Whipple, Omar and myself were all Southern Conference regulars, but the other entries were not, although they had paid their fees for the Chattanooga derby.

Except for promoter Fred Reed, who wore a suit and

necktie, the rest of us were either in sports clothes or blue jeans, and we looked as out of place in the mid-Victorian decor of the bridal suite as a honeymoon couple would have looked bedded down in a cockpit. My picturesque partner, with his wild beard and bib overalls, sat uneasily on a fragile gilded chair by the door to the bathroom. I was sharing a blue velvet love seat with Old Man Whipple, a gray-stubbled cockfighter from North Carolina whose odor would have been improved by a couple of quick runs through a sheep-dip.

Mr. Reed wiped his sweaty brow with a white linen handkerchief and continued: "Boys, when the S.P.C.A. really puts their foot down, the sheriff has to go along with 'em, that's all there is to it!

"Elections are coming up, and I just couldn't pay nobody off. But I did get to the city officials and we can stage the derby right here in this suite without interference. I know you men have all fought cocks in hotel rooms before, but you've never had a better one than this! Just take a look at this wonderful floor." Mr. Reed bent down with a broad smile on his face and rubbed the blue nylon carpet with his fingers. "Why, a carpet like this makes a perfect pit flooring for chickens! And don't worry about damages. The manager has been tipped plenty, and I promised him I'd pay any cleaning charges on the carpets. You've all got reserved rooms on this floor, and we've got the exclusive use of the service elevator to bring the cocks straight up from the basement garage.

"Frankly, boys, I think the Chattanooga derby is better off here than it is at my pit outside of town. There won't be as many spectators because of the space limitations, but I've invited some big money men, and you'll be able to place bets as high as you want to on your birds."

Old Roy Whipple, sitting beside me on the love seat, spat a stream of black tobacco juice onto the nylon carpet and then cleared his throat. "Where're we goin' to put the dead chickens, Mr. Reed?"

"That's an excellent question, Mr. Whipple," Reed replied pompously. "I'm glad you asked it. The dead cocks will be stacked in the bathtub. Are there any other questions?"

"Yes, sir. I have one," Johnny Norris said politely. "The

action will be slowed down considerably, won't it, if we have to bring the cocks up from the basement before every fight? It'll take forever to finish the derby. And what do we use for a drag pit?"

"That's another good question, Mr. Norris," Reed replied, with the deference in his voice that Johnny Norris usually received. "But these matters have all been taken into account. Except for the traveling pit, the rest of the furniture in here will be removed, and folding chairs will be set up. You'll heel the cocks in the bedroom, and the weights'll be announced far enough in advance so that there'll always be another pair waiting to pit. There's another connecting door through the bedroom to the next suite—the V.I.P. suite, the hotel calls it—and the living room of the next suite'll be used as a drag pit. With two referees, I can assure you, gentlemen, that the fighting will be as fast here as anywhere else. Are there any more questions, anything at all?"

There were no more questions.

"All right then, gentlemen. The fighting starts at ten a.m. tomorrow morning. Mimeographed schedules will be run off tonight and will be slipped under the doors to your rooms. If you'll all give me a list of your weights, I'll get started on the matching right away. By the way, gentlemen, if you don't want to dress up for dinner, you can have your meals served in your rooms. Otherwise, the hotel's got a rule about wearing coats and ties in the dining room. Your meals have been paid for, too, including tips."

Discussions began among the other cockfighters, and they started to work on their weight lists. I caught Omar's eye and jerked my head for him to follow me out into the hall. When Omar joined me in the corridor, I led the way to our room. I wrote a short note to my partner on a sheet of hotel stationery:

No good, partner. Deputies understand agrarian people and cockfighters, but city cops have a bad habit of not staying bought. There'll be a lot of drinking and a lot of money changing hands. That means women present and women mean trouble. We've got thirty of our best cocks in the basement and a confiscation raid would ruin us for the season. Get our entry fee back from Mr. Reed.

Omar read the note and then stared at me morosely with his large brown eyes. The corners of his mouth were probably turned down as well, but I couldn't see his mouth beneath his heavy moustache. "Damn it, Frank," he said, "I'm inclined to go along with you, but we'll be passing up a whole lot of easy money. Fred Reed told me personally that there were two big-money gamblers flying in from Nashville tonight, and we get fat. Really *fat!* The only entry we really have to worry about is Johnny Norris from Birmingham."

I took the note out of his hands and ran a double line under every word in it to emphasize the meaning, and passed it back.

"I'm with you, all right. Don't worry," he said earnestly. "But don't forget those eight cocks we selected to enter. They're trimmed mighty fine. If we don't fight them tomorrow they're likely to go under hack."

I nodded, thinking about the problem.

If we didn't fight our eight conditioned gamecocks, we would have to put them back on a regular maintenance diet and then recondition them all over again for the January 10 Biloxi meet. Even if they were reconditioned, they would be stale. And stale, listless cocks aren't winners.

I opened my suitcase, remembering the four-cock derby scheduled at Cook's Hollow, Tennessee. I flipped through the pages of my current *Southern Cockfighter* magazine until I found Vern Packard's advertisement for the meet. As I recalled, the derby was scheduled for the next day, December 15, at the Cook's Hollow Game Club. Vern Packard was a friend of mine, although I hadn't fought at his pit for more than four years. I circled Vern's telephone number in the advertisement, and wrote on the margin of the magazine:

> Call Packard. We're too late for the derby, but I can fight our cocks in post- and pre-derby hacks. Vern's a friend of mine. You take the truck and the rest of the cocks on to Biloxi like we planned.

Omar, cheered considerably, laughed and said: "I'll buy that, Frank. And raid or no raid, the idea of fighting cocks in a bridal suite doesn't appeal to me anyway."

Omar picked up the telephone and called Vern Packard. As I thought, I was too late to enter Vern's derby, but there were only three entries instead of four, and Vern planned "feathering the pit" hacks as well as post-derby hacks. He was happy to have me, and told Omar that he would put me up in his spare bedroom and have some coops readied for my eight cocks.

While Omar looked for Fred Reed to get our entry money back, I packed both our bags. Ordinarily, we would have had to forfeit the two hundred dollars we put up, because we had already signed the contracts and mailed them in from Ocala. But we had contracted to fight at the Chattanooga Game Club, five miles out of the city, not in a hotel suite. It was Fred Reed's hard luck that the sheriff had padlocked his pit, not ours. I repacked our bags, and by the time Omar returned to the room we were ready to leave.

As we entered the elevator, Omar said: "Fred was mighty unhappy about our withdrawal, Frank. We were the only entry to pull out. He tried his damnedest to talk me out of it. There's going to be a bar with free drinks and sandwiches all day, he said, which only proves that we're doing the right thing. By one tomorrow afternoon that suite'll be so full of smoke and drunks you won't be able to see the chickens."

Although I couldn't have agreed with Omar more, I hated to leave. There was something exciting about fighting cocks in a hotel and the prospect of winning large sums of money. It's almost impossible to resist free drinks, and there would be some beautiful women around to spend some money on. And when it comes to good-looking women, Chattanooga has got prettier girls than Dallas, Texas.

I had written to Dirty Jacques Bonin in Biloxi and arranged a deal to put Omar and me and our gamecocks up at his game farm. When he came to fight his chickens at the Ocala derby in February, we would fix him up with like facilities either at my place or Omar's.

We shook hands and parted in the basement garage of the hotel. Omar headed for Biloxi in the pickup with twenty-two gamecocks, and I drove to Cook's Hollow with Icky and the derby-conditioned birds in the station wagon.

In the heat of the fighting the next day at Vern Packard's pit, I realized how much I had depended upon Omar to look after things during the season so far. If Vern hadn't done a good portion of my talking for me, I would have had a rough time getting matches. But thanks to Vern's efforts, I managed to fight five of my eight cocks, and I won every hack. By picking the winning derby entry, and laying even money with a local gambler, I won four hundred dollars. My five hack wins added two hundred and fifty dollars more to my roll, and I was well satisfied with the outcome of the side trip to Cook's Hollow. This was a small sum compared to what we might have won at Chattanooga, but it was enormous compared to winning nothing at all.

By four that afternoon the fighting was over, and I hadn't been able to get a match for Icky. Icky scaled now at a steady 4:02 and was too light for derby fighting in the Southern Conference. All of the S.C. derby weights began at 5:00, and the only way I could fight Icky was in hack battles. In New York and Pennsylvania, where the use of short heels is preferred and smaller gamecocks are favored, I could have had all the fights I wanted. So far, Icky had only had two fights. Before he met Jack Burke's Little David at Milledgeville, I wanted him to win at least three more. He would need all of the pit experience he could get to win over Burke's Ace.

The Cook's Hollow Game Club was similar to a hundred other small southern cockpits. The pit was on Vern Packard's rocky farm, adjacent to his barn, and covered with a corrugated iron roof. There were three-tier bleachers on three sides, and the fourth side was the barn wall. A double door in the barrier provided an entranceway inside, and two-by-two coops were nailed to the interior walls of the barn to serve as cockhouses for visitors.

There was a large blackboard nailed to the outside of the barn. The fans could follow the running results of the derby as they were chalked up by the referee following each battle. Cockfighters looking for individual hacks also used the blackboard. I had written my name and the weights of all my cocks in square letters, hoping for a challenge. When three-quarters of the crowd had left, I decided to quit myself.

I was inside the barn, transferring my birds into my traveling coops, when Vern Packard introduced me to an old farmer and his son.

"Frank," Vern said, "this is Milam Peeples, and his son, Tom."

I shook hands with both men. Milam Peeples was in his late fifties, tanned and well weathered by his years of outside labor. The yellow teeth on the left side of his mouth, I noticed, were worn down almost to the gum line from chewing on a pipe. The son was a full head taller than his father, with long thick arms and big raw-looking hands. He had a lopsided smile, a thick shock of wheat-colored hair, and he wore a gauze pad over his left eye. His right eye was blue. A thin trickle of spit ran down his chin from the left corner of his slack mouth. Either it didn't bother him or he didn't notice it. I noticed it, and it bothered me.

"Glad to meet you, Mr. Mansfield," Tom Peeples said.

"I saw on the blackboard out there"—his father made a sweeping gesture with his malodorous briar pipe—"that you got a 4:02 lookin' for a fight. If you don't mind givin' me an ounce, I got a 4:03 out to my place that can take him."

"He's my cock, Mr. Mansfield," Tom broke in. "Little Joe. You ever hear of him?"

"Mr. Mansfield hasn't fought in this neck of the woods for some years, Tom," Vern answered for me. "I doubt if he has."

"Little Joe's a six-time winner, Mr. Mansfield," the old man continued, "but I've never fought him here in Vern's pit. He's crowd shy and can't be conditioned to people or noise. But if you want to drive on out to my farm, maybe we could have us a little private hack."

I nodded sympathetically. Often a gamecock is crowd shy. But I wasn't too anxious to pit Icky against a six-time winner.

"I'll tell you what," Milam Peeples said generously, "I'll give you two-to-one odds, and you can name the amount. After all, you got to fight at my place instead of here, and I want to be fair."

I agreed, holding up five fingers.

"Nope," Milam Peeples shook his head. "I ain't fightin' Little Joe for no fifty dollars. Ain't worth the risk."

I had meant five hundred dollars. I grinned and opened and closed my fist five times, as rapidly as I could.

"Five hundred dollars?" Mr. Peeples took the pipe out of his mouth.

When I nodded, he hesitated.

"Now that's getting mighty steep. If I lose, you win yourself a thousand dollars."

"You offered Frank two to one," Vern Packard reminded the old man.

"Little Joe can take him, Daddy!" Tom said eagerly.

"All right." Peeples agreed to the bet and we shook hands. "When you're ready to go you can follow us on out in your car."

"Why don't you load Mr. Mansfield's coops in his station wagon, Tom," Vern suggested. "And I'll take him up to the house to get his suitcase."

"Yes, sir," Tom said.

As soon as Vern and I entered the back door of his house into the kitchen, he dropped into a chair beside the table where we had eaten breakfast. There was an amused smile on his friendly, open face. Vern was a short wiry little man with a sparse gray moustache, and he had been a good host.

"Just a second, Frank," Vern's voice stopped me as I started for the bedroom. "It's a trick. Old Man Peeples has never heard of you, Frank, and he's taken you for a sucker. I've seen him take itinerant cockers before, and I've never said anything. Why not? Peeples is a local cocker, and most of the drifters who fight here don't come back anyway. But I don't feel that way about you. Because the local gamblers didn't know your reputation I won six hundred bucks today on your hacks." Vern laughed with genuine amusement.

"You wouldn't fight the old man anyway, once you saw his setup. He's got a square chunk of waxed linoleum in his barn for the floor of his cockpit. And that cock of his hasn't won six fights, he's won at least *eighteen* fights! He rubs rosin on Little Joe's feet, and on that slick waxed floor the opposing cock doesn't have a chance. But if you really think your cock can take him, now that you know their game, I'll give you a chunk of rosin. That way, you'll both start even."

I got my suitcase out of the bedroom. Vern rummaged through the drawers of the sideboard.

"Here," he handed me an amber chunk of rosin the size of a dime-store eraser. "You don't need very much, Frank. But don't fight him on that waxed linoleum unless you use it. If you want my advice, you're a damned fool to fight him at all!"

I winked, shook hands with Vern and crossed the yard toward the station wagon. These two peckerwoods had a lesson coming, and I had made up my mind to teach it to them. Icky was in peak condition, as sharp as a needle. They would be counting on their trick to win. With the rosin safe in my pocket, the odds were in my favor. I couldn't believe that Little Joe, despite his eighteen wins, was in proper condition to beat Icky in an even fight.

I put my suitcase in the back, checked Tom's loading of my coops, climbed into the front seat, and honked my horn to let Peeples know that I was ready to go. I followed his vintage black car out of the parking lot. The Peeples farm was some six miles out in the country, and to get there I had to follow the lurching car over a twisting, rock-strewn, spring-breaking dirt road. When the old cockfighter stopped at the entrance to his dilapidated barn, I parked beside him.

I could see the cockpit without getting out of the station wagon. The linoleum floor was a shiny, glistening design in blue-and-white checkered squares. The glassy floor was such a flagrant violation of pit regulations—anywhere—that I began to wonder if there wasn't more going on here than Vern Packard had told me. But Vern had advised me *not* to fight, so I decided to go ahead with it and see what happened.

When I leaned over the seat to pull out Icky's coop, Tom opened the front door and offered his help.

"I'll hold him for you, Mr. Mansfield."

I took my blue chicken out of the coop and passed him to Tom Peeples. He smiled, hefting Icky gently with his big raw hands.

"He feels jes' like a baseball!" Tom said, as I opened my

gaff case. "Sure does seem a shame to see Little Joe kill a pretty chicken like this one."

I cleared Icky's spur stumps with typewriter-cleaning fluid, and heeled him low with a set of silver one-and-a-quarter-inch gaffs. Holding the cock under the chest with one hand, Tom passed him back to me.

"By the way," he said, snapping his fingers, "Little Joe always fights in three-inch heels, if you want to change." Tom had waited patiently until I had finished heeling before providing me with this essential information. Another violation of form. Of course, he had no way of knowing that I wouldn't have changed to long heels anyway.

I shook my head indifferently, and he ran to meet his father who was rounding the corner of the barn. Mr Peeples had gone to the rows of chicken runs behind the barn to get Icky's opponent while Tom had helped me heel. I took a good look at Little Joe from the front seat.

The cock had been so badly battered I couldn't determine his game strain. His comb and wattles were closely cropped for fighting, and most of his head feathers were missing, pecked out in earlier battles. Instead of the usual graceful sweep of arching tail feathers, the Peeples cock had only three broken quills straggling from his stern. Both wings were ragged, shredded, in fact. Both wings had been broken in fighting, and although they had knitted, they had bumpy leading edges. As Milam Peeples sat down on a sawhorse beside the pit and turned the cock on its back for Tom to heel him, I noticed that Little Joe's left eye was missing. A blinker on top of everything else. If Little Joe had won eighteen fights, and from his appearance he had been in many battles, Icky was in for the toughest fight of his life.

Maybe his last.

Under cover from Milam and Tom Peeples, I sat in the front seat of the station wagon holding Icky in my lap and briskly rosined the bottom of his feet. I was still rubbing the feet when the old man called out that he was ready. There was only a sliver of rosin left, but I put it in my shirt pocket and joined Milam and his son at the pit.

"I'm goin' to handle," the old man said. "And if you don't have no objections, Tom here can referee."

I nodded, stepped over the low wooden wall of the pit, and took my position on the opposite score. The waxed floor was so slick my leather heels slipped on it slightly before I got to the other side. Although I figured Mr. Peeples was expecting an argument of some kind about the illegal flooring, I kept a straight face. I wondered, though, what kind of an explanation he used to counter arguments about the pit. It must have been a good one.

"Better bill 'em, Mr. Mansfield," Tom said.

We billed in the center, and Icky got the worst of the prefight session. The bald head of Little Joe and shortage of neck feathers didn't give him a mouthful of anything. The Peeples cock was the meanest and most aggressive biller I'd seen in some time. I dropped back to my score. Both sets of scores, the eight and the two feet, had been straightedged onto the linoleum with black paint. As I squatted behind my back score, Tom asked me if I was ready, and I pointed to his father.

"Get ready, then," Tom said to the old man.

Milam was forced to hold the straining Little Joe under the body with both hands. There weren't enough tail feathers for a good tail hold—and I watched Tom's lips.

"Pit!"

The fight was over.

The battle ended so quickly, all three of us were stunned. I've seen hundreds of cockfights end in the first pitting, a great many of them in fewer than fifteen seconds. But the fight between Icky and Little Joe didn't last two seconds.

I was aware that Little Joe's feet were rosined as well as Icky's. Mr. Peeples had coated them surreptitiously when he got the chicken from its coop run behind the barn. So the only way I can account for the quick ending is by crediting Icky's superior speed and conditioning and my longtime practice of releasing him first. The old man was hampered when the time came to let go, because of the manner in which he had to hold the Ace cock.

Tom's sharp order to pit was still echoing in the rafters of the barn when I released my Blue. Icky, with his sticky feet firmly planted, didn't take the two or three customary steps forward like he usually did. He flew straight into the air from a standing takeoff. Old Man Peeples scarcely had time

181

to pull his hands away from beneath Little Joe's body when Icky clipped twice and cut the veteran fighter down on its score. It happened that fast. *Click! Click!* One heel pierced Little Joe's head, and the other heel broke his neck.

As the three of us watched in silent stupefaction, Icky strutted proudly to the center of the pit, leaving white gummy footprints in his wake, and issued a deep-throated crow of victory. The expressions on the faces of Milam Peeples & Son were truly delightful to see. And then Tom Peeples's face changed from milky white to angry crimson.

"You killed my Little Joe!" he shouted.

I was still squatting on my heels when he yelled, and I was totally unprepared for the enormous fist that appeared from nowhere and caught me on the temple. I crashed sideways into the left pit wall and it was smashed flat under the weight of my body. My eyes blurred with tears. All I could see were dark red dots unevenly spaced and dancing upon a shimmering pink background. I must have sensed the darker shadow of Tom's heavy work shoe hurtling toward my head. I rolled over quickly, and his kick missed my head. Two more twisting evasive turns, and I was in the empty horse stall next to the pit. As I scrambled to my knees, my fingers touched the handle of a heavy grooming brush. I regained my feet and swung it in an arcing loop from the floor. Tom saw the edge of the weighted brush ascending, tried to halt his rushing lunge, and half turned away. The brass-studded edge caught him on his blind side, on the bump behind his left ear. As Tom fell, his arms held limply at his sides, the opposite wall of the pit collapsed under him. He was out cold.

I could see all right now, but I kept a firm grip on the brush handle as I watched Milam Peeples to see what his reaction was going to be. The old man shook his head sadly, and removed an old-fashioned snap-clasp pocketbook from his front pocket.

"You didn't have no call to hit the boy that hard, Mr. Mansfield," he said. "Little Joe was Tom's pet. He was bound to feel bad about losin' him so quick."

I tossed the brush back into the empty horse stall and rubbed my sore side. My bruised ribs felt like they were on fire. My head was still ringing, and I probed my throbbing temple gingerly with a forefinger. There was a marble-sized knot beneath the skin, and it was swelling even more as I touched it.

"Now, I'm a little short of a thousand dollars in cash, Mr. Mansfield," Milam Peeples said plaintively, standing on the other side of Tom's felled body, "but here's three hundred and fifty-two dollars in bills. You're goin' to have to take the rest of the debt out in game fowl. We'd best go on down to the runs and you can pick 'em out. I figure six gamecocks'll make us even."

I didn't. I counted the bills he handed me, shoved the wad into my hip pocket, and then held up ten fingers.

"Most of these cocks are Law Grays, Mr. Mansfield," Peeples protested. "And three are purebred Palmetto Muffs. You know yourself there ain't no better cocks than Palmetto Muffs! Take a look first, and you'll see what they're worth. I only got ten gamecocks altogether."

I followed the old man out of the barn.

Professional cockers frequently pay off their gambling debts with gamecocks instead of cash. But this kind of pay-off is normally agreed upon before a fight—not afterward. I had no objection to taking gamecocks, instead of money, this late in the season. Some hard-hitting replacements would be useful before we entered the Milledgeville Tourney, and I was on the high side of the hog when it came to settling up with Peeples.

On the way to the coop walks, Peeples stopped at the watering trough to light his pipe and to do some preliminary dickering.

"Now you seen them three Grays I fit this afternoon, Mr. Mansfield. Aces every one. You take them, and any five more of the lot and we'll be fair and square. Countin' the cash I gave you already, you're gettin' the best end and you know it."

Giving Peeples more credit than he probably deserved, I figured his gamecocks were worth about fifty dollars a head. According to my arithmetic I would be short about two hundred and fifty dollars if I only took eight cocks. Even if I took all of them I would be one hundred and fifty dollars short of the thousand dollars he had bet me. I shook my head with a positive-negative waggle.

Feet pounded on the hard-packed ground behind me. I turned. Less than twenty feet away Tom Peeples was charging toward me with a hatchet brandished in his upraised right hand. His red face was contorted and his angry blue eye was focused on infinity.

Without taking time to think I jumped toward him instead of trying to dodge his rush, twisted my body to the left, and kicked hard at his right shinbone. Tripped neatly, he sprawled headlong in the dirt. The hatchet flew out of his hand and skittered for a dozen yards across the bare ground. Before he could recover himself I had a handgrip in his thick hair and another hold on his leather belt. With one jerk as far as my knees, followed by a short heave, Tom Peeples was in the water trough. I shifted my left hand from his belt to his hair and held him beneath the water with both hands. His legs thrashed the scummy water into green foaming milk, but he couldn't get his head up. I watched the popping bubbles break at my wrists and held him under until his feet stopped churning.

"You'd best not hold his head under too long, Mr. Mansfield," his father said anxiously. "He'll be drownded!"

That was true enough. I didn't want to drown the man. I only wanted to cool him off so I could complete my business with Mr. Peeples and get back to Cook's Hollow. When I let go of Tom's head, he broke free to the surface, blubbering. He had lost the bandage in the water, but both eyes were closed. He took handholds on both sides of the tin-lined trough and brought his body up to a crouched position. He stayed that way, half in the water, and half out, his chin on his chest, weeping like a child. But he wasn't a child. He was at least twenty-two years old, and he had tried to kill me.

Mr. Peeples and I continued our walk toward his chicken runs. Although the old cockfighter complained, he helped me put the seven mature cocks into narrow traveling coops that were in the runs, and brought the three Grays that were already in coops over to my station wagon from his old car. It was easy to catch Icky, who was scratching in a horse stall. After cutting off the heels, I put him back in his coop.

"I suppose you're goin' to tell Vern Packard how you beat

me," Mr. Peeples said, as I slipped behind the wheel and slammed the door.

Looking him directly in the eyes, I nodded my head.

"If you do, Mr. Mansfield," he begged, "me or Tom neither'll be ashamed to show our faces down to the pit for two or three years."

I shrugged, and let out the clutch.

As I drove out of the barn lot, Tom Peeples was still hunkered down dejectedly in the water trough like an old man washing his privates in a bathtub.

On the return drive to Vern Packard's house I missed one of the turns and had to redouble twice before I found the way back to the main road. It was dark when I wheeled into his driveway. Vern switched on the yard lights and came outside to meet me.

"Who won?" he asked excitedly, as I got out of the station wagon.

I handed him the fragment of rosin, took the wad of bills out of my pocket and counted off one hundred dollars. Grinning, I pushed the hundred dollars into his hand. He kissed the bills, and returned the sliver of rosin.

"You keep it, Frank," he said happily. "You paid me enough for it. Come on inside and eat. I was looking for you to get back an hour ago, but I've been waiting supper on you. It's still warm though."

As soon as I was seated at the kitchen table, Vern served the plates and turned the burner up higher under the coffee to reheat it. There were rolls, baked ham and candied sweet potatoes. Vern put enough food on my plate for three men, but I dug into it.

As he poured the coffee, Vern said jokingly, "What do you carry, Frank? A rabbit's foot, a lucky magnet or do you wear a bag of juju bones around your neck?"

I stopped eating and looked at him.

Vern laughed. "Your partner telephoned about twenty minutes after you left. Mr. Baradinsky. First, he wanted to know how you made out, and I told him. Then he had some news for you about the Chattanooga derby in the Southerner Hotel."

I put my knife and fork down and waited, trying to hide

my impatience at the way he was dragging out the story.

Again Vern laughed. "No," he said, "it isn't what you're thinking, Frank. They weren't raided. The pit was hijacked, and the thieves got away with about twenty-five thousand bucks, according to your partner. He got the information secondhand, and it won't be in the papers. No chickens were lost, but everybody there—cockers, gamblers and even Mr. Reed himself—lost their pants. There were three holdup men, all with shotguns, and they knew exactly what they were doing. They made everybody take off their pants and throw them in the middle of the pit. Then one of them filled up a mattress cover with all the pants and they left the hotel suite. They didn't fool with rings or watches. Just the pants"—Vern laughed heartily—"but the *money* was in the pants! That closed the Chattanooga meet. I'll bet Fred Reed has a tough time getting an okay from Senator Foxhall for a S.C. derby next year!"

I pursed my lips thoughtfully, nodded my head, and started eating again. My swollen temple was throbbing, and I wanted to put an ice pack on it.

The next morning I left Cook's Hollow to join Omar in Biloxi, with a standing invitation to fight at Vern Packard's game club any time I felt like it. I had added $902 to my bankroll and ten purebred fighting cocks to our stake in the S.C. Tourney. But no matter what Vern Packard thought, I wasn't lucky.

At long last, my experience and knowledge of cockfighting were beginning to pay off. That, and the fact that I was using the good sense God gave me.

Chapter Fifteen

I have back issues of all five game-fowl magazines covering the Southern Conference derbies held at Biloxi, Auburn and Ocala, but I don't have to dig through them to find the results. I remember them, all of them, perfectly.

In Biloxi, we fought in the cockpit established in a warehouse near the waterfront, and we won the derby 6-3, plus three thousand five hundred dollars in cash. Icky also won his fourth hack at Biloxi over a Hulsey two-time winner entered by Baldy Allen from Columbus, Georgia. Omar, who was spelling me on handling in the pit from time to time, was awarded a wristwatch by the pit officials as the Most Sportsmanlike Handler in the Biloxi derby. My partner was as pleased with this award as I was, but he wouldn't admit it. I knew that Omar was proud of the award because he put his Rolex away, and, from that day forward, wore the wristwatch he was given at Biloxi—a cheap, $16.50 Timex.

My partner didn't attend the Alabama meet with me. The meet at Auburn on January 29 coincided with his wife's annual visit to Florida. I never met the woman, but I had seen a half-dozen snapshots she had mailed to him that had been taken at Fire Island. In the photos, all six of them taken in a crocheted bikini, she looked brittle, thin and febrile-eyed. She didn't look particularly sexy to me, but inasmuch as it was costing my partner more than twelve thousand a year to keep her in New York City, I couldn't begrudge him a week in bed with her. He was entitled to that much, I figured.

Johnny Norris of Birmingham won the Auburn derby, and I came in third. Four of my Allen Roundheads were killed during the meet, but I won two thousand five hundred dollars. A carload of arsenal employees drove over from Huntsville, Alabama, and I won most of my money from them. When it came to cockfighting, these rocket makers didn't know which way was up. In a post-derby hack, I pitted Icky against an Arkansas Traveler that ran like a gazelle in the second pitting.

Our veterans took every fight in the February 24 Ocala derby. They fought in the familiar pit as though they were defending their home territory and hens against invaders from outer space. Out of fourteen pit battles, I only carried out one bird. In order to get bets, Omar was forced to give three-to-one odds on every fight, but we still made eighteen hundred dollars on the Ocala derby and hacks.

As the weeks passed, I kept as busy as possible. My personal life, perhaps, may have seemed dull, but I loved the way I lived. On my way home at night, after a day of conditioning at Omar's farm, I often selected a book out of my partner's library. Like a lot of businessmen in New York, he had always wanted to read books, but never had enough time. When he moved permanently to Florida, he ordered a complete set of the Modern Library, including the Giants. Starting at the lowest number, I was gradually working my way through them. By March, I was up to *The Plays of Henrik Ibsen*.

Not only did I get up with the chickens, I went to bed with them as well, but I still had time for reading and for playing my guitar. My partner had asked me to stay at his house, but I declined. I liked Omar, everybody did, but we were together all day, and that was enough. Both of us were entitled to privacy, and I think he was relieved when I decided to sleep at my own farm.

Omar Baradinsky, like any man who has strong opinions, liked to talk about the things he was interested in. This was understandable, and most of the time I enjoyed the insight he revealed on many subjects. However, to listen to him every night, especially when he got a little high on John Jameson, was too much. Unable to talk back, I had to grit my teeth sometimes to prevent myself from setting him straight when he got off the track.

Against the day when my vow was over and I could talk again, I made little entries in a notebook. Someday, Old Boy, I thought, I'm going to set you straight on every one of these topics. If we hadn't separated every evening, our partnership probably wouldn't have lasted the entire season. As it happened, we were still friends after more than five months. Because we were friends, I was worried. We were leaving the next morning and I didn't want to hurt my partner's feelings or interfere in any way with his individuality. But when it came to the Milledgeville Tourney, Omar had a serious problem, and it was up to me to explain it to him.

On the afternoon of March 13 we sat across from each other at the big oak table in Omar's living room going over the ledger and our accumulated records in preparation for the tourney. We had received a telegram the week before from Senator Foxhall reconfirming our joint entry in the tournament and acknowledging receipt of our five-hundred-dollar entry fee. The wire also told us that there would be only eight entries instead of the ten originally scheduled. Two entries had forfeited.

"It's going to make a big difference, Frank," Omar said, rereading the telegram for the tenth time that day. His initial delight over our joint-acceptance—which in my mind had never been in doubt—had gradually turned to concern about whether we would win the tourney or not.

"I know we won't need as many cocks as we figured on," he continued, "but neither will the other seven entries. Every cock in the tourney will be a topflight Ace."

I nodded understandingly. Omar's concern was justified. With only eight entries instead of ten the competition would be a lot stiffer. In comparison with a derby, a major tournament is a complicated ordeal. The matchmaker for a tourney has a compounded headache. In setting up the matches for a derby, the matchmaker only has to match the cocks to be shown at the closest possible weights.

In a tournament, every entry must meet each other at least once. Not only is the matchmaking more complicated, each tourney entry must have an Ace for every weight— that is, if he expects to win.

I wanted to win the tourney just as much as Omar did, but this was my fifth try against my partner's first, and I refused to worry about winning. There was nothing more either one of us could do except pray. We had to fight the gamecocks we had, and they were in the peak of condition. To worry needlessly about winning was foolhardy.

"Do you think we've selected the right cocks?"

I nodded.

"That's it, then." Omar closed the ledger. "I'm not taking our entire bankroll, Frank. Four thousand is in the bank, and I'm leaving it there. That way, if we lose, we'll still have two thousand apiece to show for the season. I'm taking eight thousand in cash to the tourney, and I'm going to lay it fight by fight instead of putting it all down on the outcome. No matter what happens, we'll still have a fifty-fifty chance of coming home with a bundle. Now, just in case we win the tourney, how much do we stand to win?"

I wrote the information on a tablet, and shoved it across the polished table.

Not counting our separate bets—

8 entries @ $500 each	*$4,000*
Sen. Foxhall purse	*$2,000*
Total	*$6,000*

If I win the Cockfighter of the Year Award, that'll be another $1,000—

Omar dragged a hand through his beard as he looked at the figures. "Doesn't Senator Foxhall take a percentage of the entry fees like the derby promoters?" he asked.

I shook my head and smiled. The senator wasn't interested in money. He had more money than he knew what to do with, but he would still come out even and probably ahead. There would be at least four hundred spectators at the two-day tourney paying a ten-dollar admission fee each day. And the senator would make a profit from his restaurant, too. The Milledgeville cockpit was seven miles out in the country. Where else could the visitors eat?

"Do you have to win the tourney to get the Cockfighter of the Year award, Frank?" Omar asked me.

I spread my arms wide and shrugged my shoulders.

I didn't really know. Senator Foxhall hadn't given the award to anybody in three years, and it was possible that he wouldn't give the medal again this year. All I knew was that the senator awarded the medal to the man he thought deserved it. I didn't want to think about it.

I studied my partner across the table. If anything, his beard was blacker and more unkempt than it had been at the beginning of the season. He still wore his bib overalls, short-sleeved work shirt and high-topped work shoes. During our association, I had never seen him dressed differently. He was a free American and entitled to dress any way he pleased. Once a week, when he took a bath, he changed his overalls, but he wore them everywhere he went, to dinner when we ate in Ocala, and downtown when we had fought in Biloxi. Everywhere. This was my problem, and I had to tell him. I pulled the tablet toward me and began to write.

Here are some things about the tourney I have to tell you. As official entries, we'll be put up in Senator Foxhall's

home, and eat our meals there. We don't have to wear tuxes
for dinner, but we do have to wear coats and ties. Entries
and spectators alike are not admitted to the pit unless they
wear suits and ties. This is a custom of the tourney out of
respect to Senator Foxhall. But he's really a good man. He
was never a real senator, I mean in Congress. He was a
Georgia state senator in the late twenties. But for whatever
it means, he's a gentleman of the old school and we have to
abide by the customs. I don't mind wearing a suit and tie in
the pit and you shouldn't either, because it's an honor to
fight at Milledgeville.

I also have a personal problem, two of them. I've made
seat reservations for four people. My fiancée and her
brother, and for Mrs. Bernice Hungerford and her nephew.
This was several months ago. I don't know if they're com-
ing—neither woman has written or wired me. I don't care.
Well, I won't lie. I DO care. If they come, help me entertain
them. I'll be handling most of the time, and you'll have to
give them some attention for me. Neither woman has seen a
cockfight before. My fiancée's name is Mary Elizabeth
Gaylord . . .

I looked over the message, which had taken two sheets of
tablet paper, and then passed it to Omar. He scanned it
slowly, folded the two sheets, put them carefully in his shirt
pocket and entered his bedroom.

He slammed the door behind him.

I wanted to damn Omar's sensitive soul, but I couldn't.
The custom of the cockpit wasn't my doing, but I felt
ashamed. To dictate a person's wearing apparel is a violation of every human right, but I had been forced to tell my
partner about the custom or he wouldn't have been
allowed through the gate.

After fifteen minutes had passed, and Omar still didn't
reappear, I got out of my chair and knocked softly on his
door.

"I'll be out in a minute," he called out. "Fix yourself a
drink!"

I measured three ounces of bourbon into a six-ounce
glass. Every time I wrote a note of any kind, I always felt
that I was circumventing my vow in an underhanded way,

but I was sorry I hadn't written a more detailed explanation about the suit business. But I needn't have worried.

Two drinks later the bedroom door opened. I set my glass on the table, grinned at my partner and shook my head in disbelief.

Omar had cut his beard off square across the bottom with a pair of scissors, and evenly trimmed the sides. His newly cropped beard was as stiff as the spade it resembled. His heavy black moustache had been combed to both sides, and the ends were twisted into sharp points. The white smiling teeth in the dark nest of his inky beard were like a glint of lightning in a dark cloud. He wore a pearl-gray homburg over his bushy black hair, a dark gray double-knit suit, a white shirt and cordovan shoes. Hanging out for two or three inches below his beard, a shimmering gray silk necktie was clipped to his shirt by a black onyx tie bar. He looked like a wealthy Greek undertaker.

"I was saving this costume as a surprise for you tomorrow," Omar said with a pleased laugh. "My new suit arrived from my New York tailor three days ago. How do I look?"

I clasped my hands over my head like a boxer, and shook them.

"Do you know what makes my beard so stiff?" Omar said, as he mixed a drink at the table. "Pommade Hongroise. And just in case you don't know what that means, it's imported moustache wax from France."

Omar added more whiskey to my glass.

"You Southerners don't have a cartel on manners, Frank. It may come as a shock to you, partner, but I even know the correct tools to use at a formal dinner." He raised his glass. "A toast, Mr. Mansfield!"

I grinned and clinked my glass against his.

"To the All-American cockfighters, the English-Polish team of Mansfield and Baradinsky! Gentlemen, gamblers, dudes and cocksmen, each and every one!"

We drank to that.

We left Ocala at three o'clock, but it was almost two in the afternoon before we reached Milledgeville. I should have traded my old pickup in for a newer truck, but I had never gotten around to it. For Omar, trailing me all the way, the slow rate of speed on the highway must have been maddening.

When we reached Milledgeville, I waved for Omar to follow me out, and drove on through without stopping. Milledgeville isn't much of a city—a boy's military academy, a girl's college and a female insane asylum—but it's a pretty little town with red cobblestoned streets lined with shade trees.

Once we were out of town and drawing closer to the cockpit, I didn't mind driving so slowly because I liked the familiar scenery. During the summer, the highway would be bordered on both sides with solid masses of blackberry bushes draped over the barbed-wire fences. In the middle of March, the fields were iron-colored and bare. The tall Georgia slash pines were deep in rust-colored needles. The sky was a watercolor blue, and tiny tufts of white clouds were arranged on this background like a dotted-swiss design. The sun was smaller in March, but the weather wasn't cold. The clear air was sharp, tangy and stimulating, without being breezy.

Like Omar, in his new double-knit suit, I was dressed up, and we both had a place to go. I wore a blue gabardine suit that I had had for two years, but it was fresh from the cleaners. Well in advance of the tourney, I had ordered a white cattleman's Town and Country snap-brim hat from Dallas, and a new pair of black jodhpur boots from the Navarro Brothers, in El Paso. For the past seven nights I had shined and buffed the new boots until they gleamed like crystal. I wore yellow socks with my suit, and I had paid forty dollars in Miami Beach for my favorite yellow silk necktie, with its pattern of royal blue, hand-painted gamecocks.

I wasn't dressed conservatively, but a lot of my fans would be at the tourney, and they expected me to look dashing and colorful. Press representatives from all five game fowl magazines would be present, and Omar and I were bound to get our photos printed in two or three magazines whether we won the tourney or not.

A Georgia state highway patrolman waved us through the gate to the senator's plantation without getting off his motorcycle. Seeing the back of the pickup and the station wagon both loaded with chicken coops, he didn't need to check our identification cards. A mile down the yellow-graveled road, I took the fork toward the cockpit and cock-houses to weigh in and put our gamecocks away before signing in at the senator's house.

Peach Owen met us in the yards, assigned us to a cock-house, and gave us our numbers to wear on the back of our coats. We were No. 5, and before we did anything else we pinned on our numbers.

Mr. Owen was the weight-and-time official for the tour-ney, and president of the Southern Conference Cockfight-ing Association. He was a well-liked, friendly man in his mid-thirties who had given up a promising career in cock-fighting to work full time for the senator and the Southern Conference. Senator Foxhall, who was getting too old now to do much of anything, paid Peach ten thousand dollars a year to breed and take care of his flock of fancy game fowl.

"Do you want to weigh in now or wait till morning?" Peach asked.

"Let's get it over with," Omar said, handing Peach our record sheets.

"I don't need both of you," Peach winked at me. "There's a fellow up at the house who wants to see you, Mr. Mansfield."

He didn't say who it was so I stayed for the weighing-in, an almost useless precaution at a professional meet like the S.C. Tourney.

At the majority of U.S. tournaments, cocks are weighed and banded upon checking in. This banding procedure is supposed to ensure that each entry will fight only the cocks he has entered. Before each fight, weight slips are called out, and the entrants heel the cock from their assigned cockhouse according to the exact weight on the slip. If they fail to show a cock making the weight within the check mar-gin, that fight is forfeited to the other cocker who can. The metal band on the leg of the heeled cock is checked by the weight-and-time official immediately prior to the fight and then removed. If the cock wasn't banded by one of the tourney officials upon arrival, the cock is a ringer. In theory, banding upon arrival at a tourney appears to be a sound practice, but bands can be purchased from a dozen or more manufacturers of cocking supplies by anybody who wants to pay for them. The man who wants to cheat by entering a sure loser, for instance, instead of a legitimate fighter, can buy all the metal leg bands he wants to, and clamp one on a ringer in a couple of seconds.

Banding had been eliminated at the S.C. Tourney. Every cock pitted at the S.C. Tourney was a four-time winner at an authorized cockpit or game club. And all the wins were entered upon an official record sheet and initialed by the pit operator. Weighing-in at the tourney consisted of checking each gamecock against his record sheet and description and weighing the gamecock itself. Minor weight variations were taken into account by the official.

The system wasn't foolproof. It was still possible to substitute a runner for one of the checked-in fighters, but a man would be a fool to try it. Among the spectators were most of the S.C. pit operators who could recognize at sight the gamecocks that had fought in their pits earlier in the season. If one of them or one of the other entries spotted a ringer, the man who tried to pull a fast one was through with cockfighting. His name went out on a blacklist to every U.S. pit operator, and the blacklist of crooked cockfighters was published annually in the April issue of every U.S. game fowl magazine.

The four-win stipulation was a tough rule, but I was all for it because it separated the amateurs from the professionals and raised the breeding standards of game fowl. This single rule had been the biggest advance in U.S. cockfighting since the late Sol P. McCall had originated the modern tournament. Many of the fans and gamblers who attended the two-day event traveled thousands of miles to see it, but they knew they would get their money's worth. The fighting would be fast, and every cock shown had proven himself to be dead game.

After completing the weighing-in, which took about an hour, our thirty-one gamecocks were transferred to their stalls inside the cockhouse. We gave each bird a half dip of water, and I scattered a very small portion of grain on the moss-packed floor of each coop to give them some exercise after the long trip. We dropped the canvas covers over the coops to keep the birds quiet, locked the door, and drove the short distance to the senator's home to sign the guest register.

I believe that Omar was impressed by the senator's home. I had been the first time I stayed there, and it still gave me a warm feeling to see the big house as we topped the rise and parked in front of the wide veranda. The mansion was one of the better southern examples of modified English Georgian. There are many great homes like it in the southern states, but not many of them are as well tended as they should be. It takes a lot of money. Good craftsmanship had been insisted upon when the house had been constructed. All the doors, and even the windows, had ornate, carved designs. The great balustrade that led from the downstairs hall to the upstairs bedrooms had been formed and curved for the purpose from a single tree. There was enough room to sleep thirty guests, but except for the official entries, their wives, and pit officials, spectators attending the meet had to find accommodations in a hotel or motel in Milledgeville.

As we climbed the steps to the veranda, the front door opened and Ed Middleton came out and grabbed my hand. He laughed at my expression and said fondly in his deep, booming voice: "You didn't expect to see me here, did you? How's my pretty blue chicken getting along?"

In a lightweight gray linen suit, with a pink-and-gray striped tie, Ed didn't look like a sick man to me, but the brown circles under his eyes were a little darker on his pale face. He looked happy, however, and he hadn't been happy when I last saw him in Orlando. Despite his appearance of well-being, he was still liable to have a heart attack at any moment.

Still gripping Ed's hand, I jerked my head for Omar to come forward and introduce himself.

"How do you do?" Omar said. "I've seen you referee, Mr. Middleton, but I've never had the pleasure of meeting you."

"Glad to meet you at last then, Mr. Baradinsky. Evidently you've been a settling influence on my boy here. When I heard about the holdup in Chattanooga, I checked right away, and don't think I wasn't surprised when I learned that you two had pulled out before the meet! The *old* Frank

Mansfield I knew would've been right in there, reaching for the ceiling with the rest of 'em."

Omar laughed. "If there's any influencing going on, Mr. Middleton, it's Frank working on me, not the other way around."

"Well, come on in," Ed entered the hall ahead of us. "I'm not the official greeter here, Mr. Baradinsky. I'm only filling in for Mrs. Pierce. She had to go downtown for something or other." Ed snapped his fingers at a grinning Negro boy of fourteen or fifteen in a white short jacket. "Take the bags out of the station wagon to Number Five upstairs."

"Yes, sir!" the boy said quickly. He had been eager enough to get our luggage, but the three of us had blocked his way.

While Omar and I signed the guest register, Ed Middleton surprised me again.

"I'm not here as a spectator, Frank," he explained. "I'm the referee, and don't think I won't be watching every move you make in the pits." He turned to my partner. "I retired a while back from active cockfighting, Mr. Baradinsky, but I decided later that I was too young to quit."

Ed laughed, and then he looked at me, staring directly into my eyes. "I promised Martha I'd quit, as you know, Frank"—he shrugged—"but now the promise doesn't mean anything—now that she's passed away. And I know damned well she wouldn't want me sitting around all by myself."

I nodded sympathetically and smiled. Two full and active days on his feet could very well kill Ed Middleton. And yet, I was still glad to see him and delighted to learn that he was the Number One pit official. Suppose he did keel over dead? That was a much better way to go than eating his guts out with boredom while he stared at a grove of orange trees.

"Say, Frank," Ed snapped his fingers as we started to go upstairs, "did your partner ever see the senator's flock of fancy chickens?"

"No, I haven't, Mr. Middleton," Omar said, "although I've heard enough about them."

"Good! Mrs. Pierce'll be back soon, and I'll take you on the ten-cent guided tour."

We climbed the stairs to the second floor to where the Negro boy held the door open. I gave him a five-dollar bill, which was plenty, but Omar gave him a five as well. The boy was so astonished by the size of the two gratuities, he returned to our room in less than three minutes with four additional bath towels, a bowlful of ice cubes and a pitcher of orange juice.

Omar glanced critically around the room and eyed the cut-glass chandelier in the high ceiling. "I'll say this much, Frank," Omar said, "the rag rug on the floor isn't made of rags, the furniture wasn't made in Grand Rapids, and that calendar on the wall above my bed wasn't placed there by any Baptist."

I opened my suitcase on my bed and unpacked, putting my extra black button-down shirts and white socks into the high walnut dresser between our beds. Omar pushed open the double French windows and looked out, his hands clasped behind his back.

"There's a good view of the cockpit from here, Frank," he said. "The dome has turned rose in the afternoon sun. Take a look at it."

I joined him at the window. A half mile away, the dome was pink on one side, and on the other side, away from the sun, the shadows were a dark purple. The twenty separated concrete cockhouses formed a U on the southern side of the circular pit. The Atlanta architect who had built the cockpit had settled for concrete blocks, but had incorporated many of the features of the Royal Cockpit at Whitehall Palace into the structure. The long narrow windows, recessed deeply into the walls, were traditional, but they didn't let in enough light. The five strong electric lights over the pit had to be turned on for both day and night fighting.

The square squat ugly restaurant, with a white asbestos tile roof, had been added ten years after the cockpit had been finished and was connected to the pit by a screened-in breezeway. The restaurant was entirely out of keeping with the general design, and I had always thought it a pity that it hadn't been built in the first place by the original architect.

The interior of the two-story pit held circular tiers rising steeply to the rim of the dome, and seated four hundred people. The judge's box was to the right of the connecting hall to the drag pit, and the press box was directly above this exit. Including the new doorway that had been cut through the wall leading to the restaurant, there were five arched doorways to the pit.

I finished my unpacking, and slipped on my jacket again in preparation to go out. Omar turned away from the windows, and poured a glass of orange juice.

"I want to tell you something, Frank." The husky tone of his voice stopped me before I reached the door. "Whether we win the tourney or not, I want you to know that I'll always be grateful to you for getting me this far. This is truly the greatest experience of my life."

He said this so warmly that I hit him fondly on the arm with my fist. I was tempted to tell my partner about my vow of silence, but this wasn't the time to tell him. If he knew that my voice was riding on the prospect of being awarded the Cockfighter of the Year award, he would have gotten more nervous about the outcome than he was already.

"Well," he said cheerfully, clearing his throat, "isn't it about time to take a look at those fancy chickens?"

I wagged my chin and pointed to his chest. I couldn't go with him, but I knew he would enjoy seeing them. Senator Foxhall had one of the finest collections of fancy game fowl in the world. He had turned fancier, after getting too old to fight chickens in the pit. He raised purebred Gallus Bankivas, the original wild jungle fowl from which all game fowl are descended, Javanese cocks, with tails ten feet long, miniature bantams from Japan—beautiful little creatures not much larger than quail—and many other exotic breeds. If Mary Elizabeth came to the meet, I intended to show them to her. But I couldn't go with Ed and Omar right then. I had to drive into Milledgeville.

I had wired the Sealbach Hotel and reserved four rooms, but with the crowd of visitors expected the next day I knew the manager wouldn't hold them for me unless I paid for them in advance. I wrote a short note for Omar, telling him where I was going and why.

"If you want me to, I'll go with you."

I shook my head.

"Okay. But rest easy about your guests, Frank. I'll see that they're well taken care of, don't worry. Didn't I ever tell you that I was once a vice-president in charge of public relations?"

I waved a hand in his direction, and drove into town.

By seven thirty that evening all the official entries had signed in, and the great downstairs hall was crowded as we waited for Senator Foxhall to come downstairs to lead the way into the dining room. On time, the old man came down the wide stairs, clutching his housekeeper's arm tightly for support. A slight, spare man, not much taller than a fifteen-year-old boy, he still managed to hold himself rigidly erect. In his old-fashioned, broad-lapeled dinner jacket and white piqué vest, he had an almost regal appearance. His pale blue eyes, deeply recessed now in his old age, were still alert and friendly behind his gold-rimmed glasses as he passed through the crowd. Somehow, he had preserved his hair, and his ivory mane was combed straight back from his high forehead in a well-groomed pompadour.

Ed Middleton, my partner and I were standing together. When the senator reached us, Ed introduced the old man to Omar.

"Oh, yes. Baradinsky? You're a Russian, aren't you?"

"No, sir," Omar replied. "Polish."

"You look like a Russian."

"It's probably the beard," Omar said self-consciously.

"Maybe so. Anyway, you're in good hands with Frank Mansfield." The senator smiled in my direction, exposing his blue-gray false teeth. "You'll teach him our American ways, won't you, son?"

Smiling in return, I nodded my head. Omar's great-great-grandfather had emigrated to the United States, but it would have been useless to explain this fact to the senator.

Senator Foxhall nodded his head thoughtfully about twenty times before speaking again.

"Frank is a good man, Mr. Baradinsky. I knew his grand-daddy. You listen to Frank and you'll learn something about gamecocks. Did you ever hear of Polish poultry?"

"Yes, sir."

"Well, they don't come from Poland! I'll bet you didn't know that, did you?"

"No, sir, I didn't."

"I didn't think you did," the old man said gleefully. "Not many people do. Did you know that, Ed?"

"I sure did, Senator," Ed said, with a rueful laugh. "I once tried to cross some frizzle-haired Polish cocks, and after losing three in the pit, I found out that they wouldn't face when they were hurt."

"You should've come to me," the old man said. "I could've told you that and saved you some money." He turned back to Omar. "Cockfighting in Poland has never been up to standard, Mr. Baradinsky. They don't feed them right. Same thing with Ireland. Gamecocks can't fight on raw potatoes, Mr. Baradinsky."

"I'll remember that," Omar said blandly.

Mrs. Pierce, the senator's housekeeper for more than thirty years, tugged on the old man's arm. "We'd better go in to dinner now," she reminded him. As the old couple turned away from us to lead the way into the dining room, Omar shrugged his shoulders helplessly, and winked at me. I grinned and nodded my head. Actually, my partner had shown considerable restraint. The senator had been correct in everything he said. If Omar had tried to argue with him, the old man would have cut him to shreds.

Except for Omar and myself, the guests seated around the dinner table were a rather eccentric group. I had known most of them for years, but even to me it seemed like an unusual gathering of people. All of us wore our entry numbers on the backs of our coats. We needed these numbers in the pit as identification for the benefit of the spectators. But we also had to wear them at all times for Senator Foxhall. He knew our names, and he knew them well, but sometimes he had a tendency to forget them. When he did forget, he checked his typewritten list of entries against our numbers so he could address any one of us by name without embarrassment.

Senator Foxhall sat at the head of the long table, and Mrs. Pierce was seated at the opposite end. Ed Middleton and Peach Owen were seated on either side of the senator. Next to Ed was Buddy Waggoner, the second referee, who would preside over the drag pit.

By their entry numbers, the remaining guests were seated around the table, clockwise from Buddy Waggoner.

No. 1. Johnny McCoy and Colonel Bob Moore, USAF (Retired). Johnny McCoy and his partner, Colonel Bob, flew to meets all over the U.S. from their fifty-thousand-acre ranch near Dan's Derrick, Texas, in a Lear jet. Colonel Bob, although he had been retired for at least ten years, still wore his Air Force blue uniform at all times. Only two days before, this Texas partnership had fought in the Northwest Cockfighting Tourney in Seattle, Washington. From there, they had flown back to Dan's Derrick and picked up fresh, newly conditioned gamecocks. They then had flown in to Macon. The senator's limousine and private game-fowl trailer had brought them from Macon to Milledgeville.

No. 2. Pete Chocolate, Pahokee, Florida. Except for the senator, Pete Chocolate was the only male guest wearing dinner clothes. He had spoiled the effect, however, by wearing a blue-and-white T-shirt under his black tuxedo jacket. And around his neck he wore an immaculate cream-colored ascot scarf.

No. 3. Dirty Jacques Bonin, Biloxi, Mississippi. There was nothing "dirty" about Jacques Bonin's appearance. His suit was flawlessly tailored, and his spatulate nails were freshly manicured. Clean shaven and soberly attired, he looked like, and was, a church deacon. He had earned the appellation of Dirty Jacques during World War II when he had organized the gang of strikebreakers who killed or maimed eighty striking long-shoremen on the Mobile docks. He had never lived the name down, although his full-time occupation was now the breeding and fighting of Louisiana Mugs.

No. 4. Jack Burke. Dody sat beside her husband, and I sat next to her—one of Mrs. Pierce's ideas. Dody spoke to me once, and only once, during dinner.

"Jack told me to apologize for kicking you at Plant City," she whispered.

I waited politely for her to continue, but that was all she said.

Jack Burke also spoke to me during dinner, leaning forward in his chair and twisting his head in my direction.

"Let's make it an even thousand bet between Little David and your chicken, Frank. I've okayed it with Ed and Peach to have the hack immediately after the last tourney fight while the judges tote up the final scores. All right?"

When I nodded in agreement, he sat back in his chair.

No. 5. The English-Polish team of Mansfield and Baradinsky.

No. 6. Roy Whipple and his son, Roy, Jr. Mr. Whipple was the old cockfighter who had shared the velvet love seat with me in the bridal suite of the Southerner Hotel in Chattanooga. He had lost a bundle in the holdup, but it hadn't dented his bankroll. The old man owned three Asheville, North Carolina, resort hotels. Roy, Jr., was a senior at the University of North Carolina, Chapel Hill, and had obtained special permission from the dean of men to assist his father at the meet.

No. 7. Baldy Allen, of Columbus, Georgia, was the owner of several liquor stores. Breeding and fighting milk-white Doms was not only a sideline for Baldy, it was a profitable enterprise. His gregarious wife, Jean Ellen, who did his betting for him, accompanied Baldy everywhere.

No. 8. Johnny Norris, Birmingham, Alabama. Johnny was famous as a conditioner of game fowl, but I didn't consider him a first-rate handler. For fifteen years he had conditioned cocks for the late Ironclaw Burnstead. When Mr. Burnstead died, he left Johnny three hundred thousand in cash and his entire flock of game fowl. In the past three years, Johnny had gained a reputation as an all-around cocker, and this was his first entry in the S.C. Tourney.

During dinner, I listened attentively to the conversation. All I heard was "chicken talk." The only subject that any of us had in common was cockfighting, and the love of cockfighting was the distinguishing feature of every entry. Every man present had the game fowl, the knowledge, the ability and the determination to win the tourney, but only one of us could win.

I intended to be that one.

Chapter Sixteen

Out of long habit more than anything else, I drank a quick cup of coffee in the dining room the next morning and was in the cockhouse by five thirty. Gamecocks cooped for long periods in a small two-by-two stall have a tendency to get sleepy and bored. Too much lassitude makes a cock sluggish when pitted. To wake them up, I took each cock out of its coop and washed its head with a damp sponge dipped in cheap whiskey. By the time I finished the sponging at seven thirty, our gamecocks were skipping up and down inside their stalls with rejuvenated animation and crowing and clucking with happiness.

Omar joined me at eight, and a few minutes later Doc Riordan showed up at the cockhouse to wish me luck in the tourney. The pharmacist and my partner hit it off well together from the moment they met.

"I never miss the Southern Conference Tourney," Doc told Omar, "but all season long I've been chained to my desk. I'm the president of the Dixie Pharmaceutical Company, as Frank may have told you, and this year our firm is launching a new product." He reached into his coat pocket and handed Omar a small white packet. "Licarbo!" he said proudly. "Advertising is our biggest headache, although the raising of capital isn't the simple matter it used to be."

"Who handles your advertising?" Omar asked, tearing open the sample and cautiously tasting the product with the tip of his tongue.

"Unfortunately," Doc sighed, "I have to handle it myself. That's been my main trouble. But I'm a registered pharmacist, and most of the drugstores in Jax have allowed me to put my posters in their windows."

"I think you've got a good idea here in Licarbo," Omar said sincerely. "After the tourney I won't have too much to do until April, and maybe you and I can get together on this product. I used to be in advertising in New York. Perhaps Frank told you?"

"No, he didn't." Doc looked at me reproachfully. "I didn't know Frank had himself a partner until I read the account of the Plant City Main between you-all and Jack Burke. Now, that was a main I wish I'd seen! That reminds me, Frank—" Doc took a small bottle of black-and-gray capsules out of his pocket and placed it on the workbench. "These are energy capsules. I made 'em up for Mr. Burke from a formula he gave me, and they should be good. They take about an hour for the best results, but when I made 'em up for Mr. Burke's chickens, I said to myself: 'While I'm at it, I'll just make up a batch for Frank Mansfield.' "

"We appreciate it, Doctor," Omar said—and then to me, "The restaurant should be open by now. Let's get some breakfast."

Shaking my head, I opened my gaff case on the workbench and started to polish gaffs with my conical grinding stone.

"I'll have some coffee with you, Mr. Baradinsky," Doc offered.

"Fine. I'd like to find out more about Licarbo."

"Right now," Doc said, "advertising isn't quite as important as raising a little capital. However, I'd appreciate any advice you'd—"

"I'll bring you some coffee, Frank," Omar said over his shoulder. "Capital, Doctor, is simply a matter of devious stratagems worked out through a mathematical process known as pressure patterns peculiar to pecuniary people."

As soon as they were out of earshot I opened the small bottle of energy capsules Doc had given me, dumped them on the floor, and crushed them into powder with my heel. The capsules might have been wonderful, but I wouldn't take any chances with them. Jack Burke knew that Doc Riordan was a friend of mine, and that fact alone was enough to make me distrust the medicine. Perhaps Jack didn't have enough brains to plan anything so devious, but I wouldn't have used a strange product on my chickens whether Burke's name had been mentioned or not. A major tournament is not the place for experimentation.

As the parking lot filled slowly, I leaned against the locked door of our cockhouse and watched the arriving cars as they pulled in and parked under the directions of the attendants. By nine a.m., when the time came for Omar and me to go over to the pit for the opening of the tourney, there was still no sign of either Bernice or Mary Elizabeth.

Tension was building up inside me, as it always does just before a meet, and I was happy when Peach Owen disengaged the mike, and handed it to Senator Foxhall. Peach played out the extra cord behind the senator as the old man marched stiffly to the center of the pit. The senator waited for silence, which didn't take very long. This early in the morning, there were only about two hundred spectators, but by two in the afternoon, the place would be jammed.

"Ladies and gentlemen," Senator Foxhall said in his high reedy voice, "welcome to the Southern Conference Tourney! We sincerely hope that all of you will have a good time. There is only one rule that you must observe during the meet." He paused. "Conduct yourselves like ladies and gentlemen."

(Applause.)

"Before the tourney is over," he said wryly, licking his thin lips, "some of you may desire to place a small wager or two—"

(Laughter.)

"If you do, make certain you know the man you're betting with—there *may* be Internal Revenue agents in the crowd!"

(Laughter.)

The old man turned the hand microphone over to Peach Owen and returned to his chair beside the judge's box. For the remainder of the tourney he would sit there quietly, watching everything that went on with his deep-set, cold blue eyes. With those experienced eyes watching me, I knew I couldn't make a single mistake when I was in the pit.

I was elated when Peach Owen called over the PA system for entry Number Two and entry Number Five to report to the judge's box to pick up their weight slips. My tension disappeared. Now I could be busy.

The first match was 5:00 cocks. After getting our weight-slip, Omar and I double-timed back to the cockhouse to heel our chicken. Time was going on from the second we received our weight slip, and only fifteen minutes were allowed to heel and be ready for the pitting. If an entry failed to make it on time, he forfeited that fight, and the next waiting, heeled pair was called. The fifteen-minute time limit kept the fights moving along fast. Where a match was even, or after ten minutes of fighting in the main pit, the two cocks were sent to the drag pit and a new pair was started in the center pit.

From the first pitting, I knew that the fight was going to be a long-drawn-out battle. Pete Chocolate matched a Spanish cross against my Mellhorn Black, and both birds were wary and overcautious. They did little damage to each other by the fourth pitting, and just before the fifth, when Ed Middleton saw that Roy Whipple and Baldy Allen were heeled and ready, he signaled for second referee Buddy Waggoner to start the next match and ordered us to follow him into the drag pit.

In the thirty-first pitting we went to breast after the third count of twenty, one hand under the bird only, at the center score.

"Get ready," Ed Middleton said.

Pete and I faced each other across the two-foot score, both holding weary fighters with our right hand, and one foot above the ground. That's when the Indian made his first mistake.

"Pit!"

I dropped on signal and so did Pete, but Pete pushed, causing his Spanish to peck first because of the added impetus. I saw him plainly, but Ed missed it. Snapping my fingers I made a pushing gesture with my right palm and pointed to the straight-faced Seminole.

"I'm refereeing this fight, Mr. Mansfield!" Ed snapped angrily. "Handle!"

We picked up the cocks for the short rest period. I couldn't argue, but Ed had been alerted and he watched Pete closely durnig the next actionless pittings. There are no draws at the S.C.T., and I was beginning to think the fight was going to last all day when Pete just barely pushed his bird on the forty-fifth pitting. This time, Ed caught him at it.

"Foul! The winner is Number Five!"

"Foul?" Pete asked innocently. "I committed a foul of some kind?"

"Pushing on the breast score. Are you trying to argue, Mr. Chocolate?"

"I'm afraid I must, Mr. Middleton," Pete said with feigned bewilderment. Spreading his arms widely, Pete turned to the crowd of a dozen or so spectators who had followed the first fight into the drag pit. "Did any of you gentlemen see me pushing?"

"That's a fifty-dollar fine for arguing. Anything else to say, Pete?"

Pete glowered at Ed for about ten seconds, and then shook his head. We carried our birds out, returning to our respective cockhouses. The door was open and my partner was attempting frantically to heel a 5:02 Roundhead by himself when I entered.

"Take over, Frank!" Omar said excitedly. "Your drag lasted almost an hour, and we've got less than five minutes to meet Roy Whipple with a 5:02!"

I put the battered Mellhorn away, and while Omar held, I finished heeling the Roundhead. We made it to the weighing scales with two minutes to spare. During the long drag battle with Pete, three fights had been held in the main pit.

From the word "Pit!" my Allen Roundhead lasted exactly twenty-five seconds with the Whipple cock before it was cut down in midair and killed.

The fighting was just as fast for the rest of the morning. If I didn't lose during the first three or four pittings I usually won the battle. My tough, relentless conditioning methods paid off with stamina. In a long go, my rock-hard gamecocks invariably outlasted their opponents. Every fight at Milledgeville was a battle between two Aces, however, and during the first three to five pittings, when both cocks were daisy fresh, it was anybody's fight. At one p.m., when a one-hour break for lunch was called, I had lost two and won three.

Omar and I left the pit together, planning to eat at the senator's house rather than wait for service in the crowded restaurant. As we left by the side entrance, a parking attendant came running over and caught up with us.

"Mr. Mansfield, there's a lady down in the lot who asked me to find you."

"Shall I go with you, Frank?" Omar said.

I nodded, and we followed the attendant into the parking lot.

It was Bernice Hungerford. As we approached her car, she got out, slammed the door and waited. Bernice looked much prettier than I remembered. Either she wore a tight girdle, or she had lost fifteen pounds. A perky, wheatstraw, off-the-face hat was perched atop a brand new permanent, and her dark hair gleamed with some kind of spray. She wore a mustard-colored tweed suit, softened at the throat by a lemon-yellow silk scarf. The air was chilly, but it wasn't cold enough for the full-length sheared beaver coat she held draped over her left arm.

When I accepted her white-gloved extended right hand, I noticed that it was trembling.

"I had to send for you, Frank," she apologized, lifting her face to be kissed. I brushed her lips with mine, and she stepped back a pace, blushing like a girl. "I've been here for more than an hour," she said with a shy laugh. "But when I went up to the entrance and saw all those men standing around—and no women—I was afraid to go inside!"

"You'll find a lot of ladies here, once you get inside, Miss—?"

"Mrs. Hungerford," Bernice said self-consciously.

"Mrs. Hungerford," Omar said, "I'm Frank's partner, Omar Baradinsky. And I'm glad the boy caught us in time. We were just leaving for lunch, and now you can join us."

"I feel better already." Bernice smiled. "I started not to come, Frank." She took my arm, and Omar relieved her of her heavy coat. "Tommy couldn't get away, and I dreaded coming by myself, but now . . . Mr. Baradinsky," she turned impulsively to Omar on her left. "Is there such a thing as a powder room around here?"

Omar laughed. "If you can hold out for about five hundred more yards, Mrs. Hungerford, you'll be made comfortable at the house."

"Thank you. How do I look, Frank? How *does* a lady dress for a cockfight?"

"A woman as beautiful as you," Omar said, "could wear sackcloth and still look like a queen."

"Now I do feel better!" Bernice laughed gaily. "What does one *do* at a cockfight?"

"At first, I'd advise you to merely watch. But if you decide to place a wager, let me know. Frank and I will be busy, but one of us will look after you when we're free."

Thanks to my partner, the luncheon was a success. He was gracious and paternal toward Bernice, without being patronizing, and before we returned to the pit, she was no longer ill at ease or prattling with nervousness. When the fighting began, I rarely sat with her. Most of Omar's time was taken up with the placing of bets, payoffs and collections, but he joined her as often as he could.

There was another one-hour break at seven, and then the fights were to continue until midnight. According to the schedule—if everything went according to plan—the tourney would be completed by three p.m. the following afternoon. After the prizes and purses were awarded, the senator always held a free barbecue for everybody on the parklike lawn between his house and the cockpit.

We ate dinner, all three of us, in the restaurant. After dinner, Bernice begged off as a spectator from the evening fights. She was tired and bored from watching them. Without a basic understanding or knowledge of what to look for, Bernice's boredom was not unreasonable. Women rarely find cockfighting as exciting as men do.

Although I missed her friendly white-gloved wave and cheery cry of "Good luck" each time I entered the pit, I wasn't sorry to send her to the hotel in town. She promised to meet us at noon the following day, and I was relieved that I didn't have to entertain her until then.

The night fighting got bungled up.

There were two forfeits in the 5:12 weights, when Dirty Jacques Bonin and Jack Burke weren't heeled and ready on time, plus long technical arguments on both sides. To return to the cockpit after heeling, it was necessary to cross through the parking lot. Jack Burke claimed—and I think he had a reasonable point—that automobiles leaving the area after the ten-thirty fight had held him up. He failed to see why he should be penalized for a parking attendant's failure to control the traffic properly. Peach Owen brought out

210

the rules and read them aloud. The rules stated clearly that the handler was to be ready for pitting within fifteen minutes after receiving his weight slip. No provisions had been written concerning interference, so Jack forfeited the fight after being promised by Peach Owen that this provision would be discussed by the S.C.T. committee before the next season.

Due to these delays, it was after one o'clock before Omar and I got back to our room in the mansion. I had lost four fights out of twelve, but my partner, who had placed shrewd bets on every match held during the day, had added two thousand, eight hundred dollars to our bankroll.

"Are we going to win the tourney, Frank?" Omar said, as we undressed for bed.

Down to my underwear, I sat on the edge of my bed and checked over the official scorecard. Jack Burke, Roy Whipple and Johnny Norris were ahead of us, but they weren't so far ahead that we couldn't catch up with them the next day. I drew a large question mark on the blank side of the scorecard, sailed the square of cardboard in Omar's general direction and got wearily into bed. With a full day of fighting to go, the top three could just as easily be the bottom three when the points were tallied at the end of the meet.

Before Omar finished counting and stacking the money into neat piles on top of the dresser and switched off the overhead chandelier, I was sound asleep.

The next morning at eleven—during my third match of the second day—soft-spoken Johnny Norris was no longer a contender. His name was stricken from the lists, and he was barred forever from Southern Conference competition for ungentlemanly conduct.

At most southern pits, the sidewalls are constructed of wood, but the sunken pit at Milledgeville has concrete walls. At a wooden-walled pit, when two cocks are fighting close to the barrier, it isn't unusual for one of the fighters to jab one of his gaffs into a board and get stuck.

Because of this possibility, cockpits with sixteen-inch wooden walls have a ground rule "to handle" when an accident like this happens. The handler then pulls the gaff loose from the wall and, following a thirty-second rest period, the birds are pitted again.

There was no such rule at Milledgeville.

With a concrete pit, this ground rule was considered unnecessary. Unfortunately for Johnny Norris, after many years of operation, there were hairline cracks in the concrete wall. In the sixth pitting, my Claret drove Johnny's spangled Shuffler into the wall. During a quick flurry, the Shuffler hung a gaff into one of the narrow cracks. The long three-inch heel was wedged tight. The Shuffler was immobilized, with his head dangling down, about ten inches above the dirt floor of the pit.

Johnny looked angrily at Buddy and said: "Handle, for Christ's sake!"

"No such rule at this pit." Buddy shook his head stubbornly.

My Claret had backed away and was eyeing the upside-down bird, judging the distance. Advancing three short steps, he flew fiercely into the helpless Shuffler with both heels fanning. The fight was mine.

Johnny swung a roundhouse right and broke Buddy Waggoner's jaw.

After a near riot, order was restored when Senator Foxhall announced that he would stop the tourney and clear the pit if everybody didn't quiet down. Johnny Norris was taken off the S.C.T. rolls and banished back to Birmingham. Because of Johnny's forced withdrawal, the remaining seven entries had to be reshuffled and rematched by the officials. This administrative work took more than an hour.

At one o'clock, when the lunch break was called, Mary Elizabeth still hadn't put in an appearance. I had made a nuisance out of myself by writing notes and checking periodically with the box office and Parking attendants, but by one p.m. I had resigned myself that she wouldn't come.

I took Bernice to the house for lunch.

The rematching delay ruined the planned schedule. The last match between Roy Whipple and Colonel Bob Moore didn't start until three thirty. The moment the two cockfighters entered the pit, Omar and I raced for our cockhouse to heel Icky for the last hack between my bird and Burke's Little David.

When we returned to the pit, Jack Burke was already heeled and waiting. As the three of us stood in the doorway, watching the fight in progress, Jack looked contemptuously at Icky and said, "Let's raise the bet to two thousand, Frank."

Omar bridled. "One thousand is the bet, Mr. Burke. You've had Little David on a country walk all season, and Icky's had to fight to qualify. If there's any bet-changing to be done, you should give us some odds."

"Are you asking for odds, Frank?" Burke challenged, ignoring my partner.

I shook my head. Holding Icky under my left arm, I pointed to the pit with my free hand. Colonel Bob was carrying out a dead chicken, and Ed Middleton was cutting the gaff tie strings away from Whipple's winner with his knife.

We reported to the judge's booth and weighed in. Icky was at fighting weight, an even 4:02. The freedom of the long rest on a farm walk had brought Little David's weight up from four pounds to 4:03. Omar protested the one-ounce overweight immediately, and Peach Owen ordered Burke to cut away feathers until his cock matched Icky exactly.

"While the results of the tourney are being tabulated and rechecked," Peach drawled into the microphone with his deep southern voice, "there'll be an extra hack for your pleasure. The weight is 4:02, short heels, between entries four and five!"

A murmur of approval and a scattering of applause encircled the packed tiers. The majority of the people in the audience were aware of the extra hack before the announcement. Omar had laughingly told me about some of the rumors he had heard. Some people thought that the hack was a simple grudge match, while others claimed that several thousand dollars had been bet between us. The reported incident at Plant City, when Dody had kicked me in the shins, had also caused a great many rumors. Supposedly, I had made a pass at Jack's wife, or Jack Burke had taken Dody away from me, or—wildest of all—Dody had been my childhood sweetheart. How a man of thirty-three could possibly have had a childhood sweetheart of only sixteen didn't prevent the rumors. What Jack had spread about himself, or what people said about me, didn't matter. My only concern was to win the hack.

Ed Middleton examined both cocks, returned them to us, and told us to get ready.

"I've *been* ready!" Jack said.

I bobbed my head, and Ed said, "Bill 'em."

We billed the cocks on the center score.

"That's enough," Ed said, when he saw how quickly the combativeness of both cocks was aroused. "Pass 'em once and get ready."

Holding our gamecocks at arm's length, we passed them in the air with a circling movement and retreated to our respective eight-foot scores.

"Pit!"

As usual, by watching the referee's lips, I let Icky go first, beating Burke off the score. I needed the split second. The O'Neal Red, with its dark red comb, and fresh from a country walk, was faster than Icky. Despite his superb condition, the days and nights in a narrow coop walk had slowed my Blue chicken down. Icky missed with both spurs as Little David side-stepped, and my cock wound up on his back with a spur in his chest.

"Handle!"

The second I disengaged the spur from Icky's breast, I retreated to my side of the pit and examined the wound. It wasn't fatal. Using the cellulose sponge and pan of clean water furnished by the pit, I wiped away the flowing blood, and pressed my thumb against the hole to stop the bleeding until the order came to get ready.

"Pit!"

Little David was overconfident and Icky was vigilant. The Red tried three aerial attacks and failed to get above my pit-wise Blue. With mutual respect, they circled in tight patterns, heads low above the floor, hackles raised, glaring at each other with bright, angry eyes. Icky tried a tricky rushing feint that worked. As Little David wheeled and dodged instead of sidestepping, Icky walked up his spine like a lineman climbing a telephone pole. There was an audible thump as Icky struck a gaff home beneath Little David's right wing.

"Handle!"

Burke removed the gaff with gentle hands. The O'Neal Red had been hurt in the second pitting. The wound in Icky's chest no longer bled, but I held my thumb over the hole anyway, and made him stand quietly, facing him toward the wall where he couldn't see his opponent.

The third, fourth and fifth pittings were dance contests that could have been set to music. The two colorful game-cocks maneuvered, wheeled, sidestepped, feinted and leaped high into the air as they clashed. When one of them did manage to hang a heel, first one and then the other, the blow was punishing.

Prior to the sixth pitting, I held Icky's legs tight under his body to rest them, facing him toward the wall. I raised my eyes for a moment, and there sat Mary Elizabeth, not six feet away from me. I almost didn't recognize her at first. She was wearing a light blue coat with raglan sleeves, and she had a pastel-blue scarf over her blonde hair, tied beneath her chin. She sat in the second row—not in the seat I had reserved for her. Her skin was pale, and her expression was strained. As I smiled in recognition, Ed called for us to get ready, and I had to turn my back.

"Pit!"

For the first time in months I was second best in releasing my gamecock's tail. Little David outflew my Blue and fanned him down. On his back, Icky shuffled his feet like a cat. Both birds fell over, pronged together with all four gaffs, like knitting needles stuck into two balls of colored yarn.

"Handle!"

It took Burke and me almost a full minute to disengage the heels. Both cocks were severely injured and my hands were red with blood as I sponged my battered bird down gingerly with cold water. During the short rest period I didn't have time to exchange any love glances with my fiancée in the stands. Thirty seconds passed like magic.

"Get ready . . . Pit!"

Both gamecocks remained on their scores as we released them.

"Count!" Burke ordered.

"One, two, three, four, five, six, seven, eight, nine and one for Mr. Burke. Handle!" Ed said, looking up from his wrist-watch.

Both of us needed the additional thirty-second rest period. I sucked Icky's comb to warm his head, held his beak open wide and spat into his open throat to refresh him. I was massaging his tired legs gently when Ed told us to get ready.

"Pit!"

Stiff-winged, the two cocks advanced toward each other from their scores and clashed wearily in the center. Too sick and too tired for aerial fighting they buckled again and again with weakened fury. Little David fell over limply, breathing hard, and stayed there. Grateful for this respite, Icky also stopped fighting, standing quietly with his head down, bill touching the dirt.

"The count is going on," Ed announced, watching his wrist-watch and the two cocks at the same time. At the silent count of twenty seconds, when neither bird had tried to fight, Ed ordered us to handle.

I wanted to work feverishly, but I was unable to do the nursing needed to help my fighter. Rough nursing could put Icky out of the fight for good. I sponged him gently and let him rest. Icky had recovered considerably by himself from the twenty-second count.

When the order to pit was given again, he crossed the dirt floor toward his enemy on shaky legs. Little David squatted on his score like a broody hen on eggs, with his beak wide open, and his neck jerking in and out.

Icky pecked savagely at the downed cock's weaving head. An instant later, the maddened Little David bounced into the air as though driven by a compressed spring and came down on Icky's back with blurring, hard-hitting heels. My cock was uncoupled by a spine blow, paralyzed, and unable to move from the neck down. Little David's right one-and-a-quarter-inch heel had passed cleanly through Icky's kidney and the point was down as far as the caeca. On the order to handle, I disengaged the gaff and returned to my score.

I didn't dare to sponge him. There was very little I could do. Water would make him bleed more rapidly than he was bleeding already. I held him loosely between my hands, pressing my fingers lightly into his hot body, afraid he would come apart in my hands. Fortunately, Little David was as badly injured as Icky. His last desperate attack had taken every ounce of energy he had left.

After three futile counts of twenty, Ed Middleton ordered us to breast on the center score, one hand only beneath the bird.

Which gamecock would peck first?

Which gamecock would die first?

It was an endurance test. Little David had been the last chicken to fight. If Icky died first, Little David would be declared the winner by virtue of throwing the last blow. On the third breast pitting, Icky stretched out his limp neck and pecked feebly. The order to handle was given. Again we pitted, and again Icky pecked, and this time he got a billhold on the other cock's stubby dubbed comb. Little David didn't feel or notice the billhold. Little David was dead. And so was Icky, his beak clamped to the Red's comb to the last.

"I'll carry my bird out," Jack Burke said.

"You're entitled to three more twenty-second counts," Ed reminded him, going by the book.

"What's the use?" Burke said indifferently. "They're *both* dead, now."

"Dead or not," Ed said officially, "you're entitled by the rules to three counts of twenty after the other cock pecks."

Without another word Jack Burke picked up his dead gamecock and left the pit. I picked up the Blue and held him to my chest. His long neck dangled limply over my left arm. My eyes were suddenly, irrationally, humid with tears.

"That's what I call a dead-game chicken, Frank!" Senator Foxhall called out from the judge's box.

I nodded blindly in his general direction and then turned my back on the old man to look for Mary Elizabeth. She wasn't in her seat. I caught a glimpse of her blue topcoat as she hurried out through the side entrance to the parking lot. I ran after her and caught up with her running figure just beyond the closed, shuttered box office.

"Mary Elizabeth!" I said aloud. My voice sounded rusty, strangled, different, nothing at all like I remembered it.

She stopped running, turned and faced me, her face like a mask. Her lips were as bloodless as her face.

"You've decided to talk again? Is that it? It's too late now, Frank. And I know now that it was always too late for us. You aren't the man I fell in love with, but you *never* were! If I'd seen you in the cockpit ten years ago, I would've known then. I didn't watch those poor chickens fight, Frank, I watched your face. It was awful. No pity, no love, no understanding, nothing! Hate! You hate everything, yourself, me, the world, everybody!"

She closed her eyes to halt the tears. A moment later she opened her purse and wiped her eyes with a small white handkerchief.

"And I gave myself to you, Frank," she said, as though she were speaking to herself. "I gave you everything I had to offer, everything, to a man who doesn't even have a heart!"

I didn't know this woman. I had never seen her before. This was a Mary Elizabeth I had hidden from myself all these years.

I dropped my dead Blue chicken to the ground, put my left heel on its neck, reached down, and jerked off his head with my right hand. I held the beaten, bloody, but never, never bowed head out to Mary Elizabeth in my palm. I had nothing else to say to the woman.

Mary Elizabeth licked her pale lips. She took Icky's head from my hand and wrapped it in her white handkerchief. Tucking the wrapped head away in her purse, she nodded.

"Thank you. Thank you very much, Frank Mansfield. I'll accept your gift. When I get home, I'll preserve it in a jar of alcohol. I might even work out some kind of ritual, to remind myself what a damned fool I've been."

Her emerald eyes burned into mine for a moment.

"My brother's been right about you all along, but I had to drive up here to find out for myself. You're everything he said you were, Frank Mansfield. A mean, selfish sonofabitch!"

Turning abruptly, she headed toward the rows of parked cars. After only a few steps, she broke into a wobbling, feminine run. I don't know how long I stood there, looking after her retreating figure, even after she had passed from sight. A minute, two minutes, I don't know.

A voice blared over the outside speakers of the PA system: "MR. ROY WHIPPLE AND MR. FRANK MANS-FIELD. REPORT TO THE JUDGE'S BOX, PLEASE!" The announcement was repeated twice, and I heard it, but I didn't pay any attention to the amplified voice. I was immobilized by thought. I've grown up, I reflected. After thirty-three years, I was a mature individual. I had never needed Mary Elizabeth, and she had never needed me. Finally, it was all over between us—whatever it was we thought we had. My last tie with the past and Mansfield, Georgia, was broken. From now on I could look toward the future, and it had never been any brighter—

He must have made some noise, but I didn't hear Omar's feet crunching on the gravel until he grabbed my arm.

"For God's sake, Frank," Omar said excitedly. "What the hell are you standing out here for? Senator Foxhall's award-ing you the Cockfighter of the Year award! Let's go inside, man! As your partner, I'm entitled to a little reflected glory, you know."

Now that he had my attention, he smiled broadly, his white teeth gleaming through his black moustache. "Of course," he shrugged, "Old Man Whipple won the tourney, but what do we care? Thanks to Icky's victory, we're loaded!" He patted his bulging jacket pockets. "We've got so damned much money, I'm almost afraid to count it."

Smiling, I gestured for him to go on ahead of me. Omar turned toward the entrance and trotted down the short hallway to the pit.

When I reached the doorway, I paused. After the barbe-cue was over, I would ask Bernice to go to Puerto Rico with me for a month or so. If it got dull in Puerto Rico, we could swing on down to Caracas, and I might be able to pick up some Spanish Aces for next season. Omar could put our proven birds out on their Alabama walks without any assistance from me. And then, if I returned from South America by the middle of April, I would be back in plenty of time to start working with the spring stags.

Across the pit, standing behind the referee's table in front of the judge's box, the two greatest game fowl men in the world were waiting for me. Senator Foxhall and Ed Middle-ton. To the left of the table, Peach Owen was holding the leather box that contained my award.

Well, they could wait a little longer.

As I neared her seat in the front row, Bernice smiled and said, "Congratulations, Frank!"

"Thanks," I replied.

"Oh!" she said, her eyes widening with astonishment. "You—you've got your voice back!"

"Yeah," I said, grinning at her expression, "and you'll probably wish I hadn't."

"I—I don't know what you mean."

"You'll find out that I'm quite a talker, Bernice, once I get wound up. How'd you like to go to Puerto Rico for a few weeks?"

"Right now," she said, "I'm so confused that the only answer I can think of on the spur of the moment is 'Yes.'"

I laughed and turned away, joy burbling out of my throat. How good to talk again, to *laugh* again!

I jerked my jacket down in back and pushed my white hat back on my head at a careless angle. Then, squaring my shoulders, I crossed the empty pit to get my goddamned medal.

Charles Willeford was a highly decorated (Silver Star, Bronze Star, Purple Heart, Luxembourg Croix de Guerre) tank commander with the Third Army in World War II. His memoir of army life, *Something About A Soldier,* was published in 1986. He has also been a professional horse trainer, boxer, radio announcer, and painter. He studied art in Biarritz, France, and in Lima, Peru, and English at the University of Miami. The author of a collection of short stories and more than a dozen novels, including the best-selling *The Burnt Orange Heresy, Cockfighter, Miami Blues,* and *New Hope for the Dead,* the former Californian now lives in Miami, Florida, because "the crime rate—the highest in the nation—provides a writer with an exciting environment."